ALBERT EINSTEIN!
GEORG CANTOR!
DAVID HILBERT!
DONALD DUCK!

THE SECRETS OF THE UNIVERSE REVEALED!

Felix Rayman was pretty much like a lot of other folk around him. Tired of living and scared of dying. And like many of them, he turned for escape to the comforts of the bottle. That was a mistake. Because even though Felix Rayman was so much like everyone else, he was still that little bit different—and a transfinite mathematician with a propensity for out-of-the-body travel should never get drunk.

But if he does. . . .

Then maybe you'll get to meet Jesus, and the Devil. Perhaps you'll come to know Kathy the seagull and Franx the existential cockroach as you journey up Mount On, and learn what lies Beyond Going Beyond. Are you ready to be dazzled by

WHITE
LIGHT

WHITE LIGHT

or
What is Cantor's Continuum Problem?
by
Rudy Rucker

SF
ace books
A Division of Charter Communications Inc.
A GROSSET & DUNLAP COMPANY
51 Madison Avenue
New York, New York 10010

WHITE LIGHT

This book is a work of fiction, and none of the characters, other than the historical and literary figures, are intended to represent actual persons, living or dead. This book was written at the Mathematics Institute of the University of Heidelberg, with the financial support of the Alexander von Humboldt Foundation.

An ACE Book

First Ace printing: November 1980
Published Simultaneously in Canada

2 4 6 8 0 9 7 5 3
Manufactured in the United States of America

Table of Contents

PART I

"To have seen a specter isn't
everything, and there are
death-masks piled, one atop the
other, clear to heaven."

—Neal Cassady

1

In the Graveyard

Then it rained for a month. I started smoking again. Noise/Information . . . I was outside with a hat on.

Wednesday afternoon, I walked up Center Street to the graveyard on Temple Hill. The rain was keeping the others away, and it was peaceful. I stood under a big twisting tree, a beech with smooth gray hide made smoother by the rain running down it, tucks and puckers in the flesh, doughy on its own time-scale.

In the rain, under the tree in the graveyard, I was thinking about the Continuum Problem. Georg Cantor, father of our country, unearthed it in 1873 and lost his mind trying to solve it.

The light flickered and I could believe that spirits were pressing up to me. Would I sell my soul to solve the Continuum Problem, they wanted to know. Let's see the solution. Let's see the soul.

It was hard at first to tell if the deal actually came off. Four years before, I'd had a chance to ask the White Light about the Continuum Problem. It was on Memorial Day during the 'Nam war and there were guys with skinny necks and flags . . . whew! "And what about the continuum?" I'd asked, serious, pincering up a pencil with triple-jointed fingers. "Relax, you're not ready," was the answer—or more the feeling that the Answer was not going to be something I could write down in symbolic logic.

But I'd kept working at it, sharpening my inner eye so I could catch and name most of those bright glimpses . . . code the idea up in an elegant for-mulation, a magic spell which could bring the flash back. I was ready in the rain, in the graveyard, hoping to cheat the shades.

There was one stone on Temple Hill I liked particularly. Emily Wadsworth, 1793, epitaph: "Remember that you must die." I found it refresh-ing . . . this welling up of human intelligence, of the reality of existence. I'd first seen the stone a few months earlier, read it, felt happy, but then! A black flyspeck become fly spiralled up from the stone and headed for me, *If I land on you, you will die* . . . I ran.

But I was back, there by the beech tree's flowing trunk, watching the chutes and ladders, the mid-way of my mind; believing (why not) that the spirits were offering the solution of the Con-tinuum Problem to me. The patterns grew more fantastic, and I hung on, naming them quickly

and without sinking, afloat on the rising flood
. . .

The rain has picked up, I realize after a time. I look about for better shelter and pick a small mausoleum near the Wadsworth plot. I hurry over and try the door. Double doors, glass with iron grillwork. One opens, and I go in. There is an ordinary wooden door set into the floor. I tear it off the hinges and run down the staircase. More doors, I throw them behind me. Stairs, doors, black light . . . I run faster, catching up. Soon I hear the coffin, bumping and groaning down the stairs only a few steps ahead of me, I leap! And land in it, red satin, you understand, a clotted ejaculation . . .

"But this is not mathematics, Mr . . .?"

"Rayman. Felix Rayman," I reply. They are wearing dark suits with vests. Gold watch chains and wingtip shoes. The International Congress of Mathematicians, Paris, 1900.

David Hilbert takes the podium. He's talking about mathematical problems in general, leading up to his personal list of the top 23 unsolved problems.

He's little, with a pointed beard and a good speaking style. The first problem on his list is the Continuum Problem, but what catches my attention is this preliminary remark: "If we do not succeed in solving a mathematical problem, the reason frequently consists in our failure to recognize the more general standpoint from which the problem before us appears only as *a single link in a chain of related problems.*"

I search the crowd for the faces of Klein or

Minkowski . . . I'm sure they're here. But the faces are indistinct and Hilbert's German is suddenly incomprehensible. A clod of earth falls on me from the ceiling. I get up and leave.

The exit door gives into a shadowy tunnel. The catacombs of Paris. I walk on, holding a candle, and every twenty paces or so the tunnel branches. I go left, left, right, left, right, right, right, left . . . My only desire is to avoid falling into a pattern.

Occasionally I pass through small chambers where bones are stored. The monks have built walls out of the thighbones, cords of greasy fuel for the eternal fires; and behind these walls they have thrown the smaller bones. The walls of femurs are decorated with skulls, set into the stacks to form patterns—checkerboards, maps, crosses, Latin words. I see my name several times.

Some two thousand branchings into the labyrinth my mind is clear and I can remember every turn I have made. At each branching I am careful to break yet another possible rule for how I am choosing my path. If I continue forever, perhaps I can travel a path for which there is no finite description. And where will I be then? The skulls know.

I blow out my candle and sit in one of Death's chambers to listen. There is a faint, unpleasant smell and a quiet sifting of dust from the bones' imperceptible crumbling. In the labyrinth, the city of Death, it is only quiet. "We are sleeping."

Perhaps I sleep too. It is hard to tell here, but it seems that I did complete that infinite journey through the tunnels; that they drew narrower and I more flexible; and that I travelled a path which cannot be described.

As the trip ended I was an electron moving along a nerve fiber, up the spinal cord and into the brain, my brain. It was raining on my face and I tried to sit up. But my body wouldn't move. It just lay there, cooling in the October rain.

2
How I Got This Way

Being awake in a lifeless body was not an entirely new experience for me. For the last two weeks I had been having strange naps. Naps where I would wake up paralyzed and struggle through layer after layer of illusion before being able to rise. It had all come to a head the day before the graveyard.

I was fresh out of graduate school, and had a job as a mathematics instructor at a state college in Bernco, New York. Some fool or misanthrope had acronymed the college SUCAS. I was the first head to teach at SUCAS, and I felt violently out of place. In the evenings I argued with my wife and listened to the Rolling Stones' *Exile on Main Street* on my stereo earphones. In the day I slept on my office floor, asphalt tile soft with 1940's wax.

Of course it would not do for my so-called students or self-styled colleagues to see me sleeping on the floor, so I locked my door. I slept troubled by the fear that someone would use a passkey to catch me lying there, cheek slick with sleeper's drool. Frequently my mind would snap awake at the sound of a fist, a key or a claw at my door, and I would have to struggle long minutes to rouse my body.

My office-mate's name was Stuart Levin, and he'd been teaching at SUCAS two years longer than I. We had known each other faintly as undergraduates some eight years earlier—we'd lived in the same dorm at Swarthmore when I was a freshman and he was a senior.

Stuart was one of the last Zen fans and one of the first Maoists. He said he was going to be a Zen socialist playwright, and actually had a couple of odd pieces produced by the campus players. I remembered one in particular, *Thank God for Yubiwaza.* Apparently it had been based on a comic book ad for some kind of judo, and had lasted 38 seconds. I'd missed that one by stopping in the Men's Room on my way into the theatre, and had regretted the loss ever since.

What I had always admired most about Stuart back then were his wall posters of Mao and D.T. Suzuki. The Chairman was tacked to the closet door, and Suzuki was taped to the opposite wall. The fat Chinaman was waving an arm inspirationally, and the skinny old Japanese was wearing a Zen monk's garb and sitting limply on a rock. Stuart had drawn speech balloons coming out of their mouths. The Chairman was crying, "Did you WRITE today, Stuart?" and the monk was glaring across and muttering, "Today's pig, tomorrow's bacon."

I found Stuart in our office on the first day of classes. It had been eight years, and he looked middle-aged. Thinner, hair shorter, and a standard-issue assistant professor beard.

"You're going to have to watch what you say here, Rayman," was the first thing he said to me. I stepped into the office and looked around while he continued talking, the words coming out in bursts and jerks. "I just heard this summer that I'm not getting renewed." He twisted his neck around to look at me . . . accusingly, I imagined.

"You mean you already got fired?" I asked, sitting down.

Stuart nodded vehemently, "But they give you a year to find another job . . . I'm sending out 1200 letters." He handed me one from a stack on his desk. There was a misprint in the third line.

"What are you doing here anyway?" I asked. "Teaching math in upstate New York . . . where's *that* at? What happened to Zen socialism?"

His smile was like a crack in a boulder. He had the head of a man twice his size. "This was Bernadine's idea. She said that we should tunnel from within . . . coopt the System. So I decided to get a Phid in mathematics. When they want to dehumanize you they use numbers instead of names, right? Statistics instead of souls. So I studied statistics, but the only teaching job I could find was up here in cow country. And now I'm losing this job, too." Levin fell into his chair with a sigh. "I never dreamed it would turn out so fucking poor."

"Yeah," I answered. "I only went to grad school to dodge the draft. I almost got drafted anyway. But I really got into math after awhile. It's beautiful stuff . . . like really fine abstract art."

Levin snorted. "If it's so beautiful, how come no one ever looks at it. You'll be lucky if three people ever read your dissertation." He handed me a math journal. "Look at this. The fruit of five years labor."

The magazine was called the Journal of the American Statistical Association. About half-way down the table of contents I saw "Asymptotic Theory of Error Regression in Poisson Processes . . . Stuart I. Levin." I flipped to the article. It was about 10 pages long, and bristled with unfamiliar symbols.

"This looks interesting, Stuart," I lied. "Of course I'm more oriented to Logic and Set Theory, but when I get the time . . ." I decided to change the subject. "With a degree in statistics, how come you didn't get a fat job in industry? You could really undermine the system there."

He took the magazine from me and stared at his article for awhile before answering. "My teachers tricked me into caring about mathematics. When I wrote this, I thought it was going to change the whole field of statistics overnight. I figured it was so good, there was no need for me to bust my hump in a nine-to-five. I thought I'd step into a Professorship at Princeton or Berkeley. Carry the torch. Phaw. I'm going to try once more, and then I'll go to law school like I should have in the first place."

I didn't see Levin much after the first day. He had a presentiment that not one of his 1200 letters was going to be read with interest or sympathy, and he was spending all his spare time doing the homework for two law courses he was taking in night school.

I had managed to avoid telling my students where my office was . . . so most afternoons I could count on an idle peace troubled only by my guilt over April's unhappiness. When I got home April would always be lying on the couch staring at the TV with the sound off. She would just lie there in silence until I came over and asked how she was. The answer was always the same. She was pissed-off, fed-up, and dead sick of it all. The hick town, the constant baby-care, the shopping in sleazy chain stores, the problems with the car, what the neighbor lady had said today, and so on and on.

It sounded a lot worse than my life, though of course I could never admit this. Instead I laid great stress on my research (desultory), class-preparations (an hour a week sufficed), and faculty meetings (after my first I had sworn there would be no second). I had no classes Thursday, and usually stayed home with baby Iris that day in order to lessen my burden of guilt somewhat.

But the guilt was never really that bad when I was in my well-heated office with its soft, waxy floor. My classes were over for the day at noon, and after I had wolfed down my sandwich I would settle down to try to do some mathematics. My chosen field was Set Theory, the exact science of the infinite. I was attempting to work through some important new articles which had appeared. I hoped to get a new slant on Cantor's Continuum

Problem, the question of how big is the infinitude of points in space.

Off at Bernco I was isolated from other set-theorists, and the papers were very difficult to read alone. Before long a feeling of lassitude and hopelessness would overcome me, and I would lie down on the floor—telling myself it was only to relax so as to better visualize some complex set-theoretic construction.

By the clock my naps would last two, three or even four hours. But the mental time of these naps could not be measured by any system of gears and levers. My naps lasted light-years, kilograms, quantum jumps, hypervolumes . . . Space and time were fractured, shuffled, layered and re-interfaced during those fall afternoons alone with the radiator's hiss and the slow waning of the gray light.

Do you ever wake up inside your dreams? It's like the dream is going on as usual, only suddenly you feel yourself to be awake in Dreamland. In ordinary dreams one simply moves through the dreams like a blacked-out drunk. But in rare moments of lucid dreaming one remembers oneself and begins to exercise some conscious control.

These moments of strange dark clarity rarely last long—for as you move through Dreamland a thousand wrong turnings await, each one leading back to the dream-work, the visionary but mindless manipulation of hopes and fears. As soon as a dream fully engages you, the familiar hypnosis sets in, and the lucidity is over.

In the course of my naps at Bernco, I had stumbled on a method of prolonging those intervals of lucid dreaming. The trick was not to stare at anything, and to keep glancing down at my hands and body. As long as I could hold together a body in Dreamland, I could stay conscious. Sometimes I was even able to move among the bright shades till I found just the dream I wanted.

In October a bizarre side-effect began to set in. During the lucid dreaming my spirit had gotten used to moving about Dreamland in a self-generated astral body. But now, more and more often, I was having trouble clicking back into my physical body. I would come to on my office floor, but I'd be unable to open my eyes, unable to move at all. The noises in the hall would warp and loom, and I would lie there paralyzed, struggling to get control of my body.

Monday, two days before I went on that walk to the graveyard, a new phase set in. I woke up paralyzed, and as I tried to move, my astral arm swung free of my physical arm. I was lying on the floor next to the window, most of me trapped in inert flesh, but the one arm was free. I groped around, and found the radiator pipe. It was hot, but didn't hurt. On the back of the pipe I felt a place where the paint had peeled off, a spot shaped like a ragged crescent moon.

Just then Levin walked in and I woke up. "Come on, Felix, time to go home," he said as he gathered his books. "You just missed a classic Departmental meeting. We argued for an hour over whether or not to vote to change bylaw 3 of the Departmental constitution. Really stimulating stuff."

I stood up with as much difficulty as if I were climbing out of a six-foot grave. It wasn't till the next day, Tuesday, that I remembered the strange dream. When I tried to feel behind the radiator pipe, it was too hot to touch. But by putting my eye by the wall near the floor I could just make out a chipped crescent of peeled paint. But it seemed to point in a direction opposite to the one I remembered.

When I napped Tuesday afternoon I had terrible muddled dreams. Finally I woke up, paralyzed again. As before, I pulled one arm loose, then both arms. Carefully I felt my body's chest and crossed arms. I put the astral arms down on the floor and tried to push the rest of my astral body out of my physical body. There was a giving sensation, and my arms sank through the floor. I felt around a bit . . . wires, a bent nail . . . then pulled my arms back and decided to try something else.

This time I swung my astral arms back and forth to gather momentum, and then in a confused bumpy whirl I rolled free of my flesh. I was lying on the floor facing my sleeping physical body. I was out in my astral body, which was a naked mirror-image of my physical body.

For a long minute I did nothing. The room looked normal, except for a few doughy blobs which were drifting around near the window. My physical body was still breathing. I relaxed a bit and looked around the room in the hope of making a definite observation which I could check later. I had to know if this was real.

I remembered that every piece of furniture in the room had a little metal tag with a SUCAS serial number on it. I knew from touch that there was such a tag on the underside of my desk drawer . . . but I had never looked at it. I resolved to read this number and try to remember it.

I crawled over towards the desk, keeping an eye on my sleeping form. I had a terrible fear that my body would die without me in it. But I was determined to try to read the number and find out if this was more than just a crazy dream.

As I put my head under the desk, something happens to my space perceptions. Where I expect to find something like a cubic meter of legspace, I find a dark corridor that stretches through the wall and far beyond. A pair of dim red lights is moving down the corridor towards me, and I can hear labored breathing.

Quickly I look up at the ceiling, the bottom of my desk drawer. There is the metal tag. With an anxious glance at the approaching red eyes, I stretch my neck up and up to read the tag.

There are six digits, but every time I read them they change. The contours of the room are flowing, and I know I will die of fear if I see that thing coming towards me. I scrabble across the floor to my body, and somehow roll into it. A black leathery-winged creature is crawling out from under my desk. I try to scream but I'm paralyzed again . . .

I woke up with a start. It was 3:30 on Tuesday afternoon. I put my coat on and hurried home through the pouring rain.

3
Number of the Beast

Wednesday morning I stepped out of our rented house in a state of suicidal depression. Another quarrel with April. Recently she had been complaining that she never got enough sleep, so today I had struggled up from my troubled slumber to feed baby Iris when she began crying at 6:30.

The baby's delight at seeing me made getting up worthwhile. Her mouth opened wide in greeting, and I could see her two teeth. She let go of her crib railing to wave her arms in unison, and fell back onto her diaper. Her Trimfit was soaked, and I changed her, softly mimicking her coos and cries all the while.

When Iris was dressed I stood her on the table in front of her mirror with my head next to hers. I wondered how heads grow. My face surprised me—I hadn't realized what a zombie I looked like. But Iris didn't mind. "Ba-ba, Da-da," she said, giving her fat chuckle.

She began to cry loudly when I put her in her high chair. I mashed a banana and warmed up some mush. When it was ready, I spooned the paste into her mouth, shaving her cheeks and chin with the tiny spoon after every few bites. Before long she was sucking her bottle, and I could begin to feed myself. I had hardly had any supper the night before, and now I was trembling with hunger.

As I began to fry an egg, April walked into the kitchen. "I hope you didn't give her banana in that outfit," she said. "The spots are impossible to get out." I clenched my teeth and turned my egg over. The yolk broke. I cursed and dumped it into the garbage.

"What are you so cranky about?" April asked sharply.

"Go back to bed," I snarled, breaking a new egg into the pan.

"I don't know why you have to start the day out this way," April wailed. "This is my kitchen, and if I feel cheerful and like getting up, I can. It wouldn't kill you to be nice to me for once. Last night you didn't say a word to me."

I almost blurted out that I had fallen out of my body and almost been caught by the Devil, but then the yolk broke again. I scrambled the egg messily, put it on some untoasted bread, and choked the mess down with milk. April's face had that curdled look it got when she was really unhappy. I thought I was going to say something nice, but what came out was, "I'm going to have to get down to school early today, April." Suddenly I wanted to be outside more than anything. I began gathering my stuff together.

"That's right," April shouted. "Ruin my morning and leave me alone in this dump. Why can't you get a real job in the city? You're so floppy and lazy. If you wouldn't stay up all night with your pipe and earphones . . ."

Iris watched us with mild eyes. I kissed her, wiped my mouth, and hurried out the front door. April was sitting on a chair crying. "Go back to her," I told myself, "Go on." But I didn't.

Halfway down the block the pain was bearable, and by the corner I could see again. It was going to be another rainy day. The gray sky looked like it was only about a hundred meters high. But there was a certain beauty in the shadowless lighting. It looked almost like an oriental water-color, with each tree and leaf and color just so. I decided to take a long walk after lunch. After yesterday I never wanted to nap again.

I was in my office over an hour before my first class—Mathematics for Elementary Education Majors, at nine o'clock. I was a little nervous putting my feet under my desk, but of course nothing happened. I decided that my experience yesterday had been nothing more than a nightmare.

I was still not quite able to believe that five years of graduate school had led to SUCAS, and I scanned my morning mail half-hoping for some miraculous last-minute offer from a real university. But today it was just ads for new textbooks, and a nasty, cryptic memo from the Departmental Committee to the Department at large. I wished I could play lead guitar in a rock band.

I threw the mail in the trash can and picked up a book on Differential Geometry which I had recently checked out of the college library. With a

feeling of real comfort I began going over the
Frenet formulas for the moving trihedron of a
space curve.

After a few minutes something on my desk
caught my eye. It was a triangular scrap of paper
with unfamiliar handwriting on it. It must have
been under my book. I fought back a sudden conviction that the paper had some connection with
my nightmare, and picked it up.

The paper was thick, almost parchment-like;
straight on two edges and ragged on the other. A
corner torn from the page of an old book. The ink
was a reddish brown. "Dried blood," I thought
despairingly. The writing was precise enough,
but seemed to be in another alphabet. Suddenly I
realized I was looking at mirror-writing. I tried to
decipher it, but I was too jangled by now to reason
things out. I ran to my closet and held the scrap up
to the mirror on the door.

"Square my number for the tag," I read.

"It's the fault of guys like you, Rayman," a voice
said rapidly. I started violently and whirled
around. It was John Wildon, one of the full profes-
sors. He was a shy man, but obnoxious nevertheless. I rarely knew what his compacted witticisms
were about. I looked at him blankly, masking my
confusion and dislike with a cough.

. "Wage-price guidelines and a book like that
costs the library thirty bucks." He advanced to
point at the Differential Geometry book which I
had left lying on my desk. Was he complaining
that I used the library?

"It's a pretty good book," I said uncertainly,
pocketing the mysterious scrap of paper. "The
pictures are nice."

"Don't tell me you didn't know that Strunk is a Red?" Wilson inquired, sipping coffee from his mug. He had a special mug with his name on it along with the names of famous mathematicians. I hoped he would drop it some day. "Giving tax dollars to the Reds, and this county is 90% Republican." Wildon shook his head. "You'd think even a logician would know better than that." Suddenly he gave me an intense look. "You've registered?"

"To vote?" I answered, and he nodded. "Sure . . ." I was still many jumps behind him. Was Strunk the author of the book I was reading?

"Democrat?" Wildon slipped in. I nodded and he raised his mug in a silent toast. "We liberals have to look out for each other." He started out of the room. At the door he paused, "We'll get together with the wives and quaff a few."

"Fine," I said. "That would be nice."

When Wildon was gone I lit a cigarette and stared out the window for a long time. All you could see out the window was a brick wall, and above it some sky. "Square my number for the tag," the paper said. Whose number . . . what tag?

I thought back on my nightmare of the day before. I had dreamed I had left my body and crawled under my desk to read the number on the SUCAS property tag. I felt under the desk. The tag was still there. With a certain reluctance I got down on the floor and craned up. The number was 44-3556. Square my number to get the tag. What was the square root of 443,556? I took out pencil and paper.

In a few minutes I had it. The square root of

443,556 is 666. According to the Book of Revelations 666 is the number of the Beast, i.e. the Devil, i.e. the leathery-winged creature who had chased me out from under my desk Tuesday afternoon. It all fit.

I took the scrap of paper out of my pocket and examined it closely. Could I have written it myself? Perhaps I really had an astral body, had read the tag, subconsciously taken the square root, imagined the Devil by association, and had written myself this note with my mirror-reversed astral body. I held the paper tightly. If it disappeared, I'd know I was crazy. That was the second possibility. And the third? It was unthinkable.

When I heard the bell tolling nine o'clock I got up and started across the quad to Todd Hall. A fine rain was falling. On an impulse I crumpled up the triangle of paper and threw it in a litter basket. "You imagined the whole thing," I told myself, "you've just been under too much stress."

As I approached the stone steps leading up to Todd, my thoughts fell comfortably into a familiar litany of complaint. Was this really my life? What had Levin said? "I never dreamed it would turn out so fucking poor." Twenty-seven years of training, of hopes and dreams had led only to *this*, teaching arithmetic at SUCAS.

I mounted the steps, face level with the ordinary denim butt of a student several steps ahead of me. Suddenly she let out a skirling cry, kicked out her right leg, and fell down in a fit, head nodding ecstatic agreement to that old-time nerve music.

My feeling of alienation from the SUCAS community was such that I simply picked my way around her. Someone else would be eager to help . . . one of the most popular majors on campus was "Special Education." As I neared the top of the steps the door swung open and a blind student came out. I stepped aside, and he tapped past me, only to trip over the epileptic and fall onto her.

It hurt a little to see them bashing around on those stone steps, and I hesitated, on the verge of helping. Her brown hair was webbed across her spitty face, and her hand was beating his pathetically pale back, acned and exposed to light where his cheap plaid shirt had rucked up. He continued loudly to apologize. A husky blond girl came running across the quad, slipped, twisted her ankle and fell horribly at the foot of the steps. I went ahead into Todd, guilty and depressed.

I was five minutes late for class now, and the halls were practically empty. I hurried past the open doors of the classrooms where my colleagues were already hard at work—collecting homework, giving quizzes, reading from their notes. Wildon spotted me and pointedly looked at his watch.

As I neared my classroom I tried to remember what we had done in our last class, and wondered what I'd talk about today. My deaf student was waiting for me outside the classroom. "Hewwah," she said. I smiled and nodded.

"I haw a pwabwah," she continued, turning her face up to me. She was touching, but understood almost none of the material. Of course she would pass. I smiled and nodded again, embarrassed to talk.

"Yaw haw tah kahp yah han awah fwah yah

math," she said, acting out what she meant by covering her face. "I haw tah see tha lip."

"I'll try," I mouthed, and we went into the class. The class consisted of thirty girls and three dispirited males, one of whom was me.

There were three key students in this class. One, named Melanie, was a creditable likeness of the young, confused-by-her-bursting-sexuality Marilyn Monroe. Karen, the second, looked like April as a depraved seventeen-year-old. Fina, the anchor-person, had a false tooth and was so deliciously greasy that I had gone so far as to have coffee with her the week before.

Today only Karen was there, and her fat sullen lips seemed to whisper in April's voice. "I'm so unhappy. You don't love me. I want to live my own life." This was not going to be a fun class. I was glad I'd at least thrown the paper away. It was better to be crazy than to be getting letters from the Devil.

I walked over to the window, opened it, and leaned out to see how the big pile-up was progressing. I still couldn't believe it . . . three people at once. What was I doing in this zoo? The steps were clear now, but as I watched a student with greasy black hair trotted past, slipped badly, and acted out an elaborate pantomime of shock at this chance mishap. He even looked at the sole of his shoe.

I pulled my head back in and glanced at the clock. It was ten after. If I let them out five minutes early that still left 35 minutes to kill. "Well," I said, sitting down and leafing through our text, "Are there any questions about the homework?"

A dead silence. The class stared at me dully without even any of the usual flickers of lust or contempt. None of us could remember if there had ever been any homework in this course. Why were we here? "Should we have a test soon?" I ventured in desperation.

And that took care of the rest of the period. We set the test for Monday, and questions about it poured forth. Under the pressure of the situation I produced a philosophy of testing and a course outline. Finally we knew what we were there for. They left the room well-pleased.

I spent the next hour teaching Calculus II, which I genuinely enjoyed. There is something beautiful about a science which enables you to compute the volume of an egg and the surface area of a beer bottle. The students responded well, and I got off some good one-liners.

I had one other class, Foundations of Geometry, which met Tuesday and Friday afternoons. But today was Wednesday, so at 11:00 I was through for the day. It was pouring rain again, and I had to run across the quad to my office. Levin was sitting at his desk eating one of his strange-smelling sandwiches and looking through a stack of fat books.

"Hi Stuart," I said, "How's law?"

"The Law is just," he answered. "I could stand it for thirty grand a year. I keep telling myself that I'm not selling out . . . just *buying* in." He gave a short chuckle. "And you? Ready for one of your famous naps?"

"No," I said quickly. "No, no. No more naps, not after yesterday." I went on to tell him about my lucid dreams and my astral body, about the creature I'd seen yesterday, and about the note I'd found this morning. Levin quietly finished his sandwich while I talked. "Well," I concluded, "It's a relief to lay it all out like this. I guess it sounds pretty crazy when you hear it all at once."

"It does," Levin said, looking at me sympathetically. "I think if I were you, I'd try to get on a different track. Maybe even see a shrink. If you keep up like this you're going to give yourself a heart attack. Die of fear while you're sleeping."

"That's really encouraging, Stuart. But don't you think it might be real? What about the numbers?"

He shrugged. "I notice that you got rid of the note before showing it to anyone else. Offhand, I'd just have to say you're going nuts. On the other hand . . ." He thought for a minute. "I saw a book somewhere about dreams like that . . . some friend of Bernadine's had it. It was by a guy called Monroe and was called *Journeys Out of the Body*. When you've calmed down a little, you might try checking it out."

I wrote the name and title down. Another question occured to me. "You come in here late on Tuesdays don't you?" Levin nodded and I continued. "Did you see anything funny here yesterday?"

"Well," Levin said, his head splitting in that long smile, "there was this guy with red eyes and a barbed tail who wanted to see you. I told him to leave a note."

I had to laugh. "All right, all right. I'm going crazy. A lot you care." I put on my leather jacket and an old felt hat I'd gotten from my father. "I'm going to get lunch and walk in the rain."

"Think about math, Felix," Levin advised seriously as I walked out. "It'll take your mind off your nervous breakdown."

4

Bernco

I toiled up the steep asphalt to Bernco's main street, called Main Street. It was still raining hard, and water was flowing down the pavement in ruffled sheets. I had decided to eat at Sammy's, a diner run by the present mayor of Bernco. He held court in a cloud of cigar-smoke at the end of the counter while a fat woman with whiskers served the customers. This woman looked exactly like Sammy, even to the brilliantined hair. She ate things while she worked.

My breakfast had worn off quickly, and on the walk up I had already designed the ideal sandwich for today. I sat at the counter near the grill and gave the fat woman my order.

"I'd like a meat-loaf sandwich on white toast

with butter and mayonnaise, lettuce and a slice of swiss. And a cup of tea."

"Mmmm, that sounds yummy," she said, her voice sweet with saliva.

She gave me my tea, served someone a cheeseburger and an order of fries, then built my sandwich. I watched her with absorption, feeling an architect's pride. Finally it was ready, mounted on a little fluted paper plate with a spear of pickle and handful of potato chips. I sat back with a receptive smile.

But then that fat waitress turned her back to me, leaned over the sandwich, and ate it all—rapidly and in silence.

I entered a fog of rage. Expressionlessly I choked down my eventual sandwich—a juiceless cardboard replica of the consumed masterpiece. Without so much as a raised eyebrow I watched a man bring his dog behind the counter for a raw hamburger. The fat woman fed it with her spatula. Numbly I paid the check and left. The dog was barking for another round.

The rain was coming down so hard I just stood under Sammy's awning for a minute. There was a big puddle on the sagging sidewalk, and the fat drops pounded into it. Quick circles of ripples flashed into existence, moiréd, damped out. I stared into the puddle, losing myself in the patterns.

There was a bookstore down the block. A curly-haired hippie who called himself Sunfish ran the store, deserted today. He sat near the window in a beat old lawn chair shaped like two scallop shells. He was visibly depressed.

"How you gonna keep 'em down on the farm, Sunfish?"

"Felix! Got any textbook orders for me?" Business glinted in his pale bloodshot eyes.

"No, I'm just . . ."

"A useless parasite!" Sunfish cried heatedly. More New Yorker than hippie, he made a habit of starting arguments with his customers. It added texture to his life.

"I don't know why nobody seems to think I have a real job," I complained. "Just worrying about what I'll do after I get fired takes so much . . ."

"Listen to him! Next week he'll have an ulcer."

I sighed and turned to look at a rack of fantasy books. Sunfish loved fantasy. Suddenly I felt him standing right behind me.

"That's a good one," he said, pointing over my shoulder. He had dog breath.

"How come you're standing so much closer to me than I am to you?" I rapped out cuttingly.

Sunfish threw his hands up and walked back to his chair. "Eh! The guy is touchy."

I felt ashamed of myself. "I'm sorry. I have a lot of problems."

"I can believe that."

"You got any books on astral travel? There's one by a guy called Monroe?"

"In stock," Sunfish said, waving towards the back of the store. "Last shelf on the right." He went back to staring at the rain.

I spent the better part of an hour in the back of the store. A few customers came and went—mostly students seeking out this or that recommended reading. Sunfish made short work of them.

I read some of Monroe's book—particularly the passages on how to get back into your body once you're out of it. But he didn't seem to have the same problems with this that I did. There were three copies of Monroe's book, and I almost didn't notice the little pamphlet wedged behind them. I fished it out, wondering at its curious title-page:

CIMÖN and HOW TO GET THERE
F.R.

That was all. No publisher's imprint and no date. The pages were flimsy and slippery.

The significance of the initials was not lost on me, and I looked into the pamphlet with a numinous feeling of expectation. "Cimön is the land of dreams and departed spirits," the first part began.

A detailed description, with diagrams of Cimön, filled the first half of the pamphlet. It was too much for me to absorb, but the diagrams stick in my mind. One was like a thermometer. My head was swimming when I got to the second part. I hadn't moved for half an hour and my legs were cramping.

"In normal space," the HOW TO GET THERE part of the pamphlet began, "Cimön is infinitely far away. For the dreamer this poses no problem, but for the full discorporate . . ."

"You still there, Felix?" Sunfish shouted in a friendly voice.

I was ready for a break. I took the pamphlet up to him. "How much is this?"

He studied it for a minute. "What's Cimön?"

"It was behind the Monroe books."

He handed it back to me. "Is yours, amigo. I never saw it before."

"Then how did it get here?" I was thinking of the scrap of paper I'd found on my desk that morning.

Sunfish finished a yawn and leaned back in his pale-green lawn-chair. "There's always weirdos leaving stuff in here. Or the shipper threw it in." He paused, then remarked, "The Dead are going to be in the City tomorrow." Sunfish's one real enthusiasm was going to Grateful Dead concerts.

"You driving down?"

He nodded with a smile. "They'll play all night. It's for Halloween. You ought to come."

I shook my head and folded the pamphlet into my coat pocket. "My brain's already falling out."

It was still raining too hard for a walk, so I decided to go to the Drop Inn. I had enough money left for two beers. The Drop Inn was on Bernco's only non-residential side-street, and enjoyed a certain notoriety. All the heads in town drank there . . . which still left plenty of room for the odd derelict.

The only other patron at the Drop Inn today was a wizened farmhand with gum boots which reached his knees. He seemed to be chewing something.

The barmaid had a Jackson Browne record on, and was watching the rain like everyone did in Bernco. "Aren't you a math professor?" she asked me after I'd ordered a large dark draft.

"I didn't think it showed."

She smiled. "I'm Mary. I have a friend who's in

your Geometry course. Tom Percino. He says it's really far out.''

I didn't know my students' names yet, and tried to guess which one this girl would be friends with. She had lank dark hair, and a kind oval face made plain by some quarter-inch displacement of the chin. Something about her made you think of the Great Depression, the Dustbowl, Ritz Cracker Pie. I had only one Geometry student who looked like an Okie.

"Is your friend tall and with a little black mustache?" When Mary nodded I added, "Yeah, I know him." I had been talking a lot about the fourth dimension in the Geometry course, and Percino wanted to do his term paper on UFO's. He said he'd seen one that summer in Bernco.

I pulled at the tingling beer. "He's into UFO's, isn't he?"

Mary leaned across the bar. "He says you said they all come from the fourth dimension."

I chuckled cautiously, "I'm not sure I said that." My position here was precarious enough without people saying I taught about UFO's. "I don't really like UFO's," I continued. "They're too materialistic. It's like, sure, there's more to reality than just this . . ." I gestured at the barroom, the rain, Earth, "But to take your idea of something higher and just turn it into a guy in a *machine,* a machine from outer space . . . That's so pathetically materialistic. The beyond is right here all the time . . ." I ran my hand along the wooden bar, looking at the grain. I felt light-headed.

The barmaid enjoyed the rap, but was by no

means converted on the spot. "Yeah," she said. "For sure. But Tom and I really *saw* one this summer. Up on Temple Hill."

"You mean the graveyard?"

She nodded and continued. "We were sleeping-out there when we saw it. It started out like a mushroom and then grew big and flew away." She threw her hands in the air. "It was so beautiful."

I pushed my empty glass forward and she brought me another beer. "That's not the most reliable sighting I ever heard of," I said. "Or maybe you both *did* see something, but why does it have to be another damned machine? Why couldn't it have been God or an angel or living energy from dimension Z?"

"It *sounded* like a machine," she said and made a whirring noise. We both laughed. A group of students came in then and she went over to serve them. The old farmhand was still propped against the middle of the bar, staring into a shotglass of whiskey and repeatedly pursing his thin lips. I took my beer and sat down at one of the tables.

The first beer had warmed my stomach and my brain was ticking over nicely. I remembered Levin's advice and decided to think about math, about the Continuum Problem . . . a problem whose hundredth birthday was just around the corner.

On December 13, 1873, the 28-year-old Georg Cantor brought the Continuum Problem to light by proving that there are more points in space than there are natural numbers. The problem is how *much* more?

Any continuous piece of space is called a continuum. A line segment, the surface of a balloon, the space inside your head, the endless universe . . . all these are continua. Cantor discovered that viewed as sets of points all continua have the same degree of infinity, which he called c. The degree of infinity of the set of all natural numbers is called alef-null, and the next larger degree of infinity is called alef-one. In 1873, Cantor gave the first proof that c is greater than alef-null. Even if you lived forever and a day, you would not be able to assign a natural number to each and every point in space. The Continuum Problem is to decide how *much* greater c is than alef-null. Cantor thought c should be alef-one, the next infinity. But no one knows if he was right.

Sitting there in the Drop Inn. I was looking at mental pictures of alef-one and c and trying to compare them. That day alef-one looked like a whole lot of staircases . . . each of them steeper than the ones before; and c looked like a barrel. I let the staircases move out from the barrel's axis and watched to see if they could fill it up. I put lots of things . . . everything possible . . . into the barrel, sliced it into cross-sections, and drew concentric circles on the slices. I thought of a thought balloon which never stops growing, of a library with infinitely long books. I was hoping to find a proof that c is bigger than alef-one.

After awhile I noticed that there was a lull in the rain. I finished my beer, lit a cigarette and went outside. The brim of my hat kept the rain off the cigarette. I walked around town for awhile without really noticing where I was going. I had hit on what felt like a good approach to the Continuum Problem, and tried to stick with it, although my thoughts kept straying to April and to my nightmare about the Devil.

If I could only make some progress on the problem, I would be able to get a good job. If I could get a good job, April and I would be happy. If I were happy, I wouldn't keep dreaming about leaving my body.

April wanted me to go to the American Mathematical Society's annual job fair again. A hotel ball-room full of creeps behind card-tables. The petitioners were strange, quirky intelligences that had turned themselves into pretzels, adding machines, the Baseball Hall of Fame. The interviewers all wanted applied mathematicians. Whatever that meant, it didn't mean Set Theory.

For the first time I asked myself what the Continuum Problem was really about. Comparing two different things: c and alef-one. It seems fair to say that there are c possible thoughts and that alef-one is the first level of infinity which we really can't think up to. So the problem becomes: Is Everything bigger than Infinity?

The air around me was soft and luminous. I could feel CIMÖN and HOW TO GET THERE in my breast pocket. Both c and alef-one seemed like metaphysical Absolutes. Is there only one Absolute? Is the ultimate reality One or Many?

I noticed I was walking up Center Street towards Temple Hill. Bernco is on a hill which runs down to a thin gray lake. At the top of the hill is a graveyard, below that the town, below that the college, below that the elementary school, and below that the waters.

Somehow I fell asleep in the graveyard.

5

Donald Duck

After a frenzied dream of infinite catacombs I woke up with my body paralyzed again. I struggled to scream, to kick, to wave my arms. If I could only grunt, only twitch a finger . . . but I couldn't. I gave up and relaxed.

Although it was raining quite hard, I felt warm and comfortable. I wondered if I was dying. My mind strayed back to the dream. I had picked a perfectly random, utterly indescribable path through the labyrinth. There had been infinitely many choices, no last one, but now I was done with them all. In a way I had dreamed my way past alef-null. I wondered what it would be like to reach alef-one, to go on and on through all the levels of infinity, out towards the unattainable Absolute Infinite . . .

But I had to wake up! With a superhuman effort I managed to roll over, and that did it. I stood up

and began walking unsteadily out of the graveyard, looking around for that mausoleum I'd
dreamed about. I didn't see it ahead, so I turned to
look back towards the beech tree.

My real body was still lying under the tree. I
was in my astral body again. The rain was falling
right through me and I hadn't noticed.

I hesitated there for a time, torn between fear
and curiosity. I had never been so far from my
physical body before. I was scared it would die,
but I was dying to see what my astral body could
do out in the open.

I jumped off the ground and didn't fall back. I
could fly! Maybe I should whip home, see what
April was doing, zoom back here, wake up my
body, walk home and ask April if I was right. Then
I'd know whether or not this was real.

But that's how you got into trouble yesterday, I
reminded myself. I was hovering some 15 feet off
the ground. It was getting dark and I could see
people walking home from work. Most of the
houses had some lights on. The lit-up windows
looked warm and yellow . . . homey. I thought of
April and Iris, wanting only to love and be loved.
This madness had to end.

At a touch of volition my astral body floated
over to my inert flesh. The body was lying supine
near the base of the beech tree. The rain came
down through the bare branches to split into
droplets on the greasy face. Fortunately the head
was twisted to the side, and the water couldn't fill
the crooked nostrils or the slack mouth. The body
looked utterly uninviting, but I began trying to get
back into it.

I had never been out so long before. My astral

body had flowed into a blobbier, more comfortable shape, which was hard to fit to my old skeleton. The space occupied by my flesh had a clammy, icky feel to it. It was like the body cavity of a defrosted turkey, full of pimply skin, splintery bones and slippery giblets. But April needed me, and I shuffled on those mortal coils.

I tried everything then. I put steady pressure on my eyelids . . . nothing. I waited for minutes, then hit my nerves with a jolt of stored energy . . . nothing. One by one, I tried every muscle in my body. I tried to hold my breath, to wet my pants, to get an erection. Nothing doing. There was just the rhythmic weaving of my automatic body processes. Maybe I had narcolepsy.

I withdrew abruptly and hovered again in my wonderfully responsive astral body. "The hell with you," I thought as I looked down at my old body. "You'll wake up when you're ready. Meanwhile . . ."

I began testing the capabilities of my astral body . . . which looked to be made of a sort of glowing greenish jelly. Ectoplasm. I could change my size at will. One instant I towered tenuously above the beech tree, the next I was rumbling along a crack in its bark.

My light sensitivity extended as far up and down the electromagnetic spectrum as I wanted, and the sensitivity at each level could be adjusted. If I wanted to I could see by the sputtering flicker of cosmic rays.

But that was not all. I began noticing things that didn't fit into any theory of physics I'd ever heard of. There were blobs of . . . of *stuff* drifting around everywhere. Little pin-point bubbles and big dopey-looking balloons were filtering through the objects around me. With their dark wrinkles and foolish nodding, the big ones made me think of a drawing in one of Iris's Dr. Seuss books. I decided to call them bloogs like the good doctor had.

There was an arc-light near the graveyard, and it came on now. Little bloogs poured out of the light like bubbles off a swizzle-stick. Maybe they had something to do with energy. They were almost transparent, and all but imperceptible to the touch.

Wondering if I could think better now, I turned my attention back to the Continuum Problem. My mind was certainly more active than usual. Instantly I glimpsed threee or four new ways of arranging a set of c points in space. But my imagination was too active for mathematical thought. My ideas had a life of their own and refused to stand still while I contemplated them. The new arrangements of space grew legs and chased each other around the beech tree. I decided to look at them some other time.

These thoughts had brought back an unpleasant memory: Earlier I had imagined myself to be selling my soul for a solution to the continuum problem. "I didn't mean it," I whispered to the empty graveyard. "I didn't sign anything." There was no response.

I felt like doing some flying. Going to April seemed like the best bet. I looked around. It was almost completely dark now and the bloogs were thinning out. For some reason I wasn't worried that my body would die. But I was worried the police might find it and put it in jail. That had happened to me once back in college.

That time, I'd been into a fifth of bourbon at the tail end of some weeks of drinking. I was alone and it was dawn. I was sitting on the library steps watching the sun come up, and everything got warmer and lighter. Pastels shading all the way up to white as I ran to meet a being of light. Jesus. We'd talked wordlessly forever, until two cops started loading me into a paddy-wagon. "Where's the other guy?" I'd asked, and they'd exchanged a glance and answered, "He wasn't drinking."

I'd gotten suspended from school that time. Didn't really mean anything. But it would be different if the police picked me up today. Even if I wasn't drunk or stoned I looked it. And I wasn't a student anymore. I was a twenty-seven-year-old professor with, I recalled, a couple of old roaches in my coat pocket. I'd lose my job at the least and go to Attica at the worst. Rocky's bid for the presidency had left New York with the strictest drug laws in the country.

But it was really dark now, and I was nowhere near the road. The police wouldn't find me tonight. I hoped the Devil wouldn't come after me again either. I floated up, right through a big limb of the beech tree. It was partly hollow, and I could make out a pair of squirrels snuggled together in there. I was tempted to shrink down to squirrel-size and stay. But I missed April.

I floated up high above the tree-tops. I could see our house two blocks away on Tuna Street. I sped towards it.

While I was flying over, I stopped paying attention to the shape of my astral body, and it took on more comfortable lines. I angled through the roof and found myself in our hallway, near the mirror.

I was about the size and shape of a mushroom. I was hovering near the ceiling, and I could hear April vacuuming in the baby's room.

It was bright and cheerful in there, with a cluster of yellow bloogs around the light. Iris was in the crib and April was reaching to vacuum the cobwebs from the ceiling, her face up-turned. She seemed so beautiful there, her generous features relaxed, then smiling at a sound the baby made. Baby could see me. "Bah, ga bah," she said, gumming and waving her dough-girl arms my way.

I flew closer to April, and she brushed her hair back, looking through me. Things felt so right, so sane and good here in the nursery. This was where I belonged, this was the world of my heart's desire.

Wasn't there some way to just stay here? Maybe I was really dreaming, asleep on the living-room couch. I wished it with all my strength, visualizing exactly how I would look, curled up and snoozing, uncomfortable but tenacious on those purple cushions. I held on to the image and floated out of the baby's room and down the hall to the living room.

As I entered, someone lurched out the front door, slamming it behind. April ran into the living-room, alarmed by the sudden noise. "Felix?" she said, questioningly, "Felix?" But there was no answer that she could hear.

She opened the front door and looked out, but apparently it was too dark for her to see anything. When she turned back, she leaned over the hall table with a sudden exclamation of dismay. Her purse had been lying there, and someone had dumped it out and emptied her wallet.

Floating shapelessly near the ceiling I watched her refill her purse, light a cigarette and sit down. I wondered why she didn't call the police. She exhaled angrily, looked at her watch, then picked up a section of the paper, losing herself in the print.

Who had that been going out? A burglar? Or did April have a lover? I could easily have gone out to look, but I hated to leave.

After a few minutes April put the paper down, lit another cigarette and stared blankly at the dark window. Iris crawled in, smiled up at me, and pulled a stack of magazines off the table. My attention was caught by a new comic book which fell open, and I floated closer to get a better look at it.

Suddenly I am walking down a beautiful street in a world of simple colors and continuous forms. The sidewalk is smooth and unblemished, the lawn a uniform green besprent with yellow flowers, and my belly is snowy white where it sticks out from beneath my blue and black sailor suit.

I swivel my head around and admire how my neatly arranged tail-feathers sway back and forth with my purposeful waddle. My blue car with the big balloon tires is parked by the curb. I throw the key high into the air and vault over the door. With a happy, "Wak-wak-wak," I catch the key in my gloved hand.

I ease the car out into the street, and instantly I'm parked in front of Unca Scrooge's money bin. I get a suitcase out of the trunk, muttering things in a high-pitched splutter that even I can't understand. Something about a yacht.

Unca Scrooge is sitting behind his desk. "Captain Duck reporting for duty," I say, bending my beak into a long smile.

There is smoke around Scrooge's head, and he jumps straight up into the air. "It's about time, you lazy loafer!" He takes out his pocket watch and shoves it so close I almost fall over. "You're two hours late! My rival, McSkinflynt, is going to beat us to the treasure of the Lost Pyramid!"

"I was trying to finish this crossword puzzle," I explain, pulling out my puzzle book. "Do you know a nine-letter word, starting with 'D', for 'inference'?"

Scrooge is madder than ever. 'Yes," he fumes, raising his cane, "DE-DUCK-TION!" He chases me out of the building. I have the puzzle book in one hand and my suitcase in the other. My legs are a circular blur, and Scrooge is close behind.

Huey, Dewey and Louie have the ship ready, and soon we're on the high seas. I'm working on my crossword puzzle, the boys are fishing, and Scrooge is steering and scanning the horizon with his spyglass.

"What's a nine-letter word, starting with 'D', for 'airship'?" I call out. "DIRIGIBLE," the boys holler.

As I continue to work on my puzzle, a blimp hovers over our ship. MsSkinflynt leans out to taunt Scrooge. "The weather is lovely in the Yucatan this time of year."

Scrooge runs out on deck with a harpoon gun and fires on the dirigible. McSkinflynt has to crawl out of his cabin to patch up the hole. "Ta, ta," Scrooge calls as we speed off.

"What's a nine-letter word, starting with 'D', for 'tasty'?" I ask, finally looking up. Scrooge and the three boys are just staring at me over a pile of X-eyed fresh fish. I remember that I'm the cook as well as the captain, and I get to work. Before long we're all leaning back from a table covered with perfect fish skeletons. "Delicious," I observe, taking my puzzle book out of my chef's hat.

The next morning we sight land. We anchor offshore and the boys row us in under my direction. I wear my captain's hat for the ride. Scrooge just sits in the back of the dinghy worrying. As soon as we have beached the dinghy and gotten out, a dog-man comes running full tilt out of the jungle. "Don't stay here, Mr. McDuck," he says, breathlessly pushing the dinghy back into the water.

"Hold it," Scrooge hollers, "Did you find the pyramid?"

The dog-man doesn't answer. He is already rowing off. An arrow flies out of the jungle, knocking my puzzle book out of my hand. A monkey jumps out of a palm tree, grabs my book and runs off with it. I get angry and charge into the jungle after him.

Scrooge and the boys are looking at the arrow. "Aztec," Scrooge says and runs into the jungle at my heels. The boys take out a magnifying glass and look closer. There is a "Made in Japan" sticker on the arrow. "Wait," shouts Huey. "Unca," shouts Dewey. "Scrooge," shouts Louie.

Meanwhile Scrooge and I proceed to get totally lost in the jungle. Finally we sit down to rest near a stream surrounded by a clutter of vines and roots. "The ocean should be back that way," Scrooge says, pointing downstream.

"But I can hear surf over there," I say, pointing the other way.

Scrooge cocks his head and listens. Finally he leans very, very close and whispers, "Those are drums, Donald. Aztec ceremonial drums."

Just then, GLOM, a net comes down on us.

Meanwhile the boys have found a trail and have crept to within a half mile of the Lost Pyramid. They climb a tall tree and watch the goings-on. Some sort of pageant is taking place. As they watch, Scrooge and I are carried up the steps of the pyramid, bound and struggling. At the top the high priest stands behind a blood-stained altar. For some reason he is wearing sunglasses and a Western business suit.

"What is this *blood*?" I hiss to Unca Scrooge. "It's against the Code!"

But Scrooge has lost his glasses and can't see a thing. I try to tell him about the priest standing up there with a long obsidian knife in his up-stretched hands, but Scrooge just shushes me.

"McSkinflynt will save us," he says confidently. "The boys will lead him to us. Do you see the blimp yet, Donald?"

The priest's assistants lay us on the ground behind the altar. There is a sort of drain-hole under my body. I can't speak because the priest is squeezing my neck with one hand. With his stone knife he slits me open as casually as someone else would open a letter. I can't stand to look. For some reason it doesn't hurt.

When I finally open my eyes, I see my heart

raised high and pulsing in the last rays of the setting sun. Rough hands grab me and throw me down the back of the pyramid. I bounce down the steps and come to rest in some ferns at the bottom, lying on my back and unable to move.

My glazed eyes stare into the darkening heavens. I wonder what will happen to me. I have never known anyone who died. I see a dark silhouette against the dim sky. It's McSkinflynt's blimp. The boys have signalled him somehow, and are already aboard. The "Aztecs" run in terror, and Scrooge is hauled up with a rope sling.

I hear the boys' sweet voices for the last time. Why didn't I ever tell them I loved them? "Where's Unca Donald?" they ask. "We saw him disappear behind that altar."

"I didn't see," says Scrooge. "But don't worry about that rascal. He'll turn up."

The blimp drifts off and their voices fade. The nightly jungle rain begins falling, and I lie there on the wet earth as the blackness closes in.

6
Jesus and the Devil

An indefinite interval of time passed. Slowly I remembered I was not really Donald Duck. But this realization brought no change in my surroundings. It was dark and it was raining. I sharpened my senses and cast about. I was next to a cypress, there were gravestones nearby, over there was a muddy fresh grave. I was back in the Temple Hill graveyard.

With a jerk I stood up and looked around. I was still just in my translucent green astral body. I spotted the beech tree where I'd left my flesh. I went over, determined to stick with it until it woke up or the police came and got it.

The beech tree arched over me, its branches like drowned fingers. My body was gone.

I scanned the area, straining my powerful senses to the limit. But the only unusual thing I noticed was a greenish glow moving towards me across the graveyard. At first I took it for just another bloog, but suddenly the glow rushed me. I shrank into a dense globe and it surrounded me. It was all I could do to keep from being absorbed. This thing, this ghost, was all around me, squeezing, pushing, prying with tendrils of ectoplasm.

I was still whole, yet I was inside another astral being—bouncing gently like a fetus in the womb. I felt about for some signs of intelligence, and began to pick up psychic vibrations.

Blind sorrow, uncomprehending loneliness, unreasoning fear. A man's smiling face, close-up. White curtains. Rhythmic pains, harsh light on brushed steel, a gagging sweetness. A screaming yellow skull which came closer with each pain.

I tried to recall who had died in Bernco in the last few weeks. Suddenly I remembered April telling me about a woman who had died in childbirth that month. Her name had been Kathy something. This must be her ghost.

Whenever I tried to uncurl a little, the probing tendrils came at me again. I was being carried towards that fresh grave. I could feel the ghost's yearning to nestle in the coffin with me. "Come on baby," it crooned. "We go night-night."

I decided to make my move. I punched a pseudopod through the thinnest part of the creature around me and flowed out onto the ground. I planted feet and assumed a humanoid form . . . with red eyes and big black wings. I knew how scary an apparition that could be.

The ghost was swarming towards me again. I curled my wings forward, held out my hands with the palms cupped, and loosed a terrible cry. The ghost gibbered and fled back to its grave.

I felt a moment of peace then, with the night breeze blowing through me. It had stopped raining. The moon sailed through the tattered clouds like the Egyptian boat of the dead. What was that noise I had made? Sort of a scream breaking into high laughter sliding down into a coughing snarl. Highly effective. But I felt a little sorry for the ghost I'd driven off. I should have tried to talk to her, bring her back to sanity. She had been like a drowning swimmer grabbing me in deep water, and I'd treated it like a death threat.

I heard a noise behind me. I scooted my face around to the back of my head in time to see the Devil gliding in for a smooth landing, his black wings outstretched, his red eyes fixed on mine. I tensed to flee.

"Hold it right there, Rayman," the Devil said in a gravelly voice. "You can't outrun me." He looked me over slowly and spoke again with rising anger. "Impersonating the Devil. Leaving your body. Trying to black-market your soul. PK-ing those kids on the steps. Yelling at people. You think you're too good for the rules, don't you?"

Feebly I tried to protest, but he just smiled terribly and sank his taloned hand into my shoulder. "You're going to Hell, Felix," the Devil said, making his voice light and mocking. "You're going to Hell right now."

"Wait," I gasped. "You can't. I'm not dead yet."

"If you're not dead, where's your body?" the Devil spat out. He snapped his fingers and a crack yawned open in the ground before us. Far below I could see the flames and the tortured souls, writhing like heaps of maggots. Screams and a faint stench came wafting up with the heated air.

Only God could help me now. Desperately I prayed. "Dear Jesus Christ, please save my worthless ass." I reached out with that central spot of my mind which could sometimes touch God. "Dear sweet Jesus, get me out of this."

The Devil released his hold on me and strode over to the crack. "In here, Felix," he said gently. "Let's go. Jesus isn't going to answer you."

I kept on praying, more and more merged, less and less there. I put my whole attention on that central spot, the flaw, the source, the singularity, the lurking fear, the scream, the knot, the egg I never saw . . . I put my energy there and pushed. Everything got white and in the afterimage Jesus was talking to me.

"I'm here, Felix," Jesus said, "I'll take care of you."

I opened my eyes. The Devil was standing by the crack he'd opened up, looking angry but uncomfortable. Jesus was next to me. Like the Devil, He had appeared in the form I had always imagined. He had long hair, a beard, sandals and brown robes. I couldn't meet His eyes.

There was a long silence. The moon was out from the clouds. I could have counted the veins in the leaves at my feet.

"He's not dead," Jesus said to the Devil. "You know that." I gave a sigh of relief. I had been wondering.

"Where is my body?" I asked in a tight whisper. Jesus and the Devil exchanged a significant glance, but no one answered.

"You'll be seeing me again, Rayman," the Devil snarled abruptly. "Your ass is mine." He jumped into the crack in the ground. A tongue of flame shot up, and then the ground sealed back up.

I turned to look at Jesus. I was trembling all over and beginning to sob. He put His hand on my shoulder and strength flowed into me like living water. "There's no turning back now," He said quietly.

"You're going to climb Mount On, and I want you to take Kathy, that girl who died in childbirth. You're responsible for her now."

I nodded several times. "Of course, Jesus. Certainly. But what mountain do you mean? And what about my body?"

Jesus smiled. I finally had the courage to look at his eyes, filled with terrible peace. "Your body is with . . . friends. Mount On is in Cimön. It's infinite, Absolutely Infinite, but you'll find a way to the end." He took His hand off my shoulder and turned to go, then paused, looking towards the grave where I'd chased that ghost. "Kathy needs someone to help her leave Earth. Be sure you don't let her come back with you. For your own good as well as hers." He started walking off.

I stumbled after Him. There were so many questions to ask. "And what should I do then?" I called. "What should I do with the rest of my life?"

"Just don't forget me," came the answer. "I'm always here." And then He was gone.

My thoughts turned to Absolute Infinity. That was bigger than alef-null, bigger than alef-one . . . bigger than any conceivable level. I was supposed to go to Cimön and climb a mountain Absolutely Infinite in height. I wished I still had that pamphlet from Sunfish. Who had put it there for me? Probably the Devil, to lure me out of my body again.

Mount On! I figured God would be at the top. I could hardly wait to start. I might even solve the Continuum Problem on the way up.

But first I had to make friends with that crazy ghost. Suddenly gloomy, I drifted over to her grave. I really didn't feel like going down to that coffin. But, I told myself sternly, Jesus probably hadn't been particularly eager to come to Bernco just now. And He'd done it calmly and lovingly.

Slowly I managed to work myself into a feeling of love for my fellow man. That poor woman . . . dead in childbirth and out of her mind with shock. I held my nose, shrank to the size of a doll, and sank down into the ground.

As soon as I came into the coffin the ghost pounced on me with a cry. Once again I formed myself into a sphere, and her clawing fingers slid off me. I looked around a little while the hysterical wraith worked me over. I could see fairly well in the fitful "light" of the cosmic rays.

The coffin was lined with a tufted fabric which was smooth to the touch. Clearly a top-of-the-line model. The body was not as bad as I'd expected. It was well-embalmed and gave off only the faintest infra-red glow of decay. Of course the flesh had sort of puckered in everywhere and the lips had drawn way back and the eyes . . . well . . .

I stopped looking around. There was a momentary lull in the ghost's scrabbling at me. I formed a mouth and spoke up. "Kathy, Kathy, Kathy. Relax. I'm here to help you." The ghost stopped moving entirely, and I repeated my message. "I'm Felix," I added. "Felix Rayman."

"Can I go home soon, doctor?" She asked in an odd, bright voice. She had fit herself back into her body.

I plunged ahead. "I'm going to take you to where God lives," I said. "On top of a big mountain."

"Why are you talking that way," she moaned. "Jut bring me my baby. Why haven't I seen my baby?"

"Your baby is at home," I said. "Your baby is fine."

"Can I go home now?" she asked again.

"You're dead," I said bluntly. "Your only home now is with God, and I have to take you to him."

"Who says you have to," she asked in a more normal voice. "I want to stay right here."

"Look, Jesus Himself told me to get you. You could think of me as an angel of the Lord."

"You're not an angel. You had black wings before. Angels have white wings."

"I'm sorry I did that," I said. "I was scared of you. I'm just a person. But you must know where you are if you remember the black wings."

"What I think," she said in a practical tone, "is that this is the worst dream I ever had. I keep lying here and waiting to wake up."

"This is no dream," I said shortly. Squeezed into that coffin I was beginning to suffer from sensory deprivation. Odd and irrelevant images were dancing past. An alligator with a megaphone hollered at me while I caressed a carpet of naked breasts. I really didn't want to slip back into a dream. I was still depressed about poor Donald Duck. "Come on Kathy," I urged, "let's go up and get some air."

I zipped up to the surface and took on my basic nude Felix Rayman shape. The moon was down and the sky was clear. I figured it was about four in the morning. Kathy came up hesitantly. As before, her shape was amorphous . . . a blob with a few tentacles.

"Do you like my coffin?" she asked, using a crooked rip for amouth. "It's pink with red satin inside."

"It looks expensive," I said finally.

"It was. I watched them buy it. Frank wanted to just get a pine box. But my father insisted on buying the best coffin they make. The undertaker didn't even have one on hand." She made a sound that might have been a laugh. "They had to hold the funeral up for three days while they shipped the coffin here from the factory. Frank was really mad at my father."

I liked her voice. Hearing about her father and her husband made me embarassed to be naked. Modestly I retracted my penis and testicles into my body mass.

"How did you do that?" Kathy asked with interest. "And what happened to your wings?"

"I can take any shape I want. You probably can too. Try!"

Her mouth grew dripping fangs and she reached two giant lobster claws out towards me. I backed away.

"Cut it out! Stop acting like a monster."

"Why shouldn't I," she said. "I'm a ghost."

"Didn't you ever hear stories where the ghost is a beautiful lady in white?" I pointed at a nearby monument topped by a statue of a woman. She had a Roman nose and long hair flowing down to cover the nipples of her firm breasts. "How about something along those lines?"

"If I'm dead, I'm through with being a sex-object. I'm going to pick my *own* shape this time." She pulled her claws back in and hovered uncertainly.

And then she began to change. First she shrank to a compact mass. Then four lobes bulged out. Two grew long and flat, one became short and pointed, and one was short and wedgy. Her ectoplasm flowed and molded fine details until finally I could see the form she had chosen.

"A seagull," she said, cocking her head and fixing me with a bright green eye. "Just like in that great book."

"I never read that book," I said. I felt stuffy and a little foolish in my bowdlerized body. I reverted to the mushroom shape I'd used earlier. I made myself a foot high and formed a slit-like mouth on my top. "I guess I'll use this shape," I piped.

"A penis?" Kathy exclaimed with amusement. "First you make it disappear, and now that's all that's left!" She flew off laughing. I gave up and went back to the original unexpurgated Felix Rayman.

7

Let the Dead Help You

After a few minutes Kathy flew back and perched on a branch in front of me. "That was fun," she said. "That's the farthest I've been from my coffin yet. I'm glad you came along to convince me I'm dead. As long as I thought I might be dreaming, I wanted to stay near my body to take care of it."

"But now you're ready to move on?"

"I guess. What was that you said about going to see God? I'm not so sure I want to. He'll soak me right up and there'll be nothing left." She stretched out a wing and examined it. "I don't see why I shouldn't do a little travelling of my own. I've never even been to New York City."

"Oh come on," I said. "We're going to climb a mountain higher than all the infinite numbers. I've already figured out how to get started."

"That sounds like math. I hate math. Weren't you a teacher at the college?"

I nodded, then asked, "What about you?"

"I studied American literature. I read everything Jack Kerouac ever wrote, and I've never been out of Upstate New York."

"What about your husband?"

"He does construction. Kitchens, bathrooms, remodelling. He hunts, but he'll never take me on a vacation. How did you die?"

"I don't think I'm really dead. Jesus told me my body is waiting somewhere."

Kathy laughed harshly. "That's a good one. Here you are acting like you're going to be my big brother or something, and you haven't even accepted your own death."

I really didn't feel like discussing it. I was afraid she might convince me. "Forget it. Right now we've got other problems. Whether you believe the reasons or not, I've got to stick with you and help you get to God. But you want to tour the Earth. All right. We'll do some touring, see anything you like. Then we'll head out for the Beyond. O.K.?"

"We'll see."

I wondered what she had looked like when she was alive. She must have been fairly pretty to get away with being so stubborn.

"Let's start with New York," she said, flying up to a higher branch. "How do we get there?"

"Let's go up a few thousand feet and head East. When we hit the coast, we'll follow it South."

The sun was just coming up, and the sky was beautiful. There were bloogs of every color moving purposefully along twisting space curves. It was exhilarating to fly through them towards the brilliant sun.

To fly I simply pulled myself along with a certain part of my mind. It was as if I was sliding along an invisible fiber that passed through my body from head to toe. By tightening certain parts of my spine, I could accelerate indefinitely. When I released the tension I just kept zipping frictionlessly along at the same speed. Kathy kept up with me easily. Her wings served no real purpose, and she rarely bothered to flap them. At first we raced, but then we levelled off at a few hundred miles per hour. I stopped worrying about what came next and enjoyed myself.

When we hit the coast we turned right.

Before long we could see the smoke and glittering glass of a big city. I looked for the twin towers of the World Trade Center, but couldn't spot them. Then we were over the city and everything looked wrong. Manhattan is an island, but this city had a river running through it.

"Where's Fifth Avenue and the Village," Kathy wanted to know.

"I don't think this is right."

We were slowly drifting down towards a tall glass building with some of its windows missing. Suddenly I realized. "This is Boston."

"That's O.K." Kathy answered, "I've never been here either. Where are the nice stores?"

"Don't tell me you want to look at clothes. If you think I'm going to go to dozens . . ."

"No one wants you to come," she interrupted. "We can split up and meet on top of this building."

I spotted a clocktower nearby. It was around nine in the morning. "Let's meet at noon," I suggested. "The big stores are all around here, and there's a lot of stuff in Cambridge you might like too." I pointed out M.I.T. and Harvard to her and we split up.

I went over to the Boston Museum of Fine Arts with a view to visiting the Monets. At first they looked wrong . . . patchy. I was seeing too much ultraviolet. When I'd cut my vision down to normal human sensitivity, the pictures looked as beautiful as ever, but looking at them made me impatient. It seemed like a waste of time to be doing normal tourist things in my astral body.

I was beginning to wonder why I hadn't seen any other ghosts. There were just the bloogs everywhere. Maybe it was dangerous to be a ghost? I started in fear the next time a bloog nodded past me. I began speeding up and down the halls of the museum looking for another ghost.

I found one with the Greek marbles. He held himself in the traditional flowing sheet shape, and at first I mistook him for a bloog. But the light green glow distinguished him.

"Up or down?" he said as I approached. "Up or down?"

"Hello," I said. "My name is Felix."

"Your name don't matter. Up or down?"

I wasn't sure what he meant, but tried to answer him. "Well, first I'm going back downtown and then I'm hoping to go up to Cimön . . . all the way."

"Nobody lasts it out. Up or down. Up or down." He started to drift towards the entrance, and I tagged along.

"Have you seen many others?" I asked. "Many other ghosts?"

"Hundreds of 'em. Thousands. Up or down."

"Does something make them leave? How come you can stay?"

We were on the steps of the museum now. A thin student walked right through me. The old ghost chuckled unpleasantly. "You all think you're going all the way up. But it ain't so easy. You get scared and stick around. And then you get nabbed." He held up a drooping arm with two finger-like projections. The sign of the Evil Eye.

"You mean the Devil catches . . ."

"Hist!" the old ghost interrupted, looking around frantically. "Don't say it!"

Nothing happened, and my companion started talking again. "I've stuck it out fifty years."

"How do you do it? Do you pray a lot?"

"Praying's for suckers," the ghost said contemptuously. "I ain't going up and I ain't going down. I keep nice and quiet and he," again he held out the two horns, "he don't bother looking for me. He goes after the showboats." The ghost paused, looking at me with disapproval. "The way you're radiating . . ." He didn't need to finish the sentence.

"Well, I'm going to start up today," I repeated. I had a sudden paranoid conviction that this ghost worked as a spotter for the Devil.

"Where you taking off from?" he asked, as if to confirm my suspicions.

"None of your business."

"That's the way to be. You could learn to play it safe." A note of entreaty crept into the ghost's voice. "Why don't you forget that Cimön baloney and come in with me. I could show you the ropes . . ."

"Maybe later. Thanks anyway."

As I started off I could hear the old ghost repeating, "Up or down. Up or down."

I still had over an hour to kill until my meet with Kathy. My conversation with the ghost had put my nerves on edge. I wondered how long we could last here. It seemed best to keep moving.

I went back downtown and sped up and down the bloogy streets. Here and there I saw tattered old ghosts, and once a fresh ghost sped towards me as if for help. I was scared of a trick and shied away into an apartment building.

I angled through the building, cutting through floors and ceilings. On the top floor I chanced into a bathroom where a woman was about to take a shower. She had long coppery hair, big hips and full breasts. She was in her late thirties, and her body had a soft, broken-in look. I made myself small and followed her into the shower stall. As she washed herself I looked her over from every angle, finally coming to rest between her knees.

I stared up at her dripping pubic hair, at her large and small curves. She rubbed herself there with a soapy hand, and I exerted all my will to make her keep rubbing. She seemed to feel my horny vibrations. She leaned back against the wall and began using both hands. On a sudden inspiration I took on her form and fit myself into her body. When she came, I felt like I was coming too. Then she started shampooing her hair. I left through the ceiling.

In the next hour I managed to find several more attractive women in bed or in the bathroom. With the pressure of my disembodied will I was able to get two of them to masturbate while I luxuriated in their excited flesh. It definitely seemed to be possible for a ghost to influence the behaviour of a person. I could see turning into a full-time incubus.

At noon I was waiting for Kathy on top of the Prudential tower. Thirty minutes, an hour went by and she still hadn't shown. Maybe she had decided to give me the slip? Or maybe she had just lost track of the time.

I flew over Cambridge. I paused to admire the strange, polyhedral bloogs streaming out of the M.I.T. buildings, and then I began searching the streets, looking for a green seagull among the crowds of people and bloogs. Nothing.

I decided to try something different. I flew up a few hundred feet and concentrated on what Kathy's voice and vibrations had been like. I closed down my sensitivity to all other inputs and scanned all of Cambridge. Still nothing.

Tuned only to Kathy's wavelength, I swept back and forth over Boston. And then I caught something like a strangled scream. I homed in on the sensation and traced it to a storefront in South Boston. "Madame Jeanne Delacroix," a hand-painted sign in the window read, "SPIRIT HEALING. PSYCHIC SURGERY. SECRET LOVE PROBLEMS. Let the Dead Help You!"

The large window behind the sign was covered with a dingy cream curtain. You could see where lettering saying "GIANELLI'S PRODUCE" had been scraped off. Beat-looking cars were parked along one side of the street, and there was a bar and liquor-store a half block away. In a rubble-filled lot between Madame Jeanne's and the bar, some skinny black men were drinking wine on a bench they had made by ripping out a car's back seat. The sunlight was pouring down on them.

Kathy was definitely inside Madame Jeanne's. I could feel her vibrations perfectly now. She was frantic, trapped. I tried to signal her, but she was too panicky to notice. I went into the vacant lot and cautiously stuck my head in through Madame Jeanne's wall.

A big black woman in a purple robe and a dirty pink turban was sitting at a card table with her back to me. She wore several rosaries around her neck, and lying on the table in front of her was a black rooster with his throat torn out. The rooster's blood was in a bowl. Something about the warm blood was very attractive to me. I had a strong urge to bathe myself in it.

I could sense that Kathy was in a round box which rested on the table. It was decorated with Christian symbols. I guessed it was a pyx stolen from some church. Apparently she couldn't get out of it. To me, and probably to Madame Jeanne, the sound of Kathy's struggles filled the room.

Across the table from Madame Jeanne sat a slender young black woman with a limp child in her lap. A boy, about three. He seemed to be in some kind of coma or catatonic state. His breathing was even and his eyes were open, but all his muscles were slack.

"I have obtain the requisitory spirit driver for your first-born son," Madame Jeanne was saying in an island-accented voice. "Lay him down on the altar of Baal."

The young woman laid her son on the card-table, which sagged but held the weight. Madame Jeanne prepared to put Kathy into the boy's body. She dipped a long silk cord into the rooster's blood. Using a pair of plastic chopsticks she led one end of the dripping cord in through the boy's left nostril, down his throat, and back out his mouth. She attached the two ends of the cord to opposite points on the circumference of a round two-sided mirror.

Humming tunelessly, Madame Jeanne lit a candle between the pyx and the boy's head, then lifted the mirror up by the cords to a point over the candle. She pulled the cords into a taut horizontal on either side of the mirror, and began rolling the cords between her fingers. The mirror spun. The reflection of the candle danced inside the spinning mirror like a firefly in a glass sphere.

Kathy was supposed to fly into the mirror and be permanently absorbed into the little boy. Somehow I was sure it would work. Madame Jeanne looked like she knew what she was doing. I was going to have to take action.

There was no doubt that Madame Jeanne would be able to see me. But she hadn't looked my way yet. I would hide until the crucial instant when she opened the pyx.

Madame Jeanne was talking to the young mother again. "You will handle the radiation gem, sister." She handed the mirror over. "Do as I have done and likewise." The young woman began twirling the mirror over the candle flame. I came all the way into the room and edged up behind Madame Jeanne.

She was swaying slowly now and mumbling, "Amen. Ever and forever, glory the and power the, kingdom the is thine for. Evil from . . ." She was reciting the Lord's Prayer backwards. I made myself small and darted past her to hide inside the candle flame.

"Heaven in art who Father our," she concluded, and reached to open the pyx. The mirror over the candle was spinning steadily. I couldn't look at it without being drawn towards it. Silently I prayed for help.

When the pyx opened, there was an instant when Kathy was too shocked to move. Quickly I formed myself into a wall between her and the mirror.

"Come away, Kathy, come away."

She began moving through me, but then Madame Jeanne noticed me and screamed. I projected some ugly claws out towards her to make it louder.

The noise surprised the woman holding the mirror. Her spinning faltered, and the wet cord slipped out of her fingers. The mirror fell on the table and broke. Kathy was flying around the candle flame like a moth. I kept talking to her, but it wasn't sinking in.

Madame Jeanne was screaming still, but now it was words. "Black father, hah, I say to you, yeah, I say rider of the sea, the superbest blossom, be with thy servant, hah, at the altar, yeah, I priestess of the night . . ." I could see something beginning to materialize at her side. She saw it too and began screaming louder and faster. "I will it, yeah, jumby you are coming in the domicile . . ."

The form grew clearer, developing like a print in a safelit bath of chemicals. It was going to be the Devil. Kathy was stuck in the candle flame. I surrounded her and pulled.

"Frank?" she said faintly. "Can I go home now?"

"Kathy!" I blasted. "The Devil's coming. Go straight up!"

Just then he solidified next to Madame Jeanne. He bent to sniff the bowl of blood, and then he spotted me. His thick lips parted slowly.

"Follow me, Kathy," I shrilled, and rocketed through the ceiling. I didn't look back, and I didn't stop for a long time.

8

The Speed of Light

Kathy caught up with me somewhere near the edge of the Earth's atmosphere.

When I heard her calling me, I stopped. I was tense and ready to flee. The girlish seagull perched on my shoulder. I looked down through the empty miles of space beneath my feet. Nothing but bloogs following each other along invisible lines of force. It looked like the Devil hadn't bothered to chase us.

"I'm not going back there, Kathy."

She gave a delicate shudder. "But what about that poor little boy?"

"Madame Jeanne will find another soul. Or his mother will try a different doctor. I don't know." She had distracted me from the point. "We are not going back to Earth," I said firmly.

"I shouldn't have trusted her," Kathy said quietly.

"Who?"

"She was yellow. A yellow bell, and her voice echoed. I met her in Cambridge and we flew over to South Boston together. She was going to show me where she stays." Kathy's voice was distant. "She took me to Madame Jeanne's, and then they cut the rooster's neck. I was so thirsty . . ."

I interrupted. "I didn't see any yellow ghost at Madame Jeanne's."

"She lived *inside* Madame Jeanne. She said it was safer for a ghost to be inside a live person."

I told her about my conversation at the museum. "It seems," I concluded, "that if you're a ghost, you're supposed to leave Earth for Cimön."

"How?"

"Cimön is alef-null miles from Earth. Alef-null is the first infinite number. It's like One, Two, Three, . . . Alef-Null. The three dots stand for forever."

"How are we supposed to get past forever?" Kathy asked impatiently. "No matter how fast we fly, we'll never be infinitely far away from Earth."

"We keep accelerating. The first billion miles takes us 2 hours. The next takes us 1 hour. We do the third billion miles in a half hour. Each billion miles takes half as long as the one before. We can go alef-null billion miles in $2+1+\frac{1}{2}+\frac{1}{4}+\ .\ .\ .$ hours. That adds up to four hours."

"I thought no one could go faster than light," Kathy challenged.

"Neither will we. All we'll *really* be doing is accelerating up to the speed of light."

"Then how come it looks like we'll be going so much faster?"

"It's all in the relativistic time dilation. Don't worry about it."

Kathy was doubtful. "In four hours we'll be infinitely far away from Earth? Milestone alef-null?"

I nodded.

Kathy perched on my back and spread her wings. Her body trembled like a taut bow. I put my arms out ahead of me Superman style. We put the hammer down and were off in the direction of the galactic center.

The first part of the trip was dull. Although we were accelerating steadily, it still took an hour to get out of the solar system. And then we had an hour and a half of vacuum till the next star.

About three hours into our trip it began to get interesting. Objectively we were doing about .7 the speed of light. Because of our distorted time and length standards, it felt like we were doing three times that. Weird relativistic effects began setting in.

It seemed like we were looking out of a cave. All behind us and on both sides of us there was the dead absolute nothing called "Elsewhere" in relativity theory. The stars had somehow all scooted their images around to in front of us. We accelerated harder.

The thousand light-year trip across the galaxy only seemed to take half an hour. But what a half hour. I would be looking out our speed-cone at the vast disk of stars that lay ahead of me . . . most of them clinging to the edge. Slowly one of the stars would detach itself from the clustered edge and accelerate along a hyperbolic path towards the

center, then ZOW it would whip past us and go
arcing back out to the edge of our visual field.

There was a pattern to the flicker of passing
stars, and I began to get into it. It was like listening
to the clicking of train wheels. Everything but the
swooping pulses of light faded from my attention.
I pushed to make the flickering come faster.

There were patterns to the flicker . . . star clusters . . . and as we accelerated more I began to see
second- and third-order patterns. Suddenly the
stars stopped. We were out of the galaxy.

Our visual field had contracted so much that I
felt myself to be looking out of a porthole. There
was dark on all sides and I knew fear. My back was
a knot of pain, but I drove myself to accelerate
more and more, to make the porthole smaller.

A few squashed disks of light tumbled out from
infinity and whizzed back. Then more and more
came twisting past. Galaxies. I felt like a gnat in a
snowstorm. We flew through some of the
galaxies. Inside was a happy blur. We were going
much too fast to see the individual stars hurtle
past.

We pushed harder, harder. We hit a galaxy
every few seconds now, and as before I began to
detect higher-order patterns in the stroboscopic
flicker.

From then on that was all I could see . . . a
flicker which would build and build to an almost
constant flash, abruptly drop in frequency, and
then build again. At the end of each cycle we
reached a higher level of clustering and the light
became brighter.

I was on the ragged edge of exhaustion. The
strobing was building castled landscapes in my

mind. My lucidity was fading fast as I stared into the more and more involuted blur of light before me. I tried to make it come faster.

There was still a certain depth to the pattern of light ahead of us, but I noticed that the harder I pushed the accelerator, the shallower and more two-dimensional the scene in front of me became. I concentrated on flattening it out.

The energy to push no longer seemed to emanate from me or from Kathy. It was as if I were somehow ram-jetting the incoming light right through us . . . applying only a certain shift of perspective to move us ever faster.

"Come on Kathy," I cried. My voice warped and dragged. "It's just a little further. One big push!"

With a final effort we turned the universe into a single blinding point of light. I stopped pushing and the point unfurled into a flat vertical landscape. An infinite half-plane. The lower edge was sea and the upper half was an endless mountain. It looked like a tremendous painting, like Breughel's *Fall of Icarus*.

We crashed into the landscape like a starling into a billboard. And landed on a green hillside. The ground was soft, and it giggled when we hit. Thop. Gli-gli-gli-hi-hi.

My body was solid. I sat up. Kathy hopped off my back and fluttered awkwardly to land a few feet away. She needed her wings now.

There was a tingle of salt in the steady breeze. In the distance I could see a shimmering blue line of water. A sea. Was that prickly smudge a harbor?

There was something funny about the perspective here. The sea seemed to be tilting away from us. It was as if it were just a continuation of the slope we found ourselves on.

I turned and looked behind us, half expecting to see only blackness. But instead there was a mountain. Mount On. Green and yellow meadows humped and reared themselves up towards the heavens. Here and there large boulders lay in the grass. Higher up, outcroppings of rock poked through the meadows, which grew ever steeper. I peered higher. Way up there I could see jagged peaks, painfully sharp, piled one atop the other. There was no end. The mountain stretched forever into the luminous blue sky.

To the left and right were more hills leading from more sea up to more mountain. The overall perspective was very strange. It was as if the whole landscape were somehow flat, with all those cliffs and peaks an illusion. It was only that the force of gravity was trying to drag everything out to sea.

A mile up the slope from us I noticed a building. It looked like one of those huge old European resort hotels. As I stared at it I could make out more and more features. Terraces, balconies, painted window frames and whitewashed walls. Something about the upper floors seemed peculiar. It was as if there were too much there. I had noticed the same thing about the pattern of rocks and grass on the mountainside beyond. If one stared at certain spots, more and more new details kept appearing.

"Let's go look at that hotel," I suggested to Kathy. She had been staring down the slope towards the distant sea, and I had to repeat myself to get her attention.

"Seagulls don't climb mountains, Felix," she

said softly. "My path is down there. I can feel it
. . ." Her voice trailed off in a jumble I couldn't
make out.

I thought back on my conversation with Jesus.
Had it only been 12 hours ago? I had promised to
save Kathy, to bring her up from Earth. I was going
to climb Mount On. Was I supposed to drag her
along?

I sank into thought, and before long I had an
answer. Once you had escaped the Devil, you still
had to find your way to God. But there were many
ways.

I reached out towards Kathy and she flew up
and landed on my hand. Her feet were strong and
her claws pricked into me. I held her against my
chest and stroked her feathers. I could feel the
rapid beating of her heart.

"I'll miss you," I said finally. I started to say
more, but only made a sort of babbling sound
which faded into silence.

She rubbed her bill against my shoulder. "We'll
meet again," she said gently. "Over the sea,
beyond the mountain . . . we'll meet again.
Thank you, Felix. Don't forget me."

I held her up in the air and she flew off, clumsily
at first but then with growing grace. She circled
back towards me once, dipped her wings, then
wheeled and flew strongly towards the sea. I
watched the dwindling speck until it merged
with the distant blue haze. I was completely
alone.

PART II

"The actual infinite in its highest
form has created and sustains us,
and in its secondary transfinite
forms occurs all around us and
even inhabits our minds."

—Georg Cantor

9
Hilbert's Hotel

I tried to fly to the hotel, but discovered that here you needed wings to fly. I started walking across the fields sloping up towards it, circling around the larger boulders. I was naked.

The grass in the fields was short and springy. It felt nice on my bare feet. I hadn't heard a giggle since we'd landed, and I decided the ground wasn't alive after all. It was something like an Alpine meadow on Earth, except that there was no sun. The light came from everywhere.

I spotted a wiggly groove in the meadow and went over to it. It was a tiny brook, as I had hoped. I knelt to drink the water, clear and so cold that I could feel it all the way down. There had to be glaciers up there somewhere.

I toiled up the gradually steepening slope for something like an hour, and the hotel was still not much nearer. The air was very clear. I looked back. We had landed several thousand feet above the level of the sea, but surely Kathy was already on it. She was lucky to have wings.

Again I puzzled over the curious flatness of the landscape. I could feel that the slope was getting steeper, but it seemed to lie evenly with the rest of the land. I walked another half hour. The hotel didn't look any nearer at all. I sat down to rest, sucking in rapid lungfuls of the tenuous air.

Tiny yellow flowers were growing in the grass around me. I leaned close to examine one. At first it looked like a simple five-pointed star. But then I noticed that at each point of the star there was a smaller star. I looked closer. At each point of the secondary stars there were still smaller stars, tipped by tinier stars, which had . . . In a sudden flash I saw the whole infinitely regressing pattern at once.

Trembling with excitement I held a blade of grass up to the sky. Halfway down its length it forked into two bladelets. In turn, each bladelet forked into two bladelets. Which branched and rebranched, again and again . . . With a snatch of my mind I comprehended the whole infinite structure at once. No wonder the grass was springy.

I looked at the landscape around me with new eyes. Kathy and I had flown past alef-null. Out here infinity was as real as a pie in the face. And the body I had was equipped to deal with it.

I thought back on the sort of mental twitch I had used to see the infinite complexity of the flower and leaf. Maybe . . .

"La," I said, "La, La, La, . . ." I did that thing with my mind and let my voice speed up into a high-pitched gabble. A few seconds later I had finished saying alef-null "La"s.

Next I tried to count through all the natural numbers, but I got hung up trying to pronounce 217,876,234,110,899,720,123,650,123,124,687,857. I decided to use a simpler system and started over. "One. One plus one. One plus one plus one. . . ." In a minute I was done. I had counted up to alef-null.

I looked critically at the distance between me and the hotel. I sharpened my vision and began counting the boulders dotting the meadow. Sure enough there were alef-null of them to pass. No wonder I hadn't felt like I was getting any closer. If I walked past ten more or a thousand more boulders there'd still be alef-null of them left.

But my tongue had been able to do alef-null things when I'd counted out loud. Why shouldn't my legs be able to do it too? I stood up and started running. Once again there was some sort of head trick I had to do to keep speeding up. The endless energy I needed to keep moving my body faster and faster flowed into me from the landscape around me. I had a feeling that the mountain was drawing me closer, that the air was parting to let me pass, that the ground was forming footholds for me.

A minute to the first boulder, half a minute to the next, a quarter minute to the third . . . Two minutes later I was standing in the grounds of the hotel, more than a little out of breath. It had been like the trip from Earth, but without the relativistic distortions. I was in a world beyond the physics of Earth.

The hotel was built of stone. The outside walls

were covered with a rough cream-colored plaster,
and the window frames were painted a dark red.
Although the hotel was only two hundred feet
high, it had infinitely many floors. The trick was
that the upper floors got thinner and thinner. Each
successive layer of rooms was flattened enough to
use only one twentieth of the remaining hotel
height . . . so there was always room for nineteen
more floors.

The building had no roof of course. None was
needed, as each floor was protected from the ele-
ments by the floors above it. I stared up at one of
the slit-like upper windows and wondered how
anyone could use a room with an inch-high ceiling . . . let alone a room with such a low ceiling
that an electron would have to stoop to get in.

The fields beyond the hotel were open, and I
spotted several groups of strollers. A raised res-
taurant terrace was attached to the side of the
hotel, and a number of guests were lounging
there. Not many of them were human.

I made my way along a path towards the hotel
entrance. A number of trees and bushes were
planted on the grounds. They all branched endlessly into fantastic jumbles of detail. I foolishly
stuck a hand into one of the bushes, and it took me
some minutes to disentangle myself. A huge jellyfish watched me blankly from a bench. I hurried
on with a stiff nod.

To my relief the staircase leading up to the hotel
was finite. The lobby was dim and large, but not
abnormally so. I walked over to the desk-man and
blurted out the age-old question, "Where am I?"

I spoke too loudly, and a number of the guests

hanging around the lobby broke off their conversations to listen.

The clerk seemed to be human, though a full black beard concealed most of his face. He was dressed in the 1900 style, and he peered at me through gold-rimmed spectacles with little oval lenses.

"Where do you *think* you are?" He held a fountain pen poised over a little pad of paper, as if to record my answer.

"Is . . . is this heaven?"

The clerk made a quick notation. "Generally we call it Flipside. Flipside of Cimön."

The last name echoed in my ears. I'd really made it. If only I had read that pamphlet more carefully.

"How did a fresher like you get here anyway?" the clerk broke in.

"I flew."

He looked impressed. "Spontaneous? Not bad, not bad at all. I assume you want to climb Mount On?"

"Not right away . . ." I began. For some reason this drew an amused smile. I let it pass. "What's this hotel called?"

"Hilbert's Hotel."

The clerk's clothes had already nudged my memory, and when I heard the hotel's name my dream from the graveyard came back to me. David Hilbert. In his popular lectures he had often spoken of a hotel with alef-null rooms. Hilbert's Hotel.

I leaned towards the clerk in excitement. "Is he here?"

"Professor Hilbert? You might see him at tea later . . . if you could find some clothes."

I realized that I was still naked and that everybody else was dressed. Suddenly I felt the pressure of many amused stares. I pinched my buttocks together defensively. "I don't have any luggage . . . or anything . . ."

I heard a gnashing and a twittering behind me and turned around, one hand over my genitals. A man-sized beetle was swinging itself quickly across the carpet towards me. Its two forelegs were raised and waving, and streamers of fluid dripped from its mandibles. With a shriek I vaulted over the clerk's counter.

The beetle reached the counter and reared up against it. Two faceted eyes regarded me attentively, while a pool of viscous beetle-spit collected on the counter-top. "Do something," I said to the clerk in a strained voice.

He just chuckled and stepped aside so the beetle could see me better. Its forelimbs dipped in and out of the saliva repeatedly, forming tough silvery strands. Suddenly the beetle lost its footing and crashed back down to the lobby floor, pulling the wad of thickened spit along. I couldn't see it then, but could hear its legs actively clicking.

Cautiously I leaned across the counter to see what the creature was doing. All eight, or was it six, legs were darting around the silvery mass of spit-fibers. It looked as if it were spinning some sort of cocoon . . . perhaps to stuff me in while its larvae ate my flesh?

"You ought to thank him, you know," the clerk whispered to me. "His name is Franx."

"Thank him for what?"

"For that suit he's making you," the clerk hissed.

Just then the beetle finished. After a few seconds of vigorous rocking he got off his back and onto his feet. With a burst of twittering he laid a silvery jumpsuit out on the floor.

I climbed back over the counter and slipped into the silky garment. It fit perfectly and sealed up the front at the touch of a hand. It even had pockets.

I bowed stiffly. "Thank you, Franx. If there's ever anything I can do for . . ."

The twittering came again and I strained to understand it. It was actually human speech, flowery English, only speeded-up. After comprehending only a minute's worth I already felt like I had heard the story three times. Someone . . . "some benighted xenophobe" . . . had thrown an apple at him. It had stuck in his back and begun to rot. He lifted his armor-like wing-cover to show me the spot. Could I scoop out the decaying apple and flesh?

"I guess," I said hesitantly. "If I had a spoon . . ."

Franx sped across the lobby to where a woman in a black and white tailored silk suit was drinking a demi-tasse of coffee. She recoiled from him, and he snatched her cup from the low table in front of her. With his other forelimb he snagged a newspaper and came scuttling back to me.

There was nothing for it but to scoop the diseased region out of the huge insect's back. I dumped the foul-smelling globs onto the newspaper Franx had spread out, trying not to retch. I felt I was making a poor impression on the other guests, and I was relieved when I finished.

The giant cockroach had kept a stoic silence during the operation. Now he turned himself slowly around to examine the mess on the paper. Still without a sound, he lowered his head and began to feed.

I turned away. The clerk was looking at me levelly, expressionless behind the beard and glasses. "You're a kind man, Mr . . . ?"

"Rayman," I said, "Felix Rayman. Can you give me a room? I'm very tired."

"The hotel is full."

"That's impossible," I protested. "You have infinitely many rooms."

"Yes," the clerk said, his teeth flashing deep in his beard. "But we have infinitely many guests as well. One in each room. How could we fit you in?"

The question was not rhetorical. Once again he uncapped his pen to record my answer. I thought back to an Ion the Quiet story by Stanislaw Lem, and the answer was clear.

"Make the person in Room 1 move into Room 2. Make the guy in Room 2 move into Room 3. And so on. Each guest moves out of his room and into the room with the next higher number. Room 1 is left empty. You can put me in there."

The clerk made a rapid notation on his pad. "That's fine, Mr. Rayman. If you'll just sign the register while I make the arrangements . . ." He handed me a slim leather-bound volume and turned to speak into a microphone.

I riffled through the register, noticing a famous name here and there among the alien scrawls. I found a blank page and signed my name. Wondering how many pages were left, I began trying to flip through to the end of the book.

I soon became clear that there were infinitely many pages. I went into a speed-up and flipped past alef-null of them. There were still more. I peeled off alef-null more, and alef-null more again. There were still plenty of pages left.

I began picking up clumps of pages, flipping faster and faster . . . The clerk stopped me by reaching over and closing the book.

"You'll never reach the end at that rate. There's alef-one pages."

Behind me, Franx the giant cockroach had finished his little snack. I looked at him with revulsion. He had been eating his own rotten flesh.

"Come, come," he said, reading my expression. "In my father's house are many mansions, eh? When in Rome, act like the roaches! Cannibalism bespeaks, after all, nothing but the highest regard for the feastee, shall I say . . . be he even my humble servant I." He gave a squeal of laughter at his eloquence, and lowered his head to suck up the last drop of goo.

Before I could sidle away he was talking again. "Have you already qualified for a Guide? No? Good luck to you. Now it's not impossible to get a Guide, not logically ruled out, you understand . . . but the probability . . . I do assume you understand the theory of probability?"

I really wished I could get away from him. His loud and colorful speech had drawn the attention of the whole lobby. "I'm a mathematician," I said shortly.

"A mathematician! How perfectly delightful. May I ask your area of specialization?"

"I'm very tired." I took a step away from him. "Perhaps later . . ."

"Perhaps later it will be too late," the beetle cried, interposing himself between me and the elevator. "There is zero probability of getting a guide. As a mathematician you understand. Not impossible, but zero probability. Nevertheless you wish to climb Mount On. I also have such ambitions. What a team we will make. Franx and Felix!" He shouted out our names so that the whole lobby could hear. I groaned, but he babbled on. "Felix and Franx. I am a poet, Felix, a visionary, a philosopher-king. And you . . . you are a good samaritan, a mathematician, and more. Much, much more, but at the very least a mathematician with a specialization in . . . in . . ."

He wasn't going to stop until I told him. "Set Theory," I said wearily. "Transfinite numbers." I wished I had never accepted the jumpsuit.

The beetle raised its forelimbs high and made a mock salaam. "My prayers have been answered," he said. "Go in peace, my son. Render to no man evil for evil. Hold fast to that which . . ."

With a lop-sided smile frozen on my face I strode over to the elevators.

10
What is Milk?

The elevator was run by a shrimp in a blue coat with brass buttons. At least it looked like a shrimp. It had its segmented tail curled under it and sat in a contoured bucket of what might have been consommé. Instead of elevator buttons there was simply a horizontal lever which the shrimp could ease back and forth with its feelers.

I was still curious about how people could fit into those low rooms at the top of the hotel, and meant to ask about it. "I'm in Room 1 . . ." I began.

The shrimp's squeaky voice interrupted. "Don't tell the bellboys that! Thanks to you they had to move everyone!" He turned his head to stare at me with a black bead of an eye. "That suit you're wearing looks like roach-spit," he remarked after a time. The elevator had still not moved.

I was rather hurt. I had thought I looked jetsetty. "How about running me up to the top," I suggested.

"Sure thing, sport," The elevator had a glass door, and I watched the numberless hallways flicker past.

"Why aren't the ceilings getting lower?" I asked after a time.

"You tell me," the shrimp squeaked. We were speeding up and I had to keep regearing my thought processes to keep track of the floors strobing past. In many of them I saw people and creatures moving . . . creatures of every possible type. You can't be exclusive if you have alef-null rooms to fill. But the ceilings seemed to stay steady at 10 feet above the floor.

"I guess there's some sort of space distorter," I said to the shrimp questioningly. "Something that makes everything keep shrinking its height as it moves up."

"And what's going to happen at the top?" the shrimp shrilled knowingly. "Are we going to turn into Blondie and Dagwood?"

I shook my head slowly. It didn't seem like we could ever reach the top. The hotel had no roof, no last floor. If someone parachuted down on the hotel from above what would he see? I remembered the way my hand had stuck to that infinitely branching bush outside . . .

Suddenly everything went black. I could hear the shrimp snickering somewhere nearby. "This is the top, Professor. Care to get out?"

I groped around, unable to find the walls of the elevator. Was it the walls or my body which had disappeared? "Where are we?" At least my voice still worked.

"Where do you *think* we are?"

"No . . . nowhere."

"Right again," the shrimp squeaked gaily. There was a huge lurch, the lights came back on and we were zipping back down past the alef-null floors of the Hilbert Hotel.

I was shaken, and annoyed at the shrimp's rudeness. The last straw was when he tickled my ear with a sharp feeler.

"I'd like you a lot more on a skewer with mushrooms and onions," I snapped. We rode the rest of the way down in silence.

I got off at the floor above the lobby and quickly found my room. There was a bed with muslin-covered down quilt, a comfortable looking easy chair, an elegant walnut desk and a washstand. There was a red and blue oriental carpet on the floor and a few pictures on the walls.

I shut the door behind me and walked over to the window, which gave onto the mountain. As far as I could see the steep meadows stretched up, interrupted regularly by bands of rock. Counting the stripes of rock I could make out many infinite stretches. Infinitely many infinite stretches, and infinitely many infinite stretches of infinite stretches. Climbing up there wasn't going to be as easy as getting to the hotel.

I lay down on my bed to rest. Before long I slipped into a dreamless sleep.

After an indefinite interval of time I woke up with a start. I was covered with sweat, confused. The light outdoors hadn't changed. The phone was ringing and I picked it up.

It was the clerk's smooth voice. "Professor Hilbert is having tea on the terrace with some of his colleagues. Perhaps you'd care to join them. Table number 6,270,891.''

I thanked him and hung up. The terrace was reached by passing through the lobby. I spotted Franx up on the ceiling, but hurried past before he saw me. From outside, the terrace had looked fairly standard, with about fifty tables around the circumference. But now that I was on it I could see that everything shrank as it approached the middle . . . so that there were actually alef-null rings of tables around the terrace's center.

Already about ten rows in, the tables looked like dollhouse furniture, and the gesticulating diners like wind-up toys. To find Hilbert I'd have to go in better than a hundred thousand rows. Fortunately there was a clear path in, so I could run.

As on the elevator, the space distortion affected me without my feeling it. When I got to the doll-house tables, I was doll-sized and they looked perfectly normal to me. I sped towards the center, staring at the strange creatures I passed.

There was a table of rubbery carrots eating a rabbit stew. Then a whole group of liquid creatures in buckets connected by soda-straws. Then wads of feathers, coils of slimy tendrils, clouds of colored gas. I saw two toads who took turns swallowing each other whole. Some creatures were clusters of lights, others looked like sheets of paper. Some were staring into space, but most were engaged in lively conversations. A large number of them inscribed designs on the table-cloths as they talked, apparently to assist in communicating. Although I had no way of judging, they struck me as an awkward and graceless lot. Waiters whizzed back and forth on roller skates bringing platter after platter from a kitchen somewhere at the center of the terrace.

Each table had a little card with a number on it, and when I got into the six millions I slowed down a little. There were so many many creatures. The endless repetition of individual lives began to depress me . . . the insignificance of each of us was overwhelming. My vision began to blur and all the bodies on the terrace seemed to congeal into one hideous beast. I lost my footing and slipped, knocking a waiter off his foot.

He resembled a mushroom with a three-bladed propeller on top, and he wore a single roller-skate on his thick foot. He had been balancing a tray of twitching grubworms on his propeller, and now the grubs were humping off in every direction. One crawled across my bare foot. The mushroom hissed angrily and began gathering up the spilled dainties before they got away.

I apologized and continued on my way, trying to remember what Hilbert looked like. Before long I spotted three men sitting at a table, two in suits and one in shirtsleeves. With a sudden shock I realized I was looking at Georg Cantor, David Hilbert and Albert Einstein. There was an empty place at their table. I hurried over, introduced myself and asked if I could join them.

Hilbert and Einstein were absorbed in an animated and infinitely complex discussion, and merely glanced at me. But Cantor pointed to a chair and poured me a cup of tea.

"I studied Set Theory," I said to him when I sat

down. "I'm interested in the Continuum Problem." He nodded silently. He was wearing a gray suit and a white shirt with a starched collar. There was something haunted and unhappy about his eyes. He sipped his cup of tea, watching me and keeping his silence.

"It must make you really happy to be up here with all these infinities," I said coaxingly.

"I knew it would be like this," he said finally.

"I guess it goes on quite a ways?" I said, gesturing at Mount On.

"This is only the beginning of the second number class. Beyond lie all the alefs. And beyond that is the Absolute, the Absolute Infinite where, where . . ." He stopped speaking and stared into the sky.

I waited quietly for Cantor to finish his sentence. Meanwhile Hilbert ended his conversation with Einstein with a burst of laughter. He stood up to leave, giving me a small nod.

"I have certain duties. I hope that your stay here will be scientifically fruitful." And then Hilbert hurried towards the towering hotel, growing ever larger as he moved out of the field in the terrace's center.

Hilbert's remark about science made me uncomfortable. In the last year I had come to the painful realization that nothing I could ever do in mathematics or physics would remotely approach in significance the work of Cantor, Hilbert and Einstein.

But I made an attempt to appear keen and addressed Cantor again. "The mathematics must be easier here, since you can use infinite proofs. Take number theory, for instance . . ."

"*You* take it," he replied with a certain venom. "The number theorists despise to use my higher infinities as true numbers. Why should I interest myself in their myopic blunderings?"

I decided to change the subject. "Well, the . . . the beings here must certainly take infinity seriously. There must be seminars and . . ."

Cantor made an upward gesture of dismissal. "This is a tourist hotel. They live in Dumptowns on the Mainside, perfectly happy with complete finiteness. Once in awhile they come here by tunnel or sea. Most of them don't even know what they're looking at." He made the dismissing gesture again with his right arm. The arm tore loose and flew up into the sky, tumbling end over end.

"Color me gone," Cantor said, standing. "But do pay a call. You may be of use. I live with a lady on Mainside near the alef-one tunnel." He flung up his left arm. It too broke off and whizzed into the sky like a well-thrown tire-iron. He tensed his body as if for a chin-up, then suddenly turned into a ball of white light which rocketed upwards.

I stared up after him for a full minute. Perhaps that was the trick for reaching the higher infinities. Gingerly I tugged an arm to see if it would come off.

"The technique is exceptional," Einstein said, interrupting my thoughts. I had almost forgotten he was there, and turned to look at him. Einstein's face is so familiar from so many photographs, that to have him actually there gave me an extraordinarily heightened sense of reality. His deep eyes seemed to look through me. "But you're an exception too," he said after a minute. "You came here without dying. You haven't been to the Dump." He gestured towards the distant slanting sea. "I saw you land. You and a seagull."

"That was really a woman," I explained. "She just likes to look like a seagull."

"Exceptional," Einstein repeated. "Most souls arrive on the other side . . . Mainside. And they have no choice about what shape they take. Tell me, how did you do it?"

"Somehow I left my body. I saw Jesus and he told me to come here. Since it's infinitely far I used relativistic time dilation."

Einstein nodded. "That would produce the effect if continued indefinitely."

"What effect?" I asked, finally taking a sip of my tea.

"Becoming a component of the trans-dimensional radiation loss." He could see that I didn't understand, and rephrased it. "To speak in a misleading and superficial way, everything here is made of light. Cimön is a vast surface of light lying at the interface of space and anti-space. This side is called Flipside, and the other side of the surface is called Mainside. When something dies it releases a certain pulse of energy which strikes Mainside and activates an image."

"Does it usually take long? For a person to get here when he dies?"

"It can be instantaneous. In a very real sense Cimön is right next to every point in the ordinary Universe. Of course if you stay in regular space . . . like you did . . . then it's infinitely far away. But there is a trans-dimensional short-cut to

Mainside. You've used it yourself many times."

"Let me get one thing straight. Are you saying that Cimön is a big slab of light? People get here by turning into light?"

He made a cautioning gesture. "Better to call it a wave-like information pattern in a Hilbert-space energy configuration." Just then a waiter set a dish of vanilla ice-cream down in front of him. Einstein began to eat, considering each spoonful carefully.

I was wondering how I would reach the higher infinities. I was also trying to figure out how this could all be made of light . . . my body, the Mountain, the ice-cream. And what did he mean by saying I had been here many times before?

Einstein laid down his spoon and began to speak again. "Let me tell you a story I once told at a tea in Princeton. The hostess had asked me to explain relativity theory in a few words." His smile was kind, but with a hint of mischief in it. He leaned back in his chair and told his story.

'I once had a friend who had been blind from birth. One day we went for a hike in the country. It was hot, and after walking several miles we sat down to rest.

' "How thirsty I am," I remarked to my friend, "I wish I had a cool glass of milk."

' "What is milk?" my friend replied.

' "Milk? Milk is a white fluid."

' "I know what a fluid is," my friend responded, "But what is white?"

' "White is the color of a swan's feathers."

' "I know what feathers are, but what is a swan?"

' "A swan is a large bird with a crooked neck."

' "I can understand that," my blind friend replied, "Except for one thing. What is crooked?"

' "Here," I said, seizing his arm and stretching it out. "Now your arm is straight." Then I folded his arm against his chest. "And now your arm is crooked."

' "Ah! Now I know what milk is." '

At the end Einstein took hold of my arm and straightened and bent it several times. His hands felt good on me.

I thought about the story for awhile. It was about the reduction of abstract ideas to immediate experience. I tried to pinpoint the idea I had been trying to understand, the reduction I was looking for. At the table next to us a party of red-orange lawn-mowers were roaring their choppers around as the waiter set down a square yard of trembling purple sod and a quart can of motor oil.

"It's hard for me to think," I said finally. Everywhere I looked was some preposterous beast, some bizarre caper. "It's so crowded, so noisy."

"That's because we come from a universe with infinitely many inhabited star systems," Einstein said with a shrug. "And this is one of the very few nice hotels on Flipside."

He was staring at his spoon with a peculiar fixity. "I've got to be going," he said slowly and without looking up. "Back to Mainside. If I can just . . ."

Suddenly his voice and appearance changed radically. It was as if for an instant he became all men at once. His image was blurred, yet seemed to hold a sharp copy of every face I'd ever seen . . . although somehow each of those faces looked at me with Einstein's eyes.

And then he was gone in a flash of white light.

11

Epsilon-Zero

The uproar on the terrace had spilled back into the lobby. On every side of me creatures gibbered and grimaced—speeding up, slowing down, ceaselessly exchanging noisy information. I had no idea how to leave like Cantor and Einstein had. I was stuck here. I fought my way over to the front desk and tried to get the clerk's attention.

He was busy checking in an endless stream of dimpled yellow spheres. They were floating in through the front door thick and fast, and an infinite speed-up ensued. I could hear sounds of frantic activity upstairs. Finally all the smiling spheres had found lodging and the clerk turned to look at me, a little blank with fatigue.

"I want to start up Mt. On . . ." I began, but he waved me aside and spoke into his microphone for a minute.

When he had finished talking he sank onto his

stool with a sigh, took off his spectacles and began rubbing his face with both hands. "Infinitely many new guests at once," he groaned. "And they'll only eat *skagel*. Why the whole grinning sector has to come together . . ." Another groan.

"How did you fit them all in?"

For once the clerk gave me a straight answer. "We put all the old guests in the even-numbered rooms. All the new ones go in odd-numbered rooms." He had finished rubbing his nose and eyes and was working on his temples now.

"You mean all the old guests have to double up?"

The clerk looked at me pityingly. "No. You move to Room. 2. The guy in Room 2 moves to Room 4. Room 3 moves to Room 6. 4 to 8. 5 to 10. And so on. This leaves all the odd-numbered rooms vacant for the smilies."

I was embarassed he'd had to tell me. After all, I was supposed to be the expert on transfinite numbers. "I'd like to get started on that mountain," I said again. "You said something about getting a guide?"

The clerk stood up and began rummaging in a drawer. "A Guide, yes. A Guide is absolutely essential. Unfortunately we have so few of them . . . a few hundred . . ." He handed me a printed form several pages long.

"MT. ON GUIDE SERVICE APPLICATION FORM," I read and let my eye slide down the first page's labelled blanks. Name. Date and Place of Birth, Date and Place of Death, Cause, Father's Profession, Education, Employment History, Publications, Awards and Honors, Annual Income in

Last Year of Life . . . My heart sank. "I have to *apply* to get a Guide?"

The clerk spread out his hands apologetically. "There are so few of them, so many would-be climbers. We must choose the most stable, the most likely to succeed." I riffled through the form, looking at the later pages. References. MAG Scores. Purpose of Climb (150 words), Religious Beliefs, Community Services on Mainside. The clerk continued talking. "When you have completed the form you must submit it to one of the Guides through his Assistants. Do you know any Guides' Assistants?"

Of course I didn't know any Assistants. Of course my application would be rejected—one of the less promising, less stable in a pool of infinitely many. I felt like I had slid back into the horrible hopeless charade of looking for a good job. In a sudden burst of fury, I tore the application form in half and trampled it underfoot. "I don't need any stinking Guides. I don't want their second-hand God."

The clerk was unruffled. "You'll be leaving?"

I turned on my heel and walked out through the din to the hotel entrance. Something plucked at my jumpsuit, and I whirled around, ready to kill. It was Franx the giant beetle. I smiled.

"You spurn me no longer?" he twittered.

We walked out the front door together. "I saw you rending your application form. A rash act."

"Did *you* apply for a Guide?" I replied as we reached the bottom of the steps.

"I tried. I went through channels. I debased myself. But the Assistant just threw an apple at me."

" 'A benighted xenophobe' " I chuckled. "To hell with that. I'm climbing. If you come with me, so much the better."

We reached the end of the hotel grounds. Ahead of us was a grassy slope ending in the first band of rock. Mount On.

The field was mostly made of the infinitely branching grass blades. But there were also thousands of little flowers. Stars, cups, bells . . . every shape, every color. Lovely faint odors wove through the air, and tiny butterflies blundered around happily in the chemical maze.

I found the walking pleasant, paradisiacal . . . but Franx had problems. His thin legs and sticky foot pads kept getting tangled in the meadow plants, and I kept having to pull him loose. Despite his size he was not very heavy, and once or twice I actually hoisted him onto my back to get him over a particularly intricate patch of vegetation.

It took us almost an hour to reach that first band of rock. The gravity made a sudden shift in direction there . . . a ninety-degree rotation. What had looked like a fifty-foot strip of rocks turned out to be a cliff when I got onto it. Sheer and with small hand-holds. At last Franx had the advantage over me. He scuttled up the face of the cliff in less than a minute.

I began working my way up slowly, foothold by handhold. Below my feet I could see the meadow we'd crossed and the hotel. It felt like if I slipped I'd fall all the way down to the ocean, and I had to fight back a spasm of fear. I could make out a party of four moving across the meadow to my right. They looked confident and business-like. I wondered if that was a Guide in the lead. He looked like an industrial vacuum cleaner on stilts. I was so tired already. The rocks were hurting my bare feet.

I looked up the twenty remaining feet of cliff, mapping out the handholds I'd use. Franx's tiny head stared expressionlessly down at me. I looked down past my right foot to see what the Guide was up to. He was pointing a hose at me. Suddenly a flash of light blinded me. Inadvertently I shifted my right foot off its ledge.

I fell then, and had time only to wonder what would happen to me if I died here. I was in my astral body which had somehow turned solid in this kingdom of light. Could my astral body die? If it did would I move into an even more ethereal form? Would I return to Earth to live as a soulless clod? Or would it just be the end all up and down the line?

Franx caught me just as I was going to hit. He had raised up his stiff wing-covers, unfolded his iridescent wings, and flown down to snag me. The filmy wings beat frantically against the clear air, and slowly we rose up to the top of the cliff. Gravity tilted back, and he set me down in another sweet-smelling meadow.

"Why didn't you tell me you could fly? I thought you were just a cockroach."

"On my home-world Praha only the lower castes fly. A poet, a philosopher-king like myself is borne in a litter, jewel-encrusted, by tasty flying grubs. It would be more accurate to say that you, Felix, resemble such a grub. More accurate than to compare me to a cockroach."

Before I could apologize, Franx had wedged his

head under a flat rock and flipped it over. There
were a few worms and larvae and he scarfed them
right up. I still felt no hunger. It seemed that in
Cimön eating and sleeping were things you only
had to do if you felt like it.

Ahead of us lay another meadow, more tangled
than before. It ended in another cliff, smoother
and ten feet higher than the last. The Guide and
his party had angled across the meadow away
from us. It was probably easier over there. I wondered if the Guide had knocked me off balance on
purpose. More than likely. For my own safety, of
course.

I didn't see how we were ever going to make
any progress. Franx could hardly walk in the
meadows, and I could hardly climb the cliffs. No
way we could shift into an infinite speed-up at
this rate.

Franx interrupted my fretting. "By way of
amplification, let me add that I cannot fly unless I
have been in some way propelled into the air. At
festivals one hops, but this is not feasible in the
too entangling meadows."

"Why don't you just fly from cliff to cliff?" I
suggested.

"Do you think I'd have waited for you if I could?
Boon companion though you are, my soul hun-
gers after the Absolute, the One, the journey's
end. My heart leaps far, but my body lags. In fine, I
cannot fly so far." He looked at me expectantly.

It had been so easy to be carried up the cliff.
Maybe I should carry him across the meadow. He
was big, but not dense. "Get on my back," I
suggested. "I'll hop whenever we touch ground,
and you can fly us between jumps."

"I thought you'd never ask." His clinging little feet moved up my sides and his mandibles rested lightly on my neck. I gave a little shiver. What if he snapped my head off and drank me like a bottle of cherry cola?

But it worked great. I squatted and jumped into the air. Then Franx's wings buzzed and we sailed twenty or thirty feet. When we hit my legs were bent and ready, and we bounded off again. We crossed the meadow in five jumps.

On the cliff we used a sort of reverse rappel. Franx flew as high as he could, and then I grabbed hold of a ledge and shoved us higher. His wings would gain another ten or fifteen feet and I'd kick or pull against the cliff to speed us up again.

We covered dozens of meadows and cliffs that way, falling into a hypnotic rhythm. As on the approach to the hotel, the landscape began to seem alive and cooperative. We went into an infinite speed-up.

Boundless energy flowed through us out of Mt. On, and we zapped past our first alef-null cliffs. After every cliff was always a steep little meadow of about the same width . . . say a hundred feet. But every cliff was ten feet higher than the one before. We stopped to look back after those first alef-null cliffs.

It was a strange sight. There was no last stripe of rocks in the infinite pattern marching up towards us like a flattened staircase. Whenever I would try to work my way back down, my attention would suddenly dart down to some one cliff . . . say the billionth from the bottom. I could work my way back up a cliff at a time, but I could only move my attention back down in jerks.

"What do you see?" I asked Franx.

His answer was complex. Rather than looking at individual cliffs he preferred to focus on the overall pattern. He made much of the fact that each meadow was the same width, but that each cliff was ten feet higher than the one before. He pointed out that this ensured that the overall shape of the meadow-cliff pattern was parabolic, and gave a short proof of this fact. He speculated that the rate of growth of the next series of cliffs would be given by a quadratic function, leading to a meadow-cliff curve of the third degree . . .

I interrupted him. "Where did you learn all that? I thought you weren't a mathematician."

"That was poetry. Rather finely chiselled, if I do say so myself."

"Where I come from," I began. "On Earth . . ."

"I know what you call poetry. Sense impressions, emotions . . . the well-turned phrase, the fly in amber. But on Praha the equations are poetry too."

"But mathematics is supposed to be boring," I protested. "Long proofs, formal details. Of course the *idea* isn't boring, but the details . . ."

"We never do the details," Franx replied. "Because we don't care if our equations are correct. It's how they *feel* that counts."

We started up again. This time we did a sort of super speed-up, and started flicking past cycles of alef-null cliffs at what felt like one go. In each cycle of cliffs a more rapid rate of growth was embodied. Once they began to grow exponentially it seemed like I was always kicking or clawing at bare rock with Franx's wings buzzing steadily behind me. Everything glowed with light and the rocks gave off a dry dusty smell. We kept at it for a long time, folding level after level of speedups into each other, passing infinity within infinity of cliffs.

At some point I realized that we had stopped moving again. We were in a little handkerchief of a meadow with bare rock all around. Franx was lying on his back and fiddling with his legs.

"Is this alef-one?" I asked hopefully.

"I don't think so," he said. "I think it's what you'd get by raising alef-null to the alef-null power alef-null times in a row."

"You mean epsilon-zero?"

Franx gave an affirmative leg-twitch. "That's what they called it."

"Who?"

"I've spent a lot of time at that Hotel, my dear Felix. Although the Guides are reticent, the failed climbers are not. The *raison d'etre* for most climbs is the triumphant reappearance on the terrace where the new arrivals and old companions are regaled with marvellous tales of derring-do."

"And you've heard of people getting to alef-one without a Guide?"

"Indeed I have. It's not so easy as all this has been. It requires a new order of being, a new plane of existence."

"I don't see how we can top that last effort. And even if we fold speed-up after speed-up together, we're still just going to get some limit of countably many stages. Alef-one can't be reached by any countable process. We're never going to get out of the second number class."

Franx just lay there in the dry grass. There were hardly any flowers up here. I picked a blade and held it up to the sky. This leaf had ten-fold branching. I imagined labelling the branches from left to right with the ten digits zero through nine.

I noticed a tiny bug crawling up the leaf. At the first branching he hesitated, then took number 3 and continued upward. At the next branching he chose number 6, and at the fork after that he went for number 1. Then he fell into my eye.

I lidded him out, thinking about what would happen if he continued forever. His final path could be coded up by a single real number gotten by sticking his choices together: .361 . . . I realized there were just as many ways to crawl up that leaf as there were real numbers between zero and one. A whole continuum of possible paths . . . c of them.

Just then the leaf vaporized into a puff of smoke and a loud crack split the air.

It was the Guide again. He was hovering a few hundred feet away from us, carrying a humanoid climber at the end of each of his three legs. His body was squat and cylindrical. On top was a glittering dome and three snaky hoses.

One of the hoses was pointed straight up and seemed to be sucking in air rapidly enough to hold the Guide and his party aloft. The other hose was poised to shoot another energy bolt at us, and the third was talking.

"I regret that because of the small number of Guide-party openings and the unusually large number of well-qualified applicants it is now clear that we will be unable to assist you on Mount On. As you will certainly understand, public safety dictates that no unaccompanied climbers are allowed. Please return at once."

It made me sick just to look back at the cliffs we'd climbed. It looked like the next foothold was infinitely far away. Of course we could try hang-gliding it . . .

"Into the fog," Franx shrilled, scuttling away. The Guide's first energy blast had set a part of the meadow afire, and the infinite-leaved little plants were giving off a dense, almost liquid smoke. I didn't feel like jumping alone, so I took off after Franx.

Another bolt crashed into the ground at my left, and then I ran into the flames and thick smoke with my breath held. I could hear Franx twittering somewhere nearby, but the visibility was zero. White smoke tendrils twined, wrapped and re-wrapped, smeared together in a continuum. I was seeing spots, my ears rang, I had to breathe. I gasped in a lungful of the solid smoke.

I could feel it moving down into my lungs, branching through my bronchial tubes and alveoli . . . a continuous smear of off-white spreading out to a continuum of bright points in my chest. Fantastic infinite visions crowded in on me and I fell together.

12
The Library of Forms

When I came to, I was slumped over a typewriter. I had been writing, writing for a long time and slipping the completed sheets into a slit in the desk.

The desk was light gray plastic. It joined seamlessly to the walls of the tiny cubicle I found myself in. Everything in the room was white or gray. I stood up and tried the door behind me. Locked. There was a sound of machinery at work inside the desk, but the drawer was locked too.

I sat down and looked at the typewriter. It was a standard IBM Selectric, except that the typing ball was surrounded by a great deal more machinery than usual. With a practiced gesture I rolled in a sheet of paper and began typing.

A dizzy sense of *déja vu*, of multiple personalities, hit me as I began to type. I had already written everything on this machine, every variation of my story . . .

My fingers continued to dance across the keys. I was writing a description of my life, a rambling description that strolled down every leafy avenue of thought, wandered across unmarked connecting paths, and crashed through thickets of detail.

Ordinarily a writer has to leave things out. If he mentions his pen he doesn't tell you who sold it to him, what the salesgirl ate for lunch, where her tuna came from, how the ocean was formed.

To include every detail, every associated fact, leads to including the whole universe. It all sticks together like an old dish of hard candy. And to describe the whole universe, an infinity of words are needed. But alef-null was no longer a barrier for me. I could make Proust's dream come true.

I slid into a speed-up. The thoughts flowed through my fingers and onto the page. Every detail was there, every fleeting association was explained, and the whole infinity that was my life so far was there on the page.

It shot up out of the typewriter. I plucked it out of the air and scanned it with satisfaction. I had it all down in alef-null lines. There was a shrinking field in the typing ball, so that each line was 49/50 as high as the one above it. There was always room for fifty more lines.

As I used a speed-up to read through the page I again had that feeling of multiple identity. I had already written this page before . . . not once but many times, a little different each time. Just then the desk *thocked* the way a pinball machine does when you've won a free game.

The drawer-front swung down and a large book, freshly bound in leather, came sliding out.

It dropped onto the waxy linoleum floor with a thud. I picked it up and let it fall open in my lap.

The right-hand page was an infinitely detailed description of someone's life. In many ways it resembled my own. Except this guy had dropped out of college, gotten laid a lot and died in a motorcycle accident.

On the left there was no top page. The pages there seemed a little transparent, and no matter how hard I tried I couldn't seem to peel off a single last one. It was like trying to find the biggest real decimal number less than 1. .9, .99, .999?

The back of the first page I'd looked at was blank, and when I looked for the next page I ran into the same problem. There were plenty more pages, but I couldn't seem to pick up just *one* of them. What's the first real number *after* 1?

Whenever I let the book fall open I would find a single page in the middle, isolated between two topless heaps of pages. The pages were packed in just like points on a line segment. There were c of them.

I did not see how I could have written it all, but each page I looked at seemed familiar. The visions after I'd inhaled that smoke were all here. I had seen every possible variation of my life, and had proceeded to describe each one of them in endless detail. I had described a whole continuum of parallel worlds . . . somehow I had pulled the Many into One.

Occasionally I found two pages that differed from one another only in a single name, but usually the differences were much greater. In some lives the narrator could fly, in some he was paralyzed; in some he was a genius, in others he was insane. Somehow they were all me.

For awhile I searched for a correct description of my future, but it was pointless. Any mad variation, any possibility, could be found on some page . . . occasionally even beginning, "This is the true story of Felix Rayman."

Carrying the book in my hand I went over and tried the door to my cubicle again. This time it opened. I stepped out into the stacks of a library. Each bookcase was filled with books like the one I had written, each with a gold-lettered title on the spine.

I turned my book to see what I had written. "THE LIVES OF FELIX RAYMAN." You never would have guessed my name from reading the book. Each possible life was in there with each of the names I might have had. I had a dizzying feeling that in a parallel world not too far off I had just written the same book . . . except that there the title was something like THE LIVES OF VERNOR MAXWELL or THE LIVES OF COBB ANDERSON.

On impulse I squeezed my book into the shelf in front of me and looked at some of the other volumes. One called DOGS caught my eye, and I took it down. On each page there was a story about a dog. They were all alef-null words long, and sometimes made cumbersome reading. One of them really got to me though. It was sort of like *Call of the Wild,* and it was all I could do to keep from howling when I finished.

I took down another book, called FACES. On each page was a delicately shaded full-color portrait of a possible face . . . each one drawn with infinite precision. I flipped through it for awhile, hoping to see someone I knew, and eventually found a face that was almost exactly that of April's. I looked at it for a long time.

Suddenly I heard voices a few aisles away. Still barefoot, I padded quietly towards the noise to find two young women in conversation. The one talking wore her light-colored hair in a lank pony-tail. She had blank skin and thin features.

"I'm glad you drew all the lines," she was saying, "but you needn't have put in those dots."

The other woman was shorter and had curly dark hair. Her lips were thick and there was a gap between her front teeth. The short sleeves of her blouse cut into the flesh of her arms. "This is a richer book . . ." she was beginning when I appeared.

They were not too surprised to see me. "Did you write your book?" the thin-lipped one asked. I nodded and she held out her hand. "May I see it?"

"I left it back there," I said, "on the shelf by the door. It's called THE LIVES OF FELIX RAYMAN."

"I'll have to check it over before you can leave."

"Go ahead," I said, and she walked off, her heels sounding on the stone floor.

"She wants me to do mine over," the curly-haired girl said to me, handing me the book she was holding.

"SMOOTH CURVES," I read from the spine, and opened the book. The first page I saw had a sort of figure eight on it. I looked at more pages. An oval, an arc, a rounded double-you, a squiggle, a scribble. On some of the pages there were a few isolated dots as well. "She doesn't like the dots?"

"No," the girl answered with a grimace. "I don't

know why I put them in. I went white and flew
here from Truckee just to do the smooth curves
. . . there's c of them, you know, by Taylor's
Theorem . . ."

I interrupted. "Don't tell me you're a
mathematician?"

She nodded. Just then I heard the librarian calling to me. "Mr. Rayman, could you come here?
There's a problem . . ."

"There always is," the chubby mathematician
whispered to me.

"How can we get out of here?" I whispered
back.

"I think this way." She took my arm in a
friendly way and led me through the maze of
aisles to a stairwell. Surprisingly it was only one
flight down to the ground floor.

We stepped out into a high-ceilinged reading
room with windowed walls. Armchairs and
couches were placed here and there, and there
were a few people lounging in them with the thick
leather books. Some were reading, while others
simply stared out the windows at the kaleide-
scopically changing view.

To our right was a desk where a librarian dis-
pensed books, which he got from a slot in the wall.
He wore a short-sleeved white nylon shirt and
baggy black pants. You could see the loops of his
undershirt through the nylon. He motioned us
over and we approached the counter.

"SMOOTH CURVES, Judy Schwartz," he said
pointing at my companion with his ball-point.
Then at me, "THE LIVES OF FELIX RAYMAN,
Felix Rayman." His voice was high-pitched and a
little mucous. Seeing our nods of confirmation he

bent to inscribe the information on two file cards.

I looked around the room a little more. Outside was . . . uh . . . Against a yellow background, a pattern of green vortices was moving past the windows. They grew tongues, purple tongues, and began licking. Two red blobs of light flew past . . . I decided to put the view on the back burner.

In the center of the reading room was a smallish card catalog. A stooped man with a white beard was leafing through one of the loosely-packed drawers. "How many books do you have, anyway?" I asked the librarian.

"If your two books were usable, that would make it two thousand four hundred and seventy-one." I must have looked surprised, for he continued, "The Library of Forms is selective. We only house books whose theme is a basic category of human understanding, exhaustively treated. Partial, alien or idiosyncratic works are not of interest. We catalogue only those full and definitive treatments of significant forms actually occuring on Earth."

There was a hum, and a TV screen at his elbow lit up. It was the pony-tailed woman from upstairs. "The SMOOTH CURVES book is complete, and will be usable if some random dots are erased. Send Ralph up to take care of it."

"Very well." The librarian pushed a button. "And THE LIVES OF FELIX RAYMAN?"

A quick shake of the head. "Complete treatment, but of a partial topic. If he had written *all* possible lives instead of just . . ."

"But we've got that anyway . . ." the man shrugged.

"Yes. The Rayman book is only a subset of the LIVES book on shelf three twenty-eight. If he wants the service he'll have to do another."

"How about LAMPS?" the man said brightly.

The woman on the screen pursed her lips in thought. "Yes. We need a LAMPS. Pictures, don't you think?"

The man nodded once. "I'll see to it." He clicked the set off and addressed me in his wet reedy voice. "Mr. Rayman. If you'll go upstairs again Ms. Winston will give you some fuzzweed and show you where . . ."

"Look," I interrupted, "If you think I'm going to burn myself out just to draw every stupid possible lamp . . ."

"You'll have to if you want the service."

"I can use it now, can't I?" Judy Schwartz broke in.

"Well, yes. That is, as soon as Ralph . . ." He punched the button on the desk again. There was a silence. The librarian looked at us blankly, then picked up the thread. "The service, yes. You will be free, Ms. Schwartz, to use our facilities . . . our catalog, our books, our reading room. And of course you will have access to the typing and drafting rooms upstairs. The fuzzweed and the scoops are always ready."

"I'm leaving," I announced. My voice came out louder than I'd intended, and a number of readers lifted their heads to stare mildly at me.

I started uncertainly away from the desk, then turned back. "I might as well take my book . . . if you're just going to throw it away." The librarian buzzed the upstairs. In a few seconds my book plopped out of the slot in the wall. He handed it over silently.

The stairwell door opened then and a skinny man in a khaki custodian's uniform came shuffling out. He smelled strongly of volatile solvents and seemed a little dazed. He leaned against the counter, smacked his mouth several times and finally said, "Yes, Mr. Berry?"

"Ralph," the librarian said, "Ms. Winston needs you upstairs. Some erasing, I believe." Ralph nodded his loose head extravagantly and began smacking again. The librarian pointed at me. "And please see Mr. Rayman to the door." He addressed himself to me for the last time. "Just take the tunnel out, and help yourself to skis."

Ralph continued nodding, slowly bringing his head around to me. "Goin' out there again, are you," he said between two smacks. "The bum's rush." He gave a chuckle which got out of control and turned into a deep, convulsive cough.

"Are you coming?" I asked Judy Schwartz over the coughing. Outside the window rolled a peaceful country landscape, distinguished only by the presence of a few moving points of red light. But now the ground began forcing itself up into humps. The humps grew higher and thinner, became long tentacles straining out of the ground. The ends of the tentacles thickened and turned into fists, and the fists began hammering about with wild abandon. The spots of red light buzzed back and forth fretfully.

"You should draw the lamps," Judy said. "I'm going to be working on the Rieman Hypothesis here. It's just a matter of choosing the right . . ."

Ralph took my sleeve in his unsteady grip, and we walked off together. "Where'd you get that suit?" he wanted to know. "Looks like that one Elvis wore. Did you ever see Elvis?"

"Just on TV."

"I died too soon for that, goddammit all. Wound up in Truckee, got in trouble with the Godsquad, and came to work here. Here's the doors. Be sure you close the first one before you open the second."

I paused. Something Ralph had said before was puzzling me. He'd asked if I were going outside *again.*

"Was I already out there?"

He gave his slack chuckle. "The accidentals never remember." He could have been speaking to himself, and turned to go as he said it.

I grabbed him by the arm and gave him a shake. "How did I get here? I've got to know!"

"Take it slow there. I come apart easy." I released him and made a vague upward gesture. "The scoops. We pulled you in. The dreamers are no good . . . they're the red ones. But when someone goes white and wanders into Dreamland—why, if he comes within a thousand feet of us we've got us a new book."

"Is—is that 'Dreamland' out there?"

He was holding the first glass door open for me. "That's righty. Now git. I've got work to do."

I walked out the door and he let it close behind me. In front of me was the second glass door, to the outside. The tentacles of a minute ago had branched and woven themselves into a huge green basket covering the Library. I stepped outside.

It was cold . . . dry, deep-freeze cold. Right outside the door the ground was hardpacked snow, and there was a sort of path leading through the snow to what looked like a tunnel. The path, the tunnel and the Library stayed constant, but everything else was in flux. The green dome overhead tore into pieces which writhed and thickened. I wanted to get moving fast.

Attached to the Library there was a rack of cross-country ski equipment. Parkas, hats, gloves, skis, poles and shoes. I picked out a set and slipped my book into a big pocket on the parka's back. I snapped on the skis and got ready to leave.

Overhead, the pieces of green had turned into winged lizards. One flew at me. I couldn't duck in time, but it didn't matter. It went right through me . . . insubstantial as a thought. From what Ralph had said, it was a dream.

I looked around for a dreamer. A ball of red light was sportively chasing one of the lizards. It looked like it was having a good time. There were big scoops like ship's funnels on top of the Library. Some skeletons were coming around the corner of the building. They had scythes.

Keeping my eyes fixed on the strip of unchanging packed snow, I skied away from the Library of Forms and up the sloping tunnel.

13
The Truth

The other end of the short tunnel was partially blocked by drifted snow. I herring-boned over it and skied out. All around me were slopes and humps of snow. A steady wind was at work . . . pulling out a lip here, filling a hollow with ripples there, smoothing, sharpening, continuously creating. The air was filled with streaks and whorls of snow, and I couldn't see far. Looking back it was hard to pick out the hummock which hid the Library of Forms.

Except for the drifts, the snow was crusty, and I skied across it without sinking in. I fell into the familiar rhythm, kicking along and digging in my poles. The ground sloped gently downhill and I made good time. My mind went into neutral.

The windblown snowscape changed so constantly that it was hard to be sure how fast I was going. There were no landmarks, and I guided myself only by always going downhill. Skiing along, I began to feel that my regular movements were somehow sustaining the scene around me—as if I were the beating heart of this frozen world.

Occasionally a faint blush of color would bleed up through the snow from Dreamland. But I seemed to be on top of it, and there was no sign of the bizarre animations I'd seen out the Library window.

I grew hot from the exercise, and then thirsty. I paused and scooped up a handful of the snow. It was fine, powdery stuff, made of tiny dodecahedrons: crystals with twelve pentagonal faces. Each crystal flickered with an internal play of color, and when I strained my eyes I could make out tiny moving shapes and patterns inside each one. Some melted in my hand, and I lapped up the moisture.

The taste was strange, intoxicating. I began to feel myself splitting up like I had after breathing in that smoke on Mount On. Quickly I spat the liquid out of my mouth.

What had happened on the mountain anyway? The Guide had been blasting holes in the ground, and the fuzzy little plants had caught fire. I'd breathed in a lungful of smoke. Everything had gotten white and I'd had vision upon vision . . . all at once. Apparently I had turned into a ball of light, travelled through Dreamland and been scooped in by the Library of Forms. But where had the mountain gone?

As far as I could see there was nothing but snow. I wondered when it would end. Somehow I had gone beyond the countable level. The books in the Library had c pages each and Dreamland . . . perhaps still under the snow I skied across . . . Dreamland was filled with the whole continuum of possible visions.

I skied on for a long time. The wind around me waxed and waned, finally tapered to a stop. The snow underfoot became harder and harder, until finally I was skiing over ice covered by a thin coating of powder. A glacier. I saw colors flickering through the powder, and rubbed a clear window in the ice.

I was looking down on a city from above. An eerie purplish glow lit up the grid of streets, but all the buildings were dark. A spot of red light hurried down one of the avenues.

A jetliner came floating above the city, circled and headed down for a landing. It was following the red light. The space between the buildings was too narrow, but the plane kept on. One of the wings hit, scraped, broke off. Flames and smoke, and the wreckage went tumbling down towards the light, falling in frozen time.

The shapes began changing, rearticulating. The falling wreckage became a spilled bag of groceries. The jetliner a carton of eggs. The red light moved up towards me, then flew off. The eggs broke and a flock of roast turkeys flew out, headless and beating their golden safety-pin wings. They followed the red light off to the side. The dark city lay waiting for a replay.

I skied on. The sky was clear now, a blue so deep as to approach purple, and the ice field I was skiing over began to show cracks. I used my skis to get over a number of them, jumped two more, but finally came to a crevasse too wide to cross.

I took my skis off and sat down on them to rest. The crevasse was forty feet wide, and seemed to go down forever. The walls were like clear glass, and I could see all manner of things glide up to them and turn away. The ice was full of dreams. I heard water rushing far below.

There were more crevasses after this one, and the glacier ended about a mile off. It looked as if there was a city beyond the glacier. I longed to be there.

I saw no other sign of life. Only the flickering lights in the ice, and high overhead a single bird flying towards the city. I wondered briefly what had happened to Kathy. Maybe we should have stayed together. I had promised Jesus to help her. I hoped she would turn up again.

I left my skis and began walking along the crevasse. Perhaps it would get narrower. Instead it got wider and more jagged. I had just decided to turn back when I spotted something on the other side. A regular sawtooth pattern on the wall. Stairs cut into the ice. And crawling up was . . .

"Franx," I hollered. "It's Felix! Come help me!"

There was no way for me to read his expression . . . he'd told me that on Praha they did it by looking at each other's leg joints . . . but I guessed he was glad to see me. He raised his wing covers and flew over. He skidded several yards when he landed.

"The return of the prodigal," he said expansively. "But which of us has been through more?"

It was comforting to see the familiar curve of his back. I took off my hat and used it to polish him.

"It's good to see you, Franx. What happened back there anyway?"

"There was a fusillade of thunderbolts, token of the Guide's wrath at our joint success. The fuzzweed caught fire and there were holes blasted in the ground, makeshift shelters where a lesser being might have cringed and grovelled for his safety. But not I. I darted out of my hole again and again, fruitlessly struggling to save my comrade-in-arms, that noblest and mobilest set-theorist Felix Raymor." He paused to savor his words.

"The name is Rayman, Franx. But where did I go?"

"I had assumed that the Guide blasted you back to the Dump you came from. Here today, gone tomorrow. No glot, clom Fliday. Yes we have no bananas. Now you see him, now you . . ."

I broke in. "I followed you into the smoke. I held my breath as long as I could, but finally had to take in a big lungful. It felt like c particles in me, glowing white. When I came to I was at a desk . . ."

"The Library of Forms," Franx put in suddenly. "I don't believe it! You whited out! How could you . . . a raw fresher, a narrow mathematician, a crass fleshapoid."

He really seemed angry. "I've sought enlightenment for centuries—and you, you ignorant fool, you walk into a cloud of fuzzweed smoke and come out in the Library—I can't believe it, I won't! You're lying! You've just been back to the Dump that spawned you. You . . ."

I didn't know what he was talking about, but broke in anyway to challenge blindly, "I don't see where you get off calling Earth a dump. I'd hate

to see what your Praha looks like, you garbage
eater."

Franx pulled himself together and salaamed
placatingly. "A thousand pardons. You labor
under a misunderstanding. Although I never had
the pleasure to visit your fabled emerald orb, I do
not question that it compares favorably with that
insect paradise where I loved out my allotted
span. But surely your mean intellect can grasp
that I was referring to the Dump over there," he
gestured towards the city beyond the glacier. "On
the other side of Truckee?"

Einstein had said something about dumps before. I tried to remember. "I've never seen a dump
here, Franx. The way I came was to just crash in on
a field near Hilbert's Hotel."

"Extraordinary!" Franx exclaimed. "Not for
Felix Raymor the laborious pilgrimage from city
to city, across the snow and through the sea. No!
At one stroke he descends . . . or is it ascends? At
one stroke he reaches Flipside, land of promise,
land of Mount On." His legs were bunched under
him and he was staring at me intently. "One says
that those who do not pass through the Dump
were never alive . . . angels and devils is the
expression, I believe . . ." Suddenly he reared up
and seized my neck in his mandibles. "Which,
Felix? The truth!"

He had gone mad. I pushed him off me. He fell
onto his back and slid across the ice towards the
crevasse. "Look out, Franx," I called. "You're
going over."

And then he did, disappearing over the edge of
the ice-cliff with a gibber of terror. I strode forward to peer down into the abyss. Dreams were

flickering through the walls of ice, and far below a torrent of water thundered. With relief I saw Franx's bulky body spiralling upwards. He'd gotten his wings out in time.

When he rose out of the crevasse he continued to circle some twenty feet over my head. For some reason he was scared to death of me. What had I told him? Only that I hadn't started out in one of the dumps on Mainside. In his eyes that meant I'd never lived, that I was a supernatural force, possibly in league with the Devil. I cupped my hands and called up to him. "It's because I never died, Franx. Not that I never lived. My body's still on Earth. I swear I'm not a devil."

The frantic buzzing of his wings lowered in pitch and he drifted closer. "Let's hear you say the . . . the Lord's Prayer," he called suspiciously.

I recited it without stumbling or saying anything backwards, and that seemed to satisfy him. He landed near me with a thump. "The Devil does nab a few of us now and then. I apologize for my well-founded, but perhaps excessive, caution. There are press-gangs intent on shanghai. I've seen it happen, seen souls snatched up by the Evil One's minions. I'm not too sure about those Guides, for instance. And there's the flames in the Dump." He began to regain his usual expansiveness. "But if you never died, that's another matter, a different kettle of fish entirely. You have so much to learn, my dear Felix."

"Why don't you start by explaining what the dumps are?" I suggested. "And keep it simple. I'm getting cold."

"The Dump," Franx corrected. "Singular. In a word . . . the Dump is a congeries of rebirth cen-

ters. When a person shuffles off his mortal coils to
Buffalo, his essence wings to Cimön." I nodded
encouragingly. "Each species is drawn to a
characteristic spot on Mainside. These spots are
located along a line which cuts Mainside in half.
The line appears to be a, and is known as the,
Dump. Do you see how short I keep my sentences,
Felix? How crystalline my exposition?"

The sweat from my hours of skiing was
evaporating and I had started to shiver. "And you
get your body at the Dump when you come here?"

"How right you are. At the Dump you get a
body, and if that body is destroyed, it's back to the
Dump for a new one, not always of the same cut as
the redeceased, but . . ."

I had one more question. "Does a person without a body look like a spot of light? White light?"

"White or red or green," Franx said. "It depends. A dead or redead person on his way to the
Dump for a new body is green. Not a brilliant
green, you understand, just a sort of chalky dead-
fish green, a shade not unlike . . ."

"I've seen it," I interrupted, remembering
Kathy in the graveyard.

"Hasten on, O river Lethe," Franx cried dramat-
ically. "Dead people are green. You see how brief I
can be. Then there are the dreamers. They are red.
You would like to know how they get here, but
there is no time. You are in a hurry. I pass, therefore, in silence over the inter-dimensional link.
Ignorabimus . . . we will not know. But the white
lights, such as you so recently were, adrift in
Dreamland till the tireless librarians scooped you
in to squeeze a book out of you . . ."

He lost the thread of what he was talking about,

and clacked his chitinous jaws in silence for a few seconds, his forelegs frozen in mid-gesture. For some reason the thought that I had turned into a white light seemed to upset and annoy him very much. I pulled my book out of the parka back and handed it to him. "Here," I said, "you can look at it. They didn't want it."

He took the book, but didn't look at it yet. "The white lights, I was saying, are the forms of those few who can spontaneously dissolve and reform their body, travelling hither and yon during the hiatus. It is a difficult technique, although perhaps a bit more accessible to humans . . . particularly in the presence of fuzzweed. Only recently I, too . . . But what *is* this?" He turned his attention to the book. "What did you say this is?"

"It's all my possible lives," I explained. "After I breathed in that smoke and whited-out I was able to see all my lives at once. And then it was like I sat down in all the parallel universes and typed out each life in infinite detail. Somehow the Library of Forms pulled them all out of me and wrapped them up together."

Franx had opened the book at random and was reading rapidly down one of the pages, his head turned to one side. "But this is phenomenal!" he exclaimed suddenly. "This page is completely accurate. It even has me saying this sentence . . ." He read further, holding the book open with his forelimbs. "It goes on to say what happens next . . ." He read further, his compound eye twitching faster and faster. Suddenly he stopped. "Oh my," he said slowly. "How awful for me." His legs began jerking spasmodically.

I reached for the book. Had Franx actually

chanced on the one true description of my life? As I took the book a gust of wind flipped over some pages. "It was here," Franx said, flipping back a thin sheaf of pages, then another. He paused to read. "No, it wasn't this . . ." He flipped forward, backward, read and reread . . . then abruptly stopped looking. "It's no use. It *said* we wouldn't find it again."

The wind across the crevasse made a low throbbing. Behind me stretched an endless white, and above me was the clear blue sky. Had Franx read my future?

"Tell me what happens next, Franx."

"We'll run into George Cantor. He'll ask us to his house. And then . . ." His voice trailed off. His legs were twining around each other.

I resolved to go into a speed-up and flip through the whole book, but soon realized this was impossible. The one true page was lost in the continuum of possible lives. It was funny that Franx had stumbled on it. There was something paradoxical about the situation, but I couldn't quite put my finger on the paradox. I flipped a little more and read a page where I was a gunfighter in old El Paso. Yippie-tie-yay-ti-yo.

The search seemed hopeless. After all the book had c pages, and c is strictly greater than alef-null. Which meant that I could never look at every page unless I could somehow regain that white-light ability to handle the uncountable infinities. I made a remark to this effect and slipped the book back into my parka.

Franx suddenly looked up. "Now I'm supposed to say," he deepened his voice and recited portentiously, "Did you say that book has c pages? Why,

Felix, we can solve that problem you talked about
. . . the continuum problem. Come, let us take the
tunnel back to Flipside.'' His intonation was stiff
and self-mocking.

"What's the matter, Franx?"

"Don't you understand? I read the true description of everything that's ever going to happen to
you, including all our conversations and everything you see me . . ." He broke off, then resumed
with difficulty, "Even what I just said. And even
this. And even this." He stopped again in frustra-
tion. "It all seems so . . . so predictable, so
futile." He was twisting his legs in agitation, and
went on haltingly. "And—and I read that I'm
going to be murdered. It's not so terrible going
back to the Dump, I've done it before, but to have
my head viciously beaten in by a bigoted cretin of
a Godsquad thug . . ." His eyes flashed at me in
resentment. "At least after that I'll be free of your
prophecies, you . . ."

"Franx," I broke in, "Take it easy. You're rav-
ing." Suddenly the paradox I'd been looking for
jumped into relief. "It's impossible that you could
have read a true description of everything that
will happen to us. Logically impossible, given
that you don't want it. I'll prove it to you."

He stopped gnashing his mandibles and spat
out, "I know. You're going to ask me to choose
between saying 'YES' or saying 'NO'. I read that
part too."

"Just listen Franx. It has to work. I'm going to
ask you to say 'YES' or say 'NO'. You pick. But
wait! Think back on what the book said you did
. . . whether you said 'YES', said 'NO', or didn't
answer at all. Don't tell me! Remember what it

said you did, and just do something different. O.K.? Now. Say 'YES' or say 'NO."

There was a long silence. Franx seemed to be engaged in a terrible internal struggle. Several times he raised his head to speak, but only managed a dry clicking. He was lying on his stomach on the ice, and all up and down his body the little legs were waving in frenzy. Once his wingcovers started to raise, and I feared he would simply fly off to be free of my future.

But then he spoke. "No," he whispered. Then louder, "No! NO! *NO!*" He rose to his feet and chirped in delight. "I said it Felix. NO! The page said I wouldn't answer, ha, the page tried to protect itself, NO, but I've conquered it. The philospher-king has cut the Gordian knot. Let there be jubilation and great glee for I am free, I am free!" He did a little jig, kicking out his legs and rocking from side to side.

I breathed a sigh of relief. Franx certainly seemed to have gotten a little unstable. "What did you see on your climb anyway, Franx? And how far did you get?"

"I reached alef-one," he said cheerfully. "Come on, I'll take you to see it. The easy way. There's a tunnel down there that goes right through Cimön to Flipside. It really would be interesting to compare your c pages to those alef-one cliffs." He climbed onto my back and took hold with his legs and mandibles.

I jumped off the ice-cliff and into the crevasse. Franx's wings cut the air, and we angled over towards the staircase chiselled into the other side. We landed heavily.

14

At Alef-One

We started down the staircase, Franx leading the way. To the right was a sheer drop to the rushing torrent of icewater. As we went deeper the light grew fainter, and the shifting shapes in the walls of ice became more visible. Once I almost lost my footing when a ghostly catfish seemed to dart at me through the ice. The roaring of the stream made conversation impossible. I could only follow Franx's domed back. Finally we reached the bottom.

The dark frigid water went rushing past, its surface roiled in standing wave patterns. Here and there rivulets poured out of the glacier and into the torrent. Far ahead it disappeared back under the ice. Against my will, I found myself imagining how it would be to plunge into the water . . . to have every limb pulled in a different direction by the powerful currents, to be dashed against hidden teeth of ice, and finally to be sucked into black subterranean labyrinths. Why not? I was so scared of the water that I had a crazy urge to jump in and get it over with. I'd rematerialize at the Dump . . .

I shivered and pulled myself together. Franx was crouching on the bank staring at the stream. What was the matter with him? I nudged him once, twice, and he began to move again.

We walked along the stream until we came to a horizontal tunnel leading off the left . . . towards the city I'd seen. The tunnel was a man-made tube some 7 feet in diameter . . . sort of like a drainage culvert. I followed Franx in. Gradually the roaring of the stream faded.

Although the tunnel felt level underfoot, it kept looking like it was curving downhill. I couldn't see ahead of or behind us for more than fifty feet, even though the tunnel was well-lit by a luminous stripe running along the side at waist level. This was really a window into the ice, and one could see the colored dreamshapes drifting about. Here and there a door was set into the ceiling like a submarine's hatch.

"Did you come this way before?" I asked Franx.

"You didn't ask that on the page," he said brightly. "It's such a relief not to know what I'm going to say. I speak well, but speech must be spontaneous, have a little Zen in it, you understand . . ."

He had overlooked my question, and I decided to try a more interesting one. "Why is this tunnel slanting downhill when it isn't?" He paused to think that one over, and I rephrased it, "Why does it look like we're walking over the crest of a hill, when it *feels* like we're on a level path?''

"Oh that's the . . . the seriousness? I mean the gravity. I am less well-versed in physics than in other disciplines. I have read widely and well, but there are lacunae . . .'' I cleared my throat and he returned to the point. "Yes, yes, Felix. I can answer your question. I'm a little depressed and I talk more when I'm depressed. I had a rather disillusioning experience on Mount On, and I'm still finding my way, my endless weary way . . .''

We walked in silence for a while. The tunnel seemed brighter than before. We seemed always to be coming over a rise in the ground. I could have sworn that by now we were walking perpendicular to the glacier's surface, straight down into the surface of Cimön.

Suddenly Franx began talking again. "Never fear, I haven't forgotten your question. The force of gravity is variable in Cimön. Variable not so much with regard to intensity, but with regard to direction. We noticed that on the mountain, yes?''

"That's right," I responded. "The face of Mount On looks smooth, but when you climb, it's like a staircase. Sometimes gravity pushes you against the ground and it feels like a meadow, and sometimes gravity drags you back along the ground and it feels like a cliff.''

"Correct. And on Mainside. . . . I presume that you realize this is a tunnel from the Mainside of Cimön to the Flipside . . . on Mainside the gravity points almost directly into the ground and it feels like a huge plain.''

"The Library and the snow and that city are all on Mainside?''

"Of course. Now use your right-brain a little,

Felix. Think of Cimön as an infinite strip of canvas with a painting on each side. I speak concisely. The lower portion is water on both sides. One can even sail across the bottom edge. On *Flipside* the top part is mountain. Mount On. A shrinking field fits the whole Absolute Infinity in. On *Mainside* the very top part is a great desert. A bad place. Below the Desert is an endless line of garbage. The Dump. Right below that are the cities of the plain. One for each world and for each era . . . each grown up around its own characteristic part of the Dump. The gravity on Mainside points into the surface of Cimön . . . this far up Flipside the gravity points parallel to the surface. To keep 'down' underfoot, the tunnel must curve. Fill in the blanks."

There was a spot of light ahead. The tunnel ended here. What had been horizontal on Mainside was vertical on Flipside. When I tried to see it all at once I got a sick, dizzy feeling. It was like staring too long at one of those Escher interiors where staircases lead off in every direction, everting and inverting as your anxious eye clings to the billowing surface.

The tunnel ended with a stone arch leading onto a drop so sheer that the utter void of it practically sucked me off the edge. I already had vertigo from thinking about the tunnel, and I slipped lurchingly.

There was a bar across the arch overhead . . . a sort of chinning bar . . . and I grabbed onto it with both hands. No matter which way was up or how far down was, I had something solid to hang onto now, and I was able to look down without being overwhelmed.

As before, there was no next lower rock, no first step down, but now it was much worse. No infinite speed-up of alef-null eye twitches could bring my focus of attention from down there to up here. No matter how fast and how far I jumped my reference points I couldn't pull my attention back up to alef-one. It was pulling me forward. I thought to close my eyes.

When I opened them again I was staring at my hands gripping the bar across the arch. The knuckles were white and my palms were wet. Painfully I unclenched them and shuffled carefully to a spot a few feet back from the edge. I sat down on the floor and leaned against the wall. Franx had glued himself to the other wall, with his head sticking out over the abyss.

"And I thought I had reached the end," he said sadly. "One eye looks up and one eye looks down. I grow weary of looking up. Do you know how long I've been here, Felix? On Cimön?"

"I don't know. A long time."

"Twelve hundred years according to your time system. One point two millenia. One keeps track by talking to the freshers, bless their trusting hearts. Twelve hundred years and this is the farthest up Mount On I ever climbed. And any unthinking clod who cares to can stroll over here through the tunnel. Will it never end? Is there then finally no balm in Gilead?"

I wasn't sure what he was getting at. "You mean you didn't know this tunnel existed?"

"Of course I knew about the tunnel. There's lots of tunnels to alef-one, and if you're willing to chance going into the Desert you'll find tunnels to alef-two, to alef-alef-null, to the inaccessible cardinals . . . I've seen them, I've peeked up God's skirts like the others . . . gawked and gone home unchanged." He sighed heavily. "At least I really climbed alef-one. At least I have that."

I tried to boost his spirits a little. "That's fantastic, Franx, that you climbed all this way. Tell me how you did it."

"I will tell you more than that, Felix." He fixed me with one of his faceted eyes. "As a mathematician, I take it that you are relatively ignorant of . . . which is not to say unreceptive to . . . the fine points of mystical thought?"

"I'm not really a typical mathematician, Franx—whatever that means to you. I've read some Plotinus and done a little yoga. But no, I can't say that I've really . . ."

"Exactly. You have not informed yourself. So few humans are adequately prepared for Cimön. It is quite different on Praha. Even a larva, even a slave, can discourse as I now shall, with your genial permission."

"Just remember, Franx, I asked how you got up to alef-one."

"The flow of words, the give and take, how I relish it. A set-theorist. It is fortunate that we met, Felix, and not only for you, one of the first members of your race whom I can address as equal if not beetle. I would almost say you were enlightened, were it not for your lamentable delusion that you have not died. You should face facts. Accept the Dump you spring from, embrace it and only then can you cast it aside and truly move on. Already you control the white light, albeit with the aid of drugs, whereas I only recently managed . . ." He stopped talking for a minute, and then muttered, "Alef-one, just alef-one," in a bitter tone.

His mind really seemed to be slipping. I sat in silence for a few minutes thinking things over. Nobody wanted to believe that I was really still alive. I thought I was, but it wasn't clear to me how I was ever going to get back. Jesus had said I should climb to the top of Mount On, but here Franx was telling me that alef-one was the farthest he'd gotten in twelve hundred years.

I wondered how the time here fit in with the time on Earth. I'd left Earth on Thursday afternoon, flown up from Boston with Kathy. What if I got back to Earth and thousands of years had passed? My body would be long gone and it would just be back to Cimön. On the other hand, maybe the time here was sort of perpendicular to Earth time, and no matter how long I stayed it would still be late afternoon on Thursday, the thirty-first of October, 1973, when I got back.

I began thinking about April, the two-note giggle she made when she was happy. We had met on a bus back in 1965. She had short hair then, and lipstick, and listened to me as no one else ever had. She would be worrying about me, I suddenly realized. I could almost see her wheeling Baby Iris down Tuna Street in the stroller . . . the baby's blond curls, April's smooth dark hair, her head turning, looking . . .

"Well?" Franx said challengingly.

"What?" A pebble was digging into me and I shifted a little to the left.

"Don't you want to hear?"

"I'm sorry Franx. I lost track of what you were talking about." I wasn't going to bother arguing with him about whether or not I was really alive. Suddenly it occured to me that even if I was stuck here, April would die and come to Cimön in fifty or sixty years. That was something to look forward to. But by then she would have found somebody else, somebody she loved more. Franx was talking again.

"I was going to tell you how I got to alef-one, but perhaps you have lost interest?"

"No, no, I'd like to hear it." Franx seemed a little desperate, like someone who suddenly realizes there is no exit from a trap. I wondered how it would be to spend eternity in Cimön. There would be no escaping by suicide . . . you'd just be reconstituted at the nearest Dump. But wouldn't it be possible to finally reach perfect enlightenment, total union with the Absolute, the One, the ground of all being, God Himself? And there was Hell . . .

As if he sensed my unspoken question, Franx began speaking again. "There is no way out of Cimön except into the Absolute. I have sought this way for many centuries. The time for surcease has come for me, will come for you."

"Wait a minute. You say there's no way out of Cimön except into the Absolute. But what about Hell? You sounded pretty worried when you thought I was from the Devil."

"Touché. What was it the noble Vergil said? 'The road to Hell is easy, but to return—ah, there is the bring-down, there is the drag.' You can go from Cimön to Hell, but you can't come back. Only your saviour, Jesus the Christ, has managed that trick. By symmetry, one would suppose that it is possible to go to Heaven and never come back.

There should be an irreversible enlightenment, a Heaven, a union with God from which there is also no returning. There should be a losing of oneself in light as well as a losing of oneself in darkness."

I nodded and Franx continued. Talking about the Absolute seemed to salve some inner wound in him, and the frenzy and hostility which had marked his earlier utterances was fading away. "After you left I continued up the mountain. It was much easier without you to carry, and I no longer found it necessary to push off against the cliffs. I moved further out from the surface of the mountain and just flew. I could make out a sort of glow in the sky far ahead, and as I flew and stared towards the light I . . ." Franx trailed off and I had to urge him to continue.

"I became the White Light," he said finally. "You know what it's like. It doesn't faze you. I saw the One, I had it in my grasp, but then it all grew gray again, and rough rocks lay before me. I landed at alef-one."

"What did you say about white lights before?" I queried. "Red lights were dreamers, green lights were dead people, and white lights were what?"

"People who have used inner discipline or trickery to dissolve their body and reform it somewhere else. It is relatively easy for humans to do—particularly if they inhale the smoke of fuzzweed. But I do not come from a race of drug-addicts. We are poets, mystics, philosopher-kings . . ."

The frenzied tone was creeping back into his voice, and I cut him off. I was beginning to understand. "Stop me if I'm wrong, Franx, but I think I see what you're so upset about. For all these hundreds of years here you never managed to go into the White Light." He started to say something, but I talked louder, drowning him out. If I didn't put it into words, he'd spend all day circling around the point. "Then on the Mountain it finally happened. You saw the light. You *were* the light. Your years of seeking finally paid off and you stepped into Heaven." He nodded silently and I went on. "Maybe you liked it, and maybe you didn't. But you came back. You materialized again, part-way up Mount On and as far from the Absolute as ever."

Franx's legs were twitching, and he spoke in a choked whisper. "I wanted to stay there, Felix, I did. I've had enough. Time must have a stop. But now I'm scared, scared to go back. The Absolute is Everything, but it's Nothing, too."

I ran my hand over the long curve of his back. "Does *any* one ever go for good? To be with God?"

The peak of Franx's grief had passed and his legs were still again. His dry, expressionless eyes stared at me. I felt he was hiding something. "There's no way to tell. People go white and disappear, but maybe they just rematerialize somewhere else in Cimön. After all, it's infinite . . ."

He was quiet for a minute, then with a visible effort began talking again in his usual convoluted way. "Anyway, the interesting thing about our two trips, the really marvellous thing is that you reached c and I reached alef-one. You conceived of all your possible lives, and grasped them as a unity. *Fiat* THE LIVES OF FELIX RAYMAN. *Imprimatur* and *Nihil Obstat*; Annie, get the T.V. Guide. No, don't stop me, I have a point to make.

The One and the Many, Felix. You saw the Many and I saw the One." His voice cracked, but he pressed on. "I saw the One, I *was* the One, but then I clutched at it, tried to hold it. I—I killed it by looking, and ended up with alef-one."

"That's called the Reflection Principle."

"Please elaborate. This is new to me."

"The Reflection Principle is an old theological notion which we use in Set Theory. Any specific description of the full universe of Set Theory also applies to some little set inside the universe. Any description of the Absolute also applies to some limited, relative thing."

Franx made a disappointed noise. "You're just saying that the Absolute is unknowable. That's the most elementary teaching of mysticism."

"Yes, but I still don't think you see how it applies to Mount On. When you go white, and you are no longer really there, then there *is* no individual, and no conception of the Absolute. But the situation is unstable. The Absolute divides, tries to get outside itself, and *wham*, there's a beetle looking at alef-one."

My mind felt very clear. For once Franx had nothing to add. We stared out of the arch at the deep blue sky, so clear and flawless.

But there was something out there after all. A dark shape, rounded on top and with three smaller objects handing down from it. It was a Guide with three climbers.

But he wasn't flying up the mountain anymore. Instead he seemed to be moving away from the mountain, out and downward in a huge looping curve. Where were they going? I looked down past the stripes of cliff and meadow to the sea far, far below.

The sea jutted out from the flat mountainside in a gentle curve, and I had the feeling the Guide was taking these climbers there. But what was there? A sort of flickering orange light came from beyond the sea, but no matter how hard I squinted I could make out nothing more.

Looking back at the sky near us I saw something else again . . . a bright spot which seemed to be moving straight towards us. Fast. Before I could duck there was a WHOP and two arms were hanging from the bar across the arch. Two arms in the sleeves of a dark gray suit, with white cuffs peeping out. The arms swung gently to and fro.

Franx hissed menacingly and backed slowly away from the arms, his mandibles spread and ready to snap. I followed his example, and we both backed down the tunnel.

Suddenly more white light came flashing in on us. It stopped between the arms, grew irregular projections, darkened and solidified. Georg Cantor was standing there, his hands gripping the bar set into the archway. His piercing blue eyes took us in and he gave a small smile.

"Felix Rayman and . . . perhaps I've seen you somewhere?"

"My name is Franx," the beetle said, then added proudly, "I climbed up here today, all the way to alef-one. And my side-kick here has a book with c pages right in his parka. Get it out, Felix, show him." Sidekick, my ass. I began getting the book out while Franx rattled on. "Why don't we just stand here and compare the book to the cliffs.

We'll straighten out your problem right now."

Cantor stiffened a little. "You're referring to the Continuum Problem?"

I held the book out towards him. I felt embarrassed. Franx's suggestion seemed reasonable to me, but I was sure it had some stupid flaw which Cantor would cuttingly expose. "There's c pages in here," I said, smiling and nodding. "Franx was wondering why we couldn't just try matching it up page by page with those cliffs out there . . ." I trailed off lamely.

"Go ahead," Cantor said finally. "Don't let me stop you."

I went over to the edge and looked down. I was ready for it this time and felt no vertigo. I decided to move my eye up the cliffs, folding down the corner of a new page for each cliff. If every single corner was folded down by the time I finished, then I'd know that c is the same size as alef-null . . . that the Many can be reduced to the One.

But it wasn't so easy. My book had no first page and no last page. Wherever I opened it, I'd get another page, but there was never a next page. The sequence of cliffs, on the other hand, was perfectly well-ordered. Above every cliff or set of cliffs there was always a unique next cliff. The alef-one cliffs and the c pages were two different uncountable collections, each with its own natural ordering . . . and there was no obvious way to compare them. It was like dividing apples into oranges.

Half-heartedly I went into a speed-up, but I gave up after awhile. To work through all alef-one cliffs I'd have to go white again. And I didn't know how.

"I can't really handle uncountable sets," I said handing the book to Cantor. "Can you . . ."

He waves the book aside. "I'm through for the day. I'll take you to Ellie's instead. Come on." He started walking down the tunnel.

I had to trot to keep up with him. "Do you actually know the size of the continuum? Does the problem have a solution?"

"For mathematicians it is very difficult," he chuckled. "But mathematics is not everything, no? There is physics, there is metaphysics." He was walking faster than ever, and I had to run to keep up. Franx was swinging along on the ceiling just behind us. Cantor went on, "If I were still on Earth I would carry out certain experiments, certain physical tests which could very well resolve the Continuum Problem."

I could hardly contain myself. "What tests? How would they work?"

"The idea stems from my 1885 paper," he said off-handedly. "If there were a third basic substance . . . in addition to mass and aether . . . then we would know that c has power at least alef-two. But this is Cimön, and here we stick." He left it at that and redoubled his speed.

I really couldn't keep up with him anymore, and contented myself with running along behind him. I wondered what kind of experiment he meant. I made a special effort to fix the date 1885 in my mind. I'd have to look the paper up when I got back to Earth. If.

The walls of the tunnel flowed past as we ran along. It seemed farther than before. I always feel strange in tunnels. You're walking or driving along as fast as you can and nothing seems to

15
High Tea

When we were half-way through the thickness of Cimön, Cantor stopped by a round door set into the ceiling. The door was massive with a dial set into it. It looked like a safe.

He gestured to the dial. "You are a mathematician, Dr. Rayman. Perhaps you can open the lock?"

The dial had only ten markings, labelled zero through nine. I jumped to the conclusion that the combination would be a string of alef-null digits, the decimal expansion of some real number. But *which* real number?

I reached up and spun the dial slowly clockwise, pressing one hand against the door. I felt a tumbler fall at 3. I reversed direction and inched the dial counterclockwise. Another tumbler clicked at 1. There is only one familiar real num-

ber that starts with a three and a one. If my guess
was right the rest would be easy

"How I need a drink, alcoholic of course, after
the heavy lectures involving quantum me-
chanics." I recited this slowly, moving the dial
back and forth. The phrase is a well-known mem-
nonic for remembering the first fifteen digits of pi.
You list the number of letters in each word to get
3.14159265358979. A tumbler clicked with each
digit. It was pi for sure. I went into a speed-up.

An easy way to get the full decimal expansion
of pi is to sum up a special infinite series: $4/1 - 4/3$
$+ 4/5 - 4/7 + 4/9 - 4/11 + \ldots$ I started adding
and dialing in the digits as they developed. It took
me a couple of minutes and my neck got stiff from
staring up at the dial.

Finally I finished. There was a satisfying THOK
inside the heavy door. Another free game. I
pushed and the door swung open. My arms were
tired from reaching up, and I let them fall.

"Very good," Cantor said. "It's a thousand meters up." I peered into the dim shaft. I could make
out metal rungs on the side of a body-sized tube. I
wondered how we would be able to make the
climb. A thousand meters straight up is no joke for
a man Cantor's age. I said something to this effect,
but he assured me that as the gravity shifted the
climb would get easier.

If Franx was impressed by my feat he hid it
pretty well. While Cantor and I talked, the beetle
scrambled up my back and through the door—as
if I were a turkey-bone leaning against a garbage
can. Cantor took my arm.

"Where did he latch onto you?"

"Franx?" I said, stepping back with an upward

glance. I could hear him scuttling away some fifty feet up. He was still my only friend here—even though he had been acting so strangely. "He's from a place called Praha. We hooked up at Hilbert's Hotel and climbed to epsilon-zero together. I breathed in some fuzzweed there, whited out through Dreamland and reformed at the Library. Meanwhile Franx kept flying up On. He saw the One, merged in, and then used the Reflection Principle to get to alef-one. I think he's upset that he couldn't stay white."

"He could if he really wanted to," Cantor observed. "It's just across the Desert." No more was forthcoming, so I went ahead. He closed the door behind us.

The walls of the tube were metal, and the only light was what flickered through the occasional porthole cut out of the metal to expose the glowing ice of the Dreamland glacier. Our feet echoed against the rungs, and conversation was impossible. I wondered if the whole inside of the Cimön slab was made up of the crystalline dream-stuff.

As Cantor had promised, the climb became steadily easier. Although the tube was perfectly straight, it soon felt like it was inclined to the vertical.

I could see Franx far ahead when he would pass one of the light spots, and to keep up with him I had to climb without resting. The necessary movements were simple and repetitive. My body was running on automatic. Cantor followed some twenty feet behind me.

When the rungs finally ended it took me a second to notice it. The tube had widened and turned into a carpeted staircase. I crawled up several steps before I realized that I could walk up the stairs. Franx was crouched before a door at the head of the stairs. "Felix," he called, "Could you trouble yourself to ask your fellow mathematician what . . ."

Cantor's footsteps on the stairs behind me stopped. "Ring."

The staircase was carpeted with a red and blue runner held in place by brass rods. The walls and ceiling were panelled in a dark wood, and the lighting was provided by candle sconces set into the wall.

My head was clearing from the long drudgery of the climb. Franx was still turning himself laboriously around when I reached the top of the stairs. I reached over him to push the buzzer by the door.

Rapid footsteps approached and the door swung open. It was a skeletal woman in a gray silk dress. Lots of jewelery: diamonds, platinum. I assumed that she was old, but it was hard to be sure. The sutures of her skull showed on her forehead and temples, and her gums had drawn far back from her teeth. The knobs of her knees looked like galls on weedstems.

"Hello, Georg!" she said in a light, thin voice. "It's good to see you're safely back from Flipside. I'm sure you're full of new ideas . . . and much more." Her gaze fell on me. Her eyes had a strange sparkle to them.

"This is Dr. Felix Rayman," Cantor said, "and . . ."

"My name is Franx," the beetle interrupted, perhaps worrying that he would not be introduced.

"And this is Madam Elizabeth Luftballon," Cantor concluded.

She smiled and stepped back. "Just call me Ellie. And come on in. I adore meeting Georg's students." She flashed me a special smile. Despite her withered state there was something charming about her. Her smile's perfect curves and ideal symmetries reminded me of a candied slice of lemon.

Cantor led us past her and into a room off the hall. It was furnished something like Hilbert's Hotel had been, with oriental carpets and handsome antiques. There were also a number of musical instruments. Piano, violin, harpsichord.

A mullioned picture window gave onto a changing view like I had seen at the Library of Forms. Dreamland. I stared out for a minute, then turned back to the room.

Cantor was exchanging a few low words with Ellie at the door, and Franx was sniffing around. Apparently they had expected company. There was a spindly-legged little table holding tea things and a beautiful Schwarzwaldtorte.

"It's starting again," Franx twittered to me. A leg twitched in anxiety.

"What is." I drifted towards the cake. It was mostly whipped cream, and was decorated with curled shavings of chocolate. I was ready to eat some Cimön food.

Franx dogged my steps, his voice shrill with anxiety. "Your prophecies are coming true again. I read all this. This room, this cake, these words, and again a horrible death draws near on whispering wings!"

Didn't he ever think about anything but himself? I was hoping to have some interesting conversation with Cantor here, and now Franx was ready to pull another freak-out. I turned and snapped. "Do something that's not in the script. Something unexpected. And if you can't it's just too bad. Keep bugging me and *I'll* pound your head in."

Before I had quite finished he screeched, "Free," and sprang up at me. I started, lost my footing, and fell backwards with a strangled cry. On my way down I caught the tea-table with my elbow. It splintered and the tea and cake went flying.

"That wasn't in the script," Franx piped happily. I ignored him and sat up. Ellie had disappeared, but Cantor was standing in the door, watching us with an alert, interested expression.

I began gathering up the scattered tea-things. The rugs were soft and nothing but the table had broken, but hot tea and whipped cream were everywhere. Franx lost no time in burying his face in the smashed cake.

"Sorry," I said, rising. "I hope . . ."

Cantor cut me off with a wave of his hand. "It makes nothing. Ellie is happy to have guests." He raised his voice suddenly and called out, "Ellie! We've had an accident! Please bring more tea and clean cups!"

Franx was eating the last crumbs and smears off the floor. Cantor walked over and gave him a sharp nudge with his foot. "Hey! Do you want some tea?"

At the unfriendly touch, Franx spun around with a warning hiss. But then he remembered his manners and chirped, "Yes, please. In a bowl with milk and perhaps a crust of bread. Preferably a blue china bowl."

Cantor relayed the request. I took off my shoes and parka and sat down cross-legged on a purple couch with large velvet cushions. Outside the window, a pattern of colored lines was arranging itself into the envelope of a helix. A spot of red light hovered nearby. The helix solidified and began hopping about like an animated bed-spring. More helices appeared, and they began dancing with each other . . .

"What is that out there?" I asked Cantor. He had seated himself in a massive easy chair, and Franx lay on the floor, one eye on the window and one eye on us. I hoped that he wouldn't feel the need to do anything unexpected for awhile. The helices had turned into tentworms and were surrounding the spot of light with colored websheets.

"Those are the dreams," Cantor said in his deep voice. "The spots of red light are the dreamers."

"That's what everyone keeps telling me. But does that mean that the spots of light are creating the whole . . ." I broke off, groping for a word. The colored tent had grown in size. There was a hole in the side, and you could see the spot of light moving tenderly up and down the body of a huge, moist grubworm.

"Felice!" Franx exclaimed, moving towards the window with a start. "My precious one!" The white grub's body rippled, and a sort of mouth extruded from its near end. The spot of ruby light hovered there like a bee at a flower. Franx had reared up against the window now and was twit-tering incomprehensibly. A pair of erectile hairs protruded from his rear. A big drop of milky fluid slid along them, hung trembling, dripped onto the rug.

Suddenly the tent collapsed and the spot of light shot off the left. Sheets of colors rippled past and angry faces began forming. Another spot of light moved in the distance. Franx slid down from the window and sniffed the wet spot behind him without embarassment. "She looked like my mate. That dreamer must have been from Praha."

Cantor nodded. "The dreamers usually seek out visions appropriate to them. But," he wagged his finger at me, "the dreamers are not creating the visions out there. They observe them, they experience them, but the visions will still be there when every dreamer is gone. Like with sets, is it not?"

Outside the window a circle of mushrooms had grown. They had cruel, mocking faces. A red light moved about uncertainly in their midst.

"Let me get this straight," I said. "All the possible dreams are out there. When someone has a dream he really turns into a spot of red light and comes to Dreamland. By some kind of instinct he picks out a few dreams which are appropriate, experiences them and then goes back to his regular body?"

Just then Ellie came in with the tea. She frowned a little when she saw the shattered table. "You'll have to get me another one, Georg. There's a new antique store in Truckee."

"Still more?" he sighed. "Is it really so . . ."

Before he could expand on his objections, Ellie started talking again. "And these are your students? That will be good for you to teach them.

You're almost due for one of your terrible depressions, I can tell."

Cantor waved his hand in a feeble dismissive gesture. "No more students, Ellie. Only God can teach. But they are certainly welcome to stay." He glanced at me questioningly. I nodded and he continued, "Mr. Rayman will be needing a bed." He frowned at Franx. "And what about you?"

"I'll use the floor in Felix's room. No, the wall. I mean the . . . the ceiling." He stopped there, apparently having foiled the prophecies once again.

"Will that be in order, my sweet?" Cantor said to Ellie.

"Of course, Georg. It will do us both good to have the company." She gave me a strange look, holding eye contact longer than felt comfortable. "Would you like some brandy as well?"

"Well sure. That would be nice."

She left the room again and Cantor turned his attention back to me. "There was something . . . yes. The spots of light. A sleeping person reaches here with a spot of light he carries in his pineal gland. They are like eyes, these red lights. Eyes that can freely move across the trans-dimensional bridge from Earth to Dreamland. And after death there is only the light and a little more."

"But this doesn't feel like a dream," I protested. "A-and the room isn't changing."

There was a high giggle in the kitchen, followed by a crash.

"Ellie!" Cantor hollered, "Are you all right?" There was a faint answer. Cantor looked at me again. "Of course this isn't a dream. If it was my dream I wouldn't be living in such a woman's house. The dreams are out there." He gestured at the window. "As you must know by now, Cimön is like a huge pancake. Mainside, Flipside, and the filling is Dreamland. In most places it's covered up with dirt and rocks, but around here it reaches right up to the surface. The snowstorms feed the glacier, and the glacier is Dreamland."

Ellie brought in the brandy bottle and three glasses. She leaned over to pour, and seemed to make a point of bumping me with her withered behind. Could such a woman possibly have sexual thoughts? She seated herself next to me on the couch. I poured some brandy into Franx's bowl, and we all sipped in silence for a minute.

There was another question bothering me. "It doesn't seem much different here from Hilbert's Hotel. I could handle countable infinities then, and I can handle them now. But what about alef-one and c? And the higher infinities? When will I really see them?"

"It depends what 'you' means," Cantor said. I raised my eyebrows questioningly, but he shook his head. "It would do no good for me to try to explain. You still think like a mathematician. Only trust in God." He poured himself a little more tea. "Do you play?" he said suddenly.

I didn't know immediately what he meant, but Franx piped up, "I flute tolerably well. Perhaps we could play a duet?" Cantor smiled at him for the first time.

"A little Scarlatti, Ellie?"

"Oh yes, Georg. One of the concertos." She walked over to seat herself at the harpsichord, and Franx followed her. She handed him a pamphlet of music which he rapidly scanned through and returned.

"I am at your service," Franx declared. "Do you prefer the Cimön or the classical style?"

"Oh, give me the overtones," Ellie said, gaily fingering a chord. She struck with her fingers and the tart notes hung in the air. Franx stretched his head forward and emitted a perfect C, richly rounded and burnished with a light tremolo.

They started playing then. Cantor gave a sigh of contentment and leaned back in his chair with his eyes closed.

Ordinarily my appreciation of music doesn't go back much earlier than Robert Johnson, but with Cimön ears it was different. Franx was piling endless sequences of overtones onto each note, and Ellie was flicking in zillions of extra little grace notes between every beat Scarlatti wrote. The pattern shimmered around us and filled my senses. Good, harmonious thoughts filled my mind.

They played for a long time, maybe forty minutes. Somewhere toward the end Cantor fell asleep. It was easy to notice, since a dull red light oozed out through his closed eyes. For an instant I thought he was bleeding, but then the light formed itself into a ball which hovered near his head. Cantor's astral dream eye. It winked at me and glided across the room, through the window glass. It hovered out there for an instant, then sped off in search of the perfect dream.

PART III

"Within the context of neo-rock
we must open up our eyes
and seize and rend
the veil of smoke which man calls order."
—Patti Smith

16
Inflatable Love Doll

Cantor's body was still in the chair, but just barely. Clearly most of him had gone into that dream eye. In his chair there was only a motionless husk, translucent, greenish, unreal. I wondered if he would be gone long. There were still so many questions.

Franx and Ellie finished the duet with a quick arpeggio of alef-null notes, and I clapped lightly. "That was really lovely. But the professor seems to have fallen asleep." I felt a little stiff, alone with the beetle and this skinny lady.

She seated herself next to me again and poured herself a fresh brandy. Franx held forth at some length on the subtleties of Scarlatti's composition, and she listened attentively. But even though she seemed to be concentrating only on what Franx said, she was constantly brushing against me in a perhaps unconscious flirtation.

There was no question of making love to a
woman like this . . . she would snap like a stick.
But my mindless male instincts urged me to assert
myself, to win her attention.

As soon as Franx paused for a breath I seized the
reins of the conversation. "It's too bad he fell
asleep. I wanted to ask him more about the Continuum Problem. He suggested that it might be
possible to physically test it on Earth."

Ellie stared into my eyes while I spoke, and my
tongue grew thick. What was it about this woman? By any sane standard she was repulsive . . .
almost a freak . . . but there was some aura of
sexuality around her . . .

"You can't always take Georg too seriously,"
she was saying. "I've heard him prove that Bacon
wrote Shakespeare's plays and that Joseph was
Jesus Christ's natural father. He likes to astound
people."

"He also said that there is a metaphysical approach to the Continuum Problem," I continued.
She had such a lovely smile. "Do you . . . do you
know anything about that?"

"Yes," she began. "He says you must *become*
the . . ."

Franx's harsh chirp interrupted. "I realize I risk
the high crime of *lèse majesté*, but how can you
set-theorists be so sure that c really is larger than
alef-null? Surely this is just poetry. All infinities
are really the same. Why shouldn't there be a
mapping from the natural numbers onto the
points in the continuum . . . a mapping which
has simply been overlooked. To be human is to be
erroneous, Felix." He chuckled condescendingly.

I felt almost sure he didn't believe what he was saying.

But I was glad at the question. I knew just how to answer it, and I was eager to have a chance to shine. I took my book out of my parka pocket. "Look, Franx, this has c pages. To prove that c is greater than alef-null, I need only demonstrate that no matter how you go about picking alef-null pages, I can always carry out a procedure for singling out at least one page which you will miss."

"Wait," Ellie said, rising. "Don't use the book. I have something nicer." She walked across the room, found a pasteboard box, and came back. She had a mincing walk that made her whole body sway, and I had to remind myself again that she was little more than a skeleton.

"Georg won't let me take these out when he's around." She handed me the box. It was a pack of cards. As I slid out the deck she stared at me, watching hungrily for my reaction. I looked at the top card.

A dark-haired woman with full lips and hair under her arms. The back of a man's head. My heart beat faster. Franx hoisted himself up on the couch arm and stared. I cut the deck. A full derierre, and up in the corner a face puffed with passion. Cut. A man, a kneeling woman. Cut. Two women standing and . . . Hmmm.

Franx's voice broke in. "Is that a seed catalog? We have those too."

The veins of my neck were engorged and it was a little hard to talk. I nodded and set the deck down on the table. Ellie was still staring at me.

Slowly she licked her lips. I couldn't meet her gaze.

"Are there supposed to be c of them?" Franx inquired blandly. "All right, let's see your trick for finding a card different from any alef-null cards I pick."

With an effort I ignored the pictures. I still wasn't sure what sort of reaction Ellie expected from me. Perhaps this was just some complicated way of ridiculing me.

I cut the deck and set the two halves on the table. "Now Franx, we'll go into a speed-up. You'll pick alef-null cards in a row, and when you're done I'll have singled out a card which you didn't pick."

Franx drew a card from the left-hand packet and I cut the right-hand packet again. "Pick another." This time he took a card from one of the right-hand packets, and I recut the packet he hadn't picked from yet. We kept it up like that. I kept recutting the untouched packet, which grew thinner, but never vanishingly so.

After alef-null steps, Franx had picked what looked like every blonde in the deck, and the untouched packet still held a card. A cheeky girl lying demurely on a white bed. For a second I thought it was April.

Before Franx could say anything, Ellie spoke up. "Would you like to go to bed now, Dr. Rayman?" She stood and began unbuttoning the front of her gray dress. There was something funny about her navel. "Look," she said, fingering it. "I blow up."

I backed up warily and stepped on Franx, who was pressing forward in curiosity. I slipped and when I had regained my footing, Ellie had pulled an air-hose out of the wall. She fastened it to the valve in her navel. "Say when, Felix."

She began to swell. First her breasts. They grew and grew so that she had to shed her dress and bra. A sad old pair of cotton drawers hung on her bony hips. The breasts continued to grow, quickly going beyond the attractive and into the grotesque.

She reached out and squeezed the immense milk-bags. Some of the air went down into her hips and legs. She held the breasts down until her lower half had inflated properly. Now the skimpy cotton panties were strained tight by her broad pelvis and full buttocks.

She unhooked the hose and turned to smile brightly at me with those thin lips and withered gums. "Your face," I said numbly. "You forgot that."

Ellie giggled and then squatted to compress her body. Slowly her features swelled. The gums crawled back down the teeth, the lips pouted out, the cheeks grew firm . . . even her hair thickened. She looked like one of the women in her deck of cards. Perhaps she had posed for the pictures.

"I noticed which cards you liked," she said softly. She took me by the hand. "Come . . ."

"I shouldn't," I said weakly. She pulled me to the bedroom.

Franx watched us from the ceiling, occasionally twittering in surprise. When we had finished I started to drift into sleep, but Ellie shook me awake. "Take me out, Felix. I want to dance."

"On the mountain? It's just rocks." I really

didn't feel like going back through the tunnel.

She gave me another hard shake and pulled some strange clothes out from under the bed. "Not the mountain, the city. Truckee. There's a nice supper-club I know."

Ellie was fully dressed in a few minutes. She wore pink toreador pants and a rubber top which looked more or less like a hose coiled around her. I slipped my jumpsuit back on, and Franx crawled down the wall.

Ellie said it was summer outside, so I left my ski-shoes and the parka. But I went back to the sitting room and got my book. After all, there was no telling if we'd be back this way again. Cantor was still resting lightly in his chair. He looked like a dried leaf. I saluted him silently and went out into the hall.

"Don't show that to anyone out there," Ellie cautioned, when she saw I had my book.

"Why not?"

"They don't have many infinities here." She sounded so cautious.

"Would they be upset if they saw some?"

"A lot of the people in Truckee are . . . frightened. But it's not like that at the club." The three of us stepped outside.

I had half expected to find myself on Mount On or in Dreamland, but the front door gave onto a residential city street lined with beat old parked cars. The city sloped away from us. It was twilight and the yellowish street-lights were on. There were trees, and a warm breeze rustled the leaves. Shadows danced on the pavement and on the stone walls of the houses lining the street. We started off. It was quiet and our footsteps echoed.

"Where's Dreamland?" I asked Ellie.

She tossed her head, shaking out her long wavy hair. "That's out the back door. I live here because it's a triple point. Truckee in front, Dreamland in back, and Mount On right through the tunnel."

We still hadn't seen anyone else. It was my favorite time of day . . . that time when gray light suffuses the city and everything glows with its own luminous significance. Ellie seemed to know her way. We followed her around corners and down the empty tree-lined streets. Here and there a garbage can had overflowed, and Franx snatched up this or that tidbit.

The neighborhood was mostly houses, but there were a few large buildings that could have been temples. They were lit up, and one could hear voices from within. I wondered what sort of religion the citizens of heaven practiced.

I fell into step next to Franx. He was being unusually quiet. "What do you think of this, Franx? Have you seen Truckee before?"

"I shouldn't be here," he said somberly. "They're going to smash my head in. I should do something, but I'm so tired, Felix, the current of history is too strong for me . . ."

For the first time I believed him. "I'm going to miss you."

"I'll see you again." I started to ask another question, but he cut me off. "There's not much time left. There's something you ought to know. You'll begin to notice it soon. Everything is alive. Don't forget." He paused to scoop up a half-eaten sandwich from the gutter.

"What are you trying to tell me, Franx?"

His answer was muffled. "You'll see. Keep your

eyes open. I'm going to fill up while I can." He darted over to another garbage can.

The light was fading and Ellie kept walking faster. Occasionally a car drove by, leaving a wake of foul exhaust. We passed a few people on the sidewalk, but when they saw Franx their faces tightened. Apparently they weren't used to aliens.

I grabbed Ellie's arm to slow her down. "What's the rush? And how come people look at Franx that way?"

She answered in a low rushed voice. "It's just around the corner up there," she said. "Where we're going. It's like a speakeasy. I'll explain there." She tried to twist out of my grip.

Franx had raised himself onto the rim of a garbage can to examine the contents. The can slipped out from under him now, and rolled into the street. Slowly he moved along the trail of garbage, picking and choosing. A man in an undershirt appeared at a window, frowned at us and picked up a phone receiver.

"Come on," Ellie begged. "We've got to get under cover before . . ."

A '52 Ford with writing on it turned the corner and pulled up next to us. A spotlight hit me in the eyes, and a rough voice spoke out of the glare. "Godsquad. Let's see some I.D."

I heard a hissing sound behind me. Thinking it was Franx, I turned and whispered, "Take it easy. I'll talk."

The car door opened, slammed, and a heavy hand fell on my shoulder. Ellie began screaming, and the spotlight moved off my face. I was dazzled and it took me a second to make out the scene.

Franx was on the pavement by the half-empty garbage can, looking up at us with his expressionless faceted eyes. "Don't worry, I'll clean it up," he was saying, but it was hard to hear him over Ellie's screams.

I looked at her then. She had let the air out of her navel. She looked like any other scrawny old woman. She was pointing at Franx and yelping, "The Evil One! Oh, save me, save me!"

The car door slammed again, and a figure in black ran over to Franx and jumped on him with both feet. I tensed myself for the *goosh*, but the huge beetle's resilient exoskeleton just bounced the man off to land in a heap on the sidewalk.

Franx twittered something I couldn't make out, something about talking cars. "Fly, Franx!" I shouted. "Get out of here!" The man holding me hit me hard in the stomach. I slid to the ground.

Through a red haze I saw Franx scramble around, lift his wingcovers, and take an awkward hop into the air. His wings began to buzz, and I cheered weakly. The second Godsquad man took out his gun. I shouted a warning. The pistol fired. Franx jerked in the air and fell heavily to the street.

The man who had hit me pulled a short club out of his belt. He hurried around the car into the street. I could hear him pounding Franx's head in. It crunched, at first.

Then it was over. A patch of green light winged up from the street and across the sky. "He's gone for now," the man in the street called with a deep chuckle.

The man with the gun was standing over me. The pistol was aimed at my head. "Hey Vince!

How about his friend? The devil lover." His voice
was high-pitched, self-righteous, angry.

"Don't shoot him against the car," Vince
cautioned.

Ellie spoke up then. "He's a good boy." Her
voice was old and quavering. "He's just come
here, you know. I've taken him under my wing."

The man with the gun looked down at Ellie
with a sneer on his face. He was tall and had short
dark hair combed into greasy waves. A high-
school bully. "So! You took it on yourself to process a fresher. You alone?" Ellie nodded meekly.
"And what if he's from the Evil One, too? That
hell-bug might have been his familiar! I ought to
shoot him. I ought to shoot him right now. If he's
human he'll *probably* come back through the
Dump just the same." Ellie began sobbing.

"Put the gun away, Carl," the other man said.
He was short and heavy set. Balding. "You can go,
ma'am." He grabbed my arm and helped me stand
up. "We'll just check this fellow out for you."

He shoved me into the back seat of their car.
Ellie came over to stick her head in the door.
"Now you come back, Felix." I started to say
something, but she cut me off with a frown. Her
withered lips silently mouthed a word. Please.
Then she stepped back onto the sidewalk.

17
Urban Terror

Vince drove and Carl sat next to him. The back doors had no handles on the inside, and there was a grill between the front and back seats. They hadn't bothered to look at my book.

I wished there were a gun hidden inside it.

"I haven't done anything."

Carl turned and looked at me scornfully. "You didn't have time, did you?"

I tried a new tack. "This is ridiculous. We're only here in astral bodies. What are you so scared of?"

"You hear that, Vince? You hear that occult talk?"

Vince grunted. There was more traffic now and the streets were brightly lit. We passed a few stores here and there. All of them seemed to have used, broken-down merchandise. For that matter, the Ford I was in seemed to be at least third-hand.

Springs poked through the seat, and there was a bad shimmy in the front wheels. The car didn't seem capable of going over thirty.

We cruised in silence for a while. More stores and people. We were near the center of Truckee . . . if it had a center. I was surprised to see an immense dump where one might have expected a city park. Scores of people were climbing about on the mountains of junk. Some rooted feverishly, and others just looked around expectantly. There were small fires here and there, fires which everyone avoided.

As we drove by, a rusted-out '56 Chevy suddenly appeared. A handful of people scrambled up the shifting scree to claim possession. It looked like a stocky man in a T-shirt had won, but suddenly a TV set materialized where his head had been. He began running around and waving his arms. Two tough-looking black women elbowed past him to get at the car. He tripped and rolled down a moraine of beer-cans.

We drove along next to the Dump for block after block. It seemed to stretch on forever, cutting Mainside in half like Franx had said. Battered objects were appearing on it constantly. None of the people swarming around the Dump brought anything, but everyone left with something. Occasionally you would see a person come crawling out of the garbage like a maggot squeezed out of a pork chop.

One of these new people came staggering out of the Dump and into the street. He looked like he had died of drink-insult to the brain. Vince ran over him without even slowing down. The wheels thumped one-two over the drunk, and I looked out the back window. A ragged green light was fluttering towards the Dump, folding on itself like a sheet of windblown newspaper.

"I ran that guy down last week, too," Vince said with a wheezy chuckle.

"Is it bad for him?"

"They say it hurts like hell."

"And a discorporated spirit like that is easy pickings for Satan," Carl chimed in. "As if you didn't know."

"What do you mean?"

"You see those fires? Each one of them goes straight to Hell. You go through the Dump once too often and, brother, that's all she wrote."

The car wheeled around a corner and pulled up in front of a white-painted cast-iron building. There was a billboard two stories high on the front of the building. The billboard looked like a car-lot advertisement, with a hyper-real color portrait of the boss. The boss was "Bob Teeter." The inevitable teeth and checked sport coat. But he wasn't selling cars.

"GOD CHOSE JESUS! JESUS CHOSE BOB TEETER! BOB TEETER CHOSE YOU!" the billboard read. Carl and Vince led me into the building.

It looked like any other police station. "Got a fresher, Sarge," Vince said to the officer behind the desk. Without looking up, the sargeant held out a form.

"We found him on the loose," Carl added. "With a giant cockroach."

The sargeant glanced at me with a flicker of interest. He wore a tie. He had a well-trimmed blond beard and flesh-colored glasses. You could tell he considered himself to be an intellectual. "What did you bring with you?" His voice was low and insistent. His eye fell on the book I was carrying, and he held out his hand. "Let me see."

"I don't think . . ." I began, but Carl gave me a hard shove and wrenched the book from my grasp. He tossed it onto the desk with an illiterate's contempt for the printed word. One of the corners stubbed, and the book landed face down with some pages folded under.

The sargeant read, "The Lives of Felix Rayman," from the spine. He scanned a page, squinting as the print got smaller. He flipped and glanced at some other pages. "How come all the pages end up in a blur like that?"

"It's not a blur," I protested. "There's alef-null lines on each page." They looked blankly at me. "There's infinitely many lines on each page, and there's a larger infinity of pages."

The sergeant's face clouded over. Too late I remembered Ellie's warning that infinity was not a homey concept in Truckee. Carl twisted my arm up in a hammer-lock. A pistol dug into my ribs.

"I think you got a live one," the sargeant said. 'Take him upstairs, and don't hesitate to shoot."

I was tempted to slug Carl and get it over with. If they killed me here, I'd just reappear somewhere in the Dump. Intellectually I knew this, but emotionally I wasn't ready to take a bullet in the gut. It would hurt while I died, it would hurt a lot. If my luck was bad it might take days. And if I landed on one of those fires I'd go to Hell. I decided I was curious to see what Bob Teeter would have to say.

As it turned out, Teeter had gone home for the

day. They locked me in a cell for the night. I tried to meditate and turn into a white light again, but nothing came of it. After seeing the way Cantor had looked while dreaming, I didn't really want to fall asleep, but before I knew it I had.

My dreams were the usual kaleidescopic blur at first, but at some point I snapped into consciousness. I could sense, for the first time, that I was a red ball of light. When I tried the old trick of looking at my hands, the ball obligingly extruded two. I let the hands snap back and began looking around.

The dream I had just been having . . . of working in a tuna cannery . . . was still playing all around me. Silver scales, sluices of salt-water. I walked out of the factory and surprised a fellow worker in the act of enjoying homosexual intercourse with a soft-drink machine.

With a twitch I entered a new dream space. People yelling at me. Twitch. A final exam. Twitch. Driving to Florida. I went into a speed-up then, searching all over Dreamland. I didn't know what I was looking for until I found it.

It was a drunk lying on a hot summer sidewalk. Spit all over his face. His wallet is lying next to him, inside out. He looks familiar. Another dreamer was already there. Glowing red light as usual, but formed into the shape of a woman's body, also familiar. April.

She leans over the drunk and tries to wake him. He looks just like me. This was April dreaming that I was hurt and drunk, and that she was trying to help me.

The drunk stands up then and looks at April with bleary hate-filled eyes. Curses drip from his cracked lips, and he pushes April away. He falls and hits his head on the sidewalk. It bounces. She backs off, sobbing.

I went up to her then, touched her. "April, baby, it's me."

That wasn't part of her dream, and she ignored it. I tried to pull her away, but she slipped out of my grasp, leaned over that slob on the sidewalk. Did she really think I could ever sink that low? He'd wet his pants, for god's sake.

If only I could get a message to her, tell her I was all right. Suddenly I knew how. I began zooming through Dreamland again, looking for the right dream. I didn't have much time, and had to settle for a rough approximation of what I wanted. I noted where it was and whipped back to April's dream.

The guy on the sidewalk seems to have died now. A dog noses at him, takes a tentative first nip out of his cheek. Nobody could have nightmares like April. She sobbed broken-heartedly while the dog had lunch.

Finally her nightmare ended, and she drifted away. This was the moment to act. I squeezed up against her and began pushing her along. She didn't resist, and pretty soon I'd brought her to the dream I wanted her to see.

It is the cockpit of an airplane, World War One style. A guy who looks something like me is flying the plane, his teeth bared in a grin. The Earth has dwindled to a ball far below. The radio crackles. "White lightning, white lightning, do you rrread me?" The voice is zealous, fruity.

The pilot speaks into the microphone. "I'm high all right, but not on false drugs. All I need is a clean windshield, powerful gasoline and a shoeshine.''

The line came from a Firesign Theatre record that April and I had often listened to together. She'd recognize it. Every time she left the dream, I gently forced her back to see it again. I wanted to make sure she remembered.

Pushing her back into the dream over and over, I fell into a light trance. Then I lost control, drifted through endless rickety buildings, and awoke. I was still in my cell.

They brought me some food after awhile. Scrambled eggs on a paper plate. They slid it in under the bars. For the first time since leaving Earth, I ate.

A little later I heard a deep, authoritative voice. Carl and Vince came and took me down the hall. Bob Teeter had an office there with silent air-conditioners plugged into both windows. All the furniture was scratched and wobbly. One leg of his desk was held on with wire.

There were more of the TEETER CHOSE YOU posters on the wall, some with four-color Sunday School illustrations of Jesus shaking hands with Bob while God's glowing eye beamed approvingly in the background. There was a map with pins in it, and a box half-filled with copies of THE HEAVENLY LAW, by Bob Teeter.

Teeter was a big white-haired man who looked like he might have once been a bartender in Pittsburgh. His head was enormous. His eyes were the size of hard-boiled eggs. A born leader.

Vince gave him a quick run-down, threw my book on his desk and went back downstairs. I stood in front of the desk, and Carl stood behind me with a .38 against my temple.

Bob Teeter looked at the book uncomprehend-
ingly, and then turned those huge eyes up at me.
"Did you find this on the Dump?"

His voice was deep and melancholy.

"I've never been to the Dump." Teeter looked
shocked. Carl cocked his pistol. I'd said the wrong
thing again.

"You're from the Evil One." It was not a question. The pistol was digging into my right temple.

I didn't answer, and Carl nudged me even harder with the gun. Suddenly I didn't care if they
killed me or not. I snapped my head down to the
right and hooked my left arm up, hoping to make a
blind catch. I was lucky and grabbed onto the
pistol with my pinky jamming the action. I
yanked down and continued to turn. The gun
came free.

I took a quick step back and Carl rushed me. I
just had time to switch the gun to my right hand.
He pinned my arms to my sides in a bear hug.

His doughy face looked down at me with a
contemptuous expression. "We're going to kill
you slow, devil."

I pushed my face forward and bit his face as
hard as I could. My teeth sank in. Part of his cheek
came off.

He screamed and his hug loosened enough so
that I could pull up my left hand and push myself
loose. I had a good grip on the pistol now, and
when he came for me again I shot him between the
eyes.

He staggered back, twirled and fell. The back of
his head looked like a spaghetti dinner. His body
shrivelled and pulled together. In seconds it had

turned into a wad of green light, which moved out through the window and towards the Dump.

Teeter was pushing a button on his desk. I levelled the pistol at him. Footsteps were pounding up the stairs. I stepped towards him with a snarl. "You got about ten seconds to live, Bob."

"Let's not be hasty!" he cried in his deep voice.

"All right." I stepped around behind him and locked my forearm against his neck. "Get me out of here alive."

When they kicked the door in I was crouched behind Teeter with the gun on him. I told him what to say. The Godsquad did it. In ten minutes Teeter and I were in Vince's Ford. Teeter was locked in back and I was driving. I had two pistols and a machinegun on the seat next to me, not to mention my book and a complimentary copy of THE HEAVENLY LAW. It had been easy. The next thing I wanted to do was go white and get out of Truckee.

18
Pig Spit

The Godsquad had promised not to come after me for half an hour. I planned to ditch the car and head out on foot before then. I hadn't decided yet whether or not to shoot Bob Teeter.

"Give me one reason why I shouldn't kill you."

"They need me here," the sepulchral voice responded.

"Before I came . . . that was twenty-five years ago . . . there was no city, no centralized authority. I've given them that, and more. I've given them something to believe in." His voice softened. "Felix . . . I know you're scared here . . . you never thought . . . you never thought heaven would be like this . . ."

"This isn't heaven. Not if there's police. And don't call me Felix."

Teeter chuckled indulgently. "I'm old enough to be your father. You got a tough break coming here so young, and I'm not surprised that you're feeling bitter and rebellious. And no, this isn't the real heaven . . . this is just a way-station, a rest stop."

We had entered a crummier part of Truckee. There were lots of people hanging around on the sidewalks, most of them old. They looked poor, and I was struck by the fact that no one was consuming anything . . . no eating, no drinking, no smoking, not even any gum chewing. They were just standing around looking blank, dressed in whatever they'd picked off the Dump. Occasionally someone would recognize Teeter in the back seat and wave frantically.

"If it's just a way-station, then why have you been here for twenty-five years?"

"These people need me. I built this city for them."

I was beginning to get the picture. "You mean that when you first came here there was no city?"

"Just the Dump. Where everything goes when it dies."

The Dump. It wasn't just people that recorporated there. I had seen cars and TV sets appearing too. "What happened to the people here before you built Truckee?"

"They just wandered off," Teeter said mournfully. "Off into the wilderness."

And probably found God, I added to myself. But now Teeter had built this bottleneck, this monument to himself, and people were getting hung up here . . . possibly forever. I shuddered at the thought of standing around on a downtown Truckee sidewalk in slippers for the rest of time.

Word must have been passing down the

sidewalks faster than our ancient Ford could
drive, for more and more people were standing at
the curb and waving as we cruised past. Teeter
beamed kindly out the window and kept his right
hand gently oscillating in benediction. You
would have thought I was his chauffeur.

"But why do they stay here?" I asked. "What's
in it for them?"

"They're scared," Teeter said simply. "Truckee
is like home to them. And some day the Lord will
take us into his great mansions."

I was loath to start talking about Jesus with this
man. I was sure I had seen Jesus in the graveyard,
but maybe Bob Teeter had seen Him too. Who was
I to say? Still, there was one thing . . . "Why do
you have the Godsquad? I can't believe that God
would want you to torture and kill people."

"You killed Carl," Teeter said accusingly. "He
had a wife and four children here. They came here
in their Winnebago six years ago, and there wasn't
a finer citizen of Truckee than Carl. Who knows if
he'll recorporate safely?" Teeter sighed sorrow-
fully.

"That's not an answer. I killed Carl because he
was going to kill me. It was self-defense."

"But if you kill me, it won't be self-defense,
Felix. It'll be murder. Can't you see that I'm your
friend? I want to help you."

The crowds had thinned out again. We seemed
to be in a junk and wine neighborhood now. There
was a bar on every corner, and what people you
saw were either lying on the sidewalk or slowly
sliding down the walls they leaned on. Teeter was
right. I wasn't going to be able to kill him. Killing

Carl had felt good, but snuffing this old fraud would feel bad.

"I'm going to let you out here, Bob." It was impossible not to use his first name. "But answer my question first."

"What question was that, Felix?"

"Why the Godsquad? Why the Gestapo tactics?"

"For beings like you," he said simply. "I don't even know that you're human. You don't come from the Dump. I know there's other parts of the afterworld. Good parts and . . . evil parts. I have to protect my people." I stopped the car and Teeter concluded, "I have nothing against you personally, Felix, but you'd better go back where you came from. I can't vouch for your safety."

I picked up a pistol and got out to open his door. "Keep it up, and you'll crucify Jesus one of these days."

He unfolded himself and looked down at me unflinchingly. "You're not Him."

I got in the car and drove another couple of blocks. The Godsquad was going to be coming soon, and Teeter would tell them where to look. I had to get rid of the car. I spotted a bar that looked a little flashier than the others and pulled up next to it. It was called the Gold Diamond. There were two women in miniskirts and halters leaning against the wall.

I slid the .38 into my jump-suit's big pocket and walked into the bar. I had my book in my left hand and the machinegun in my right.

Inside it was mostly black guys in sharp clothes. I squeezed a burst of machine-gun fire into the floor and the room fell silent. I hoped no one would shoot me. I held my gun level, sweeping it slowly back and forth.

"Who wants to buy this machine-gun?" I shouted.

When the import of what I had said sank in, a few of them started laughing. A long, skinny man in an outsize red cap waved me over. "Come here, you bad muthafukka."

He introduced his friend, who had a shaved head and totally white eyeballs. "This here Orphan Jones. What you want for the piece?"

I wasn't sure what the values here were. "I don't know. Couple hundred bucks?"

Orphan Jones nodded, and the skinny man said, "Right on time." Conversation at the other tables had resumed.

"One other thing," I said. "I've got a car outside. It's hot. Godsquad. I need someone to drive it off."

Orphan Jones stood up and spoke in a deep raspy voice. "Key in it?"

"Yes. But . . ."

"I can see," he said, anticipating my objection. "And I can drive. Good God, can the onliest Orphan Jones drive." He walked rapidly across the room and out the door. He took the machine-gun with him, and flicked off a burst as he stepped outside. "Kill, kill, *kill*," he rasped in a rising intonation. And then I heard the car-door slam and the tires squeal.

"He gone," the Orphan's partner said to me, then added, "They call me Tin Man."

"Felix," I said extending my hand. We shook and I remembered to slide past the handshake into the brotherhood clasp. But Tin Man had added further embellishments to his handshake, and I ended up feeling honkie just the same.

"Where you from?" he asked.

"New York."

"I'm from the South Side."

I nodded. He still hadn't given me the $200. "What kind of dope do they have here anyway?" I figured if I got the right stuff I could white out of Truckee.

"Dip and dab?"

"I don't think so. Weed?"

"White boys. You go see Speck. Speck fix you up." He lapsed into silence and leaned back in his chair. He stared vacantly across the room and began slowly working his jaw from side to side.

"Well I guess I'll go," I said uncertainly. "But you'll have to . . . to give me the money and tell me where to find Speck."

"Speck everywhere." He continued to move his jaw. His eyes were glazed with disinterest.

I took the .38 out of my pocket and laid it on the table with the muzzle pointing at him. "Come on, Tin Man. I don't have the time."

He pulled two hundred-dollar bills out of his pocket without taking his eyes off the bottles behind the bar. "Fourty-three One-ten," he said, as if to himself.

I thanked him and walked out of the Gold Diamond. The sky outside was bright. It was hot. I heard an engine roaring towards me and stepped around the corner of the building. A Godsquad car sped past. Vince was driving and Carl was riding shotgun. He didn't look any the worse for wear. I was ready and willing to kill him again, if it came to that.

The street I was on was 128th Street. I went over
a few blocks and started walking back downtown
towards 110th. If I'd understood Tin Man right,
I'd be able to get some weed there.

I was still wearing my jumpsuit, but I had left
my shoes at Ellie's. There were spots of sun-
softened tar on the cracked sidewalk. They felt
nice under my feet. Cimön has no sun, but the sky
was so bright that I began to sweat a little. Now
and then an old jalopy would chug past, leaving a
thick cloud of fumes. Many of the buildings had
no glass windows, only holes in the walls. People
leaned out here and there. There was lots of broken glass around, and I had to watch where I
stepped.

I ran my fingers across my forehead and tasted
the sweat. It was hard to believe that this was only
an astral body. A strange idea began nagging at
me, an idea I didn't want to face. I passed a liquor
store then. On a sudden reckless impulse I went in
to get a half-pint of whisky.

None of the bottles had seals on them, and many
of the labels were torn. I picked a bottle whose
contents seemed less cloudy than the others and
took it over to the counter. A wiry old lady ran the
store. She had white hair and a lot of pink lipstick. "Seventy-eight," she said.

"Huh?"

"Seventy-eight dollars." I fumbled out one of
my hundreds, trying not to look too surprised.

She smiled as she took the bill, and I decided to
ask a question. "Where is this whiskey made? I
don't believe I've seen any distilleries here in
Truckee . . ."

She looked at me sharply. "You *are* a fresher aren't you?"

"But I've registered," I added hastily. God forbid she should call the Godsquad on me.

She nodded and laid my change on the counter. "My husband works the Dump. He pours together the drops that are in the bottoms of the bottles that pop up. This is real good whiskey." She looked at me appraisingly. "He could use an assistant, if you're looking for work."

I avoided a direct refusal. "Sounds interesting. But does *all* the garbage from Earth always . . . pop up?"

She folded her lips in a smile. "Just the things that have a soul. Things that once meant something to someone, but got lost in the shuffle. Bob Teeter says that we're all here together because of love. Have you picked your temple yet?"

I backed towards the door. "Maybe later. Right now I want to get drunk."

She nodded approvingly, and sang out, "Come back real soon."

The whiskey didn't have much bite. Probably cut with water or worse. But I could feel it hitting me as I padded along the warm concrete. It was hard to believe this wasn't Earth. Cleveland maybe, or Detroit. A pick-up loaded with furniture tooled past.

Hard to believe I wasn't on Earth. That was the idea I didn't want to face, the idea that had driven me into the liquor store. What if I *was* on Earth . . . if everything since the graveyard had just been dreams and hallucinations. I thought back carefully.

I had had a couple of beers at the Drop Inn, walked up to Temple Hill and fallen asleep. I'd left my body and met Kathy, flown to Cimön, gone up Mount On, whited out, skied across Dreamland, walked through some tunnels to Ellie's house. And then I'd walked out of her house to find myself in this city.

But what if. What if I had just gotten dead drunk at the Drop Inn and imagined everything since. Or maybe Mary the barmaid had dosed me . . . put STP in my beer. It wasn't impossible. There was a Trailways bus stop right outside the Drop Inn. Maybe I had stumbled into it and was just now coming to in Cleveland.

I took another slug of the thin whiskey and realized I'd killed the bottle. I threw it high into the air and watched it break on the street. It was pretty the way the shards of glass caught the light. I wanted a cigarette. I felt in my pocket. There was just the .38 and a hundred dollar bill. I'd left my change on the counter at the liquor store. No wonder she'd been so friendly when I left.

I realized I was carrying something in my left hand and looked to see what it was. Oh yes. The book. Seeing it, I couldn't decide if I wished I were on Earth or not. In any case here was the proof. I flipped it open and scanned down a page to see if it really had alef-null words.

But I couldn't read past the fiftieth line. From there on it was just a blur of ink. My heart sank. I realized then how much I didn't want this to be Earth. I didn't want to lose what I'd been through, didn't want this to turn into just another crazy trip. It had to be the whiskey clouding my vision.

I craned up past the buildings at the sky. It was

bright, but there was no sun to be seen. No sun in Cimön. "There's glory for you." I said it in a deep, Humpty-Dumpty voice. It sounded so funny I had to laugh. Since my head was tilted way back, the laugh came out a silly gurgle. I laughed harder, and a lot of mucus ran out of my nose—which made it even funnier.

There was a sudden jolt and I fell down. I'd walked into someone from behind, an old man with a cane and a heavy overcoat.

He stood up stiffly, and I yanked at a corner of his coat. "Take that coat off, man. That's non-sense."

"Get your hands off me," he cried, knocking my hand loose with a blow of his cane. He walked off.

My whole face was squeezed shut in laughter. My stomach was cramping. "Wait," I managed, "What I wanna know. What I wanna. Wawa. Wawaw. Wawawawa . . ."

It was interesting to feel my jaw moving. I kept moving it and letting noise come out of my throat. The vibrations from my voice-box resonated in my sinuses. More mucus ran out and I began to giggle again, lying there on the sidewalk.

"Pig spit," I said. I got hung up on the last vowel. "Spispi, Spispispispi . . ." I made the sound higher and twisted it into pig squeals. I knew I could stop any time, but there really wasn't any reason to. No reason at all.

19
Candy Hearts

It was the sidewalk that woke me up. "BUZZ OFF," it said, bouncing me up and down. I sat up with the feeling that some transcendent revelation had been cut short. Or waking up had *been* the revelation. Something about the One and the Many . . . I couldn't catch it. My pants were wet. It was still daytime . . . or daytime again. Late afternoon.

I assessed the damages. My money and the .38 were gone, of course. My book was still there. It muttered, "PIG BOY," when I picked it up.

I stood unsteadily and looked around. Something had definitely changed while I was gone. Everything was alive. I don't know exactly how I could tell. It still looked pretty much like the same old Truckee. But everything I looked at reminded me of a face . . . even blank walls.

"HOO DOO," the wall next to me said firmly.

"I go," I muttered, and started walking. Tin Man had said Speck was at 43 110th Street. Maybe Speck could help me get my head back together.

An empty bottle winked up at me and sniggered, "U BET." I walked on. The sidewalk was soft and billowy. It was like walking on a water bed.

There was a steady buzz of conversation from all the objects around me. I was pretty sure that this wasn't Earth.

I felt loose and shaky all over. That stuff I'd drunk must have been drugged or even poisoned. Maybe that old woman had poisoned me so she could steal my gun and my hundred dollars. "Real good whiskey." I felt like I had flat-out *died* on that sidewalk.

What had happened after the pig squeals? Spiralling, spiralling through a dark red tunnel lined with T.V. screens, each one with a different face talking, talking, talking. And then I'd been out in the light, the White Light. There was something I had realized just when the sidewalk woke me up . . . something important . . .

"DO TELL," the signpost next to me remarked. I looked up. 110th Street.

"Which way to Speck's?" I asked the post. "He lives at 43."

"NO DICE," the post responded. I gave it a kick and turned right. Now and then a car chuffed past, but I hadn't seen anything of the Godsquad since I'd left the Gold Diamond. Maybe they didn't even exist in this revised Truckee I'd woken up in.

After a block and a half I spotted a three-story building marked 43. "BOMB SHELL," the steps said as I walked up. When I pushed the doorbell marked Speck it said, "DREAM MALE."

There was a clatter and a wheezy voice to my right called, "Who's there?" I stepped back onto the steps and saw a fat guy with greasy hair leaning out the window.

"SHOW ME," the steps said, and I added, "Tin Man sent me."

"*That* crooked son of a bitch." Speck looked me over. "Just a minute." He disappeared and I could hear him walking heavily to the front door.

"Come on in," Speck said, and I followed him into his apartment. A tall, skinny guy with a walrus mustache and balding black hair was slouched in a battered armchair. On a blue couch shiny with grease sat a girl with wavy hair. She had round cheeks with faint acne scars. "This's S-Curve and Kathy," Speck said.

"I'm Felix," I said, sitting down next to the Kathy. "SHE DOES," the couch said matter-of-factly. Speck sat down on a folding chair and leaned over a low wooden table.

On the table there was a fat lit candle, a mound of green leaves on a sheet of newspaper, a red plastic bong, a wind-up car with a spring sticking out, several empty matchbooks, a flimsy tin ashtray full of burnt matches, a big pair of tweezers, a kitchen knife, five empty beer bottles, and a wrapper from a pack of Twinkies. Everything was covered with fine gray ash. I'd come to the right place.

"We're gonna do a tune," S-Curve said to me. "You in?" I nodded and my book said, "A-OK."

Speck was processing a few of the leaves. They were like fern fronds and seemed to be pretty tough. He would cut off a piece with the knife and then hold it over the candle until it dried out a little. He was making a little pile of the dried-out bits. The girl next to me continued to stare at the candle. She hadn't even glanced at me yet.

"I came to Cimön with a girl called Kathy," I said to her.

"Felix Rayman," she crooned in a far away voice. "Felix Rayman."

"DIG IT," the couch exclaimed, and the table added, "ONE TOO."

"Kathy!" I said, laughing in pleased surprise. "Is it really you?"

She took her eyes off the candle then and looked at me with a smile. "It worked," she said.

"What?"

"I just made you appear. I pulled you out of the flame." "BIG FISH," the candle added. Kathy patted me on the knee. "I got here a while ago," she said. "I was hoping you would show up."

"Reunion," S-Curve said. He got up and put on a record. They had a tiny record player and three scratched records with no jackets. This was side two of *Exile on Main Street*. The familiar music filled me with well-being. *"And I hid the speed inside my shoe,"* sang Jagger.

Speck had charged up the bong and gotten it lit. He left the bong sitting on the table and leaned over it, sucking in the smoke. As he started to exhale, his body outline blurred and brightened.

He shrank together into a ball of white light which hovered motionlessly for a few seconds. Then colors bled into the light, the ball grew projections, the intensity dimmed, and it was just Speck again, standing there with his yellow teeth showing in a loose smile.

"BE MINE," said the bong, and I leaned over it, fitting my mouth into the opening. I sucked in the smoke. My sphere of awareness rapidly shrank to a point. There was a mandala in front of me. I buzzed back and forth as I fell towards the nectar-laden center. I hung there for an instant, and then there was a silent explosion. I was rushing out the center, filling up like a nipple-end prophylactic, squeezed in . . .

"YOU WHO," the couch called as I fell back into it. There had been an instant, right when I moved through the center . . . an instant when I had been able to see the One, the Absolute, to grasp that YES is the same as NO . . . that Everything is Nothing . . .

And then I'd come back. Just like that. There was something about the shift from total enlightenment to ordinary consciousness that seemed to be the real core of the experience. Something about moving through the interface. The interface between One and Many, between being and becoming, between death and life, between c and alef-one . . .

Kathy took a hit off the bong, contracted into a ball of light, bounced back. Then it was S-Curve's turn. He was clearly a heavy user. He inhaled for a long time while the little pipe-bowl glowed and hissed, "HOT DOG."

S-Curve was a blob of light now, but more dumbell-shaped than spherical. When he snapped back there were two of him. He was so skinny that both of him fit into the armchair.

"God *damn*, S," Speck said. "One of you's gonna have to leave. I ain't turning both of you on."

"Be cool," the one S-Curve said. "We'll make a run tomorrow." the other added.

"LET'S GO," the bong urged. The bowl had burned out.

"What is this stuff?" I asked.

"They call it fuzzweed," Kathy said. "It grows all over that mountain . . . Mount On?"

"There's a tunnel about fifty miles from here," S-Curve said in his slow, inflectionless voice. "Nice big field of the stuff. All you have to do is drive there and walk through."

"Does the Godsquad bother you?" I envisioned the usual growers vs. *federales* scenario.

"The what?" Kathy and S-Curve looked like they didn't know what I was talking about.

"You know. Bob Teeter's personal army?"

Speck laughed his wheezy laugh and hawked up a marbled gob of phlegm. "*Those* douchebags. Ain't but about ten of them."

"But I thought Teeter ran this city. He said he built it twenty-five years ago."

The wall behind me snorted, "NO WAY."

"You talking about the guy with the big head?" an S-Curve put in. "Has a couple of temples?" I nodded and he grimaced in contempt. "Phaw! That's just for old people. Still looking to see St. Penis and the pearly gates." He started refilling the bowl of the bong. "Hell, I see God every time I get high. You can't stay there is all. Once you're all white you're the same as their God. But you always come back somewhere."

"But what if you didn't?" I said as S-Curve fired up the pipe. "What if you just stayed there. With the One."

The S-Curve I'd been talking to had turned into

a ball of light again, and his twin took the bong hastily. "Ten seconds ain't no different than forever," he said quickly, before fitting his mouth to the bong. Just as he faded into a ball of light, the first S-Curve came back and finished off the bowl.

"Stop hogging!" Speck shouted and lunged across the table to get the bong. A bumpy fart tore out of him and his chair creaked, "HOT LIPS."

Speck and the S-Curves started laughing like maniacs at that. I was having trouble absorbing it all. "Take a little walk?" I murmured to Kathy. She nodded and we stood up. I still had my book.

"I think we'll go out for some air," I said.

"Speck was leaning over his work-table. "Whatever. Get some cigarettes. And a six-pack."

We went out, and the steps muttered, "IT FITS."

"Do you hear that?" I asked Kathy. "Do you hear the way everything talks all the time?"

"NO DOUBT," a garbage can put in. Kathy nodded. "Like those candy valentine hearts. They don't make much sense."

It was evening again, and we walked in silence for a few minutes. The concrete was still warm from the heat of the day. It felt nice on my feet.

Kathy came up to my shoulder and was wearing a loose dress made out of an Indian bedspread. She didn't look like I had expected her to. She wasn't deformed or anything, but she wasn't beautiful either. Still, there was a nice roundness to her cheeks, and her eyes reminded me of my own. The greasy quality of her skin was somehow attractive to me. "SHE DOES," the couch had promised.

She felt me looking at her, and stared back with

a little hostility. "What's the matter," she said. "Don't I live up to your fantasies?"

"HOT STUFF," a lamp post chuckled nastily.

I was embarassed, at a loss for words. "I . . . I just didn't know what you looked like. You look fine . . . just fine." Awkwardly I put my arm around her. Her waist was slim and flexible.

"What happened to the seagull?" I asked after a minute. "What happened after we split up?"

"I flew to that harbor, you know?" I nodded and she went on. "There were all kinds of things there. Like monsters. They went in and out of the water a lot. There weren't any other seagulls, and I started across the sea alone. It was curved."

I was starting to feel awkward with my arm around her. How well did I know her, really? I put both hands behind my back and paced along next to her while she talked. "MAMMA'S BOY," a garbage can rattled at me, and I whacked it with the side of my foot.

"The sky was funny," Kathy was saying. "At first I could see way up Mount On when I looked back, but then I'd moved around the curve of the sea and there was only sky. But there was fire."

"You mean the sea was on fire?"

"No, no. The sea was boiling, and the fire was in the sky. Looking into the sky was like looking down . . . down into a pit of fire?"

We had walked a few blocks from Speck's. I saw what looked like a grocery store down one of the side streets, and took Kathy's arm to steer her that way. Her voice was the same as ever, husky and a little tentative. She really wasn't unattractive.

"NEW LOVE," a manhole cover opined as we walked over it.

I raised my voice to drown it out. "Were there people there? In the fire?"

"Yes. There were things moving in the fire and little screams. And . . . there were creatures bringing more people all the time. Big things that looked like you did in the graveyard when you scared me?"

"Devils," I said slowly.

"Yes," Kathy went on, "and there were machines bringing people there too . . . domed machines carrying three people at a time."

It all made sense. "Those were Guides," I exclaimed. "They must work for Satan. That must have been Hell you saw up there . . . or down there . . ." I began waving my hands in the air to show her what I meant. "I think Cimön is sort of like a folded piece of paper. We started out on the side with Mount On, and now we're on the other side. In between is Dreamland and at the fold is the sea. That fire you saw must have been Hell, off in space below the fold."

"I don't really know what you're talking about, Felix." Her deep brown eyes looked up at me through a wing of hair. "Let me finish my story."

We had come to the grocery now, and I realized that I had no money. But I didn't want to bring that up yet. I seated myself on the midnight-blue fender of a sleek '52 Hudson Hornet. Kathy sat down next to me.

It was night now. Yellow light spilled out of the grocery and onto the sidewalk. Inside were a couple of guys flirting with the girl behind the counter. I could hear music floating out of someone's window. The air was still and warm, filled with faint smells of garbage and cars. I wished this evening would never end.

"MOON CALF," the car whispered. Kathy resumed her story.

"I didn't want to go back to the harbor . . . I wanted to see what lay across the sea. But there was fire and monsters in the sky and the sea was boiling as far as I could see. The water went up into the sky in big clouds of steam and then rained down. Useless heavy rain driving into the sea forever." She glanced at me, then went on. "I decided to swim under the boiling part. I dove and swam all the way down to the bottom. I was flying through water . . . like a penguin. There was ice at the bottom, ice with colored lights in it, and I swam along the bottom until I couldn't any longer. When I came up I was past the boiling part."

I was playing with her fingers while she talked. "Were there any fish in the sea?"

"Not fish exactly. Little glowing things like jellyfish."

"Maybe the unborn souls," I suggested. But she went on with her story, reciting it slowly.

"It was windy, and I let the gale carry me towards the other shore. I don't know how long that part took. I was confused, and seeing things."

"What things?"

"Patterns . . . lines and colored dots. There were so many of them. Too many." She paused, searching for words, then gave it up. "Anyway it got colder and the sea froze. The wind kept blowing and there was snow. It was hard to fly. Later the sky got clear and I was over a glacier. There was a big crack near the end."

"I think I saw you!" I exclaimed. "I was at the crevasse near the end of the glacier with Franx, and I saw a bird fly over."

"Will you let me finish, Felix? I flew to the end of the ice, and then I saw a huge plain with a row of cities. Cities and then a desert."

"But how did . . ."

"I'm just coming to that." She held both hands in the air before her, holding her vision. "I saw a clearing with big heaps and mounds. There were green lights landing, and I thought I saw birds. I started to land and there was a man pointing a stick at me. But it wasn't a stick."

"You mean someone shot you?"

She ran her hands slowly wonderingly, over her face. "I—I think so. Something hit me and it was like in the hospital . . . the funny feeling and turning green. At first I thought I was in my coffin again. But I was too squeezed, and Daddy got me a big coffin, you know, all with pink taffeta . . ."

I took one of her hands down from her face. "I remember, Kathy."

She pulled her hand back from me. "I didn't want this body back! When I crawled out from the garbage and realized . . . I wanted to die. But I can't. We're all stuck here forever, Felix, do you know that? S-Curve explained it to me. I don't know what I'm going to do here forever. I don't know what I'll do!"

"FLY ME," suggested the car we were sitting on.

20
Talking Cars

The keys were in the ignition. "Let's do," I said to Kathy.

"Do what." We were sitting on a midnight blue '52 Hudson. It had a slit of a windshield—like a tank's.

"Let's take this car. You heard it, it invited us to." I patted the fender.

"COME ON," the car said opening a door encouragingly.

Kathy hesitated a minute, then nodded once. "All right," she said. "Why not? I've only known those guys for a day anyway. But let me get some beer and cigarettes first."

"Groovy." I stepped down into the driver's seat and sank into the soft dusty cushions, setting my book down next to me. "One thing," I said to the empty seats, "You're going to have to start talking in sentences more than two words long. I'm not

asking for rational social intercourse, mind you
. . . just no more of these cute da-DAH phrases.''

"CAN DO," the car said. I sighed.

Kathy came out with a whole case of beer bottles, corked and unlabelled. Speck must have
given her money. "For what?" an ugly part of my
mind wanted to know.

"Do you think that's really beer?" I asked as she
opened the other door and set the case on the back
seat.

"NAPALM BALM," the car said, and Kathy got
in with a laugh. She looked happy.

The car started up with no trouble and pulled
off down the street. No one ran out to stop us—for
all I knew the car didn't *have* an owner. Franx had
said something about talking cars just before he
died. I wonder if he'd recorporated, and in what
form.

The heavy warm air beat in through my open
window. I realized that the car was content to
drive itself, and let go of the steering wheel.
"ZERO COOL," it remarked.

I reached back and got two beers. They were
cold, and the taste was not off, like the whiskey's
had been. Maybe they brewed their own in Cimön.

"It's good to be moving again," Kathy said.
"I don't ever want to stop. Just now, standing
there . . ."

"I know," I said, thinking of the people waving
to Bob Teeter. "It's like the only thing worse than
death is eternal life."

"Oh, don't say that." She leaned her face into
the wind. "Anything's better than nothing."

We were on a main thoroughfare now, and

lights were streaming past. There were plenty of parked cars, but not too many were driving. A sudden doubt crossed my mind. "Do you need gas?" I asked the car.

"I GOT A TOMBSTONE HAND AND A GRAVEYARD MIND," the car said in a unique burst of loquaciousness, "I'M JUST TWENTY-ONE AND I *DON'T* MIND DYIN'." Only later would I realize what this meant. But I assumed there was enough gas. I flicked on the radio. The dial glowed for a minute, warming up. I wondered what would be on.

There were no numbers on the dial, but when Kathy twisted the right-hand knob, a pointer moved back and forth in the little rectangular window. Suddenly there was a crackle and the sound came on.

A saxophone playing in short bursts. It stopped and a man with a faint Boston accent recited a haiku: *"Useless, useless. Heavy rain driving into the sea."* More saxophone, more haiku. After awhile a piano took over, and the reader launched into a longer piece, ending with the line: *"I wish I was free of that slaving meat-wheel and safe in Heaven dead."* He gave an embarrassed chuckle.

Kathy had slouched down in her seat. She'd lit a cigarette and her face was slightly turned away from me. She reached out, jiggled the radio knob, and the first haiku came back again. *"Useless, useless. Heavy rain driving into the sea."* She sighed and the saxophone segwayed out into a jumble of loosely strung guitars.

"What is that, Kathy?"

"What I wanted to hear." She was still staring into the beating night air. "Speck's car has a radio like this. Everything is on all the time."

A different man's voice was talking over the randomly plucked strings. His voice had a ranting, confident quality. It was hard to make out what he was saying. Lots of dates, numbers. *"I knew I should have worn more paisley."*

"That's Neal," Kathy said. "There's not much of him on."

"I still don't . . ."

"It's a record of Cassady and Kerouac doing a jazz reading. My big brother gave it to me in high school and I used to listen to it a lot. It's how I got interested in Kerouac in the first place."

The first voice, Kerouac, was on again, talking about death, about the Void, about enlightenment and bald artists with black berets hanging reality on iron fences in Washington Square. He had a strange little chuckle he'd slip in here and there. Kathy's lips moved with the words. I began to feel jealous.

"I guess you'd like to find him and sit at his feet," I said.

"It's a thought," she said, flicking her cigarette out the window. "Either that or find a way to get back to Earth." Then she relented and smiled at me. "You want to hear something else?"

"Sure. What else is on?"

"Anything you want. Just twist the knob and it'll stop on whatever you have in mind."

I turned the knob through a babble of possibilities, not quite sure what I really did want to hear. Somehow I ended up with the Led Zep doing "Whole Lotta Love." The exaggeratedly heavy beat seemed like just the thing for cruising

Truckee. I threw my empty beer-bottle out the window and opened another.

We were driving along the road next to the dump now. The green lights falling down into it were clear against the starless night sky. A figure tottered out into the street ahead of us. A hitch-hiker. I thought of the way Vince had run a man down, and braced myself. But our car stopped, snapped on the dome light and opened a back door.

"You don't *have* to get in," I called to the figure in a futile effort to maintain some control over the flow of events.

"Felix?" the ragged man answered, "Is that you?" He stuck his head in and looked me over. It was a man with tufty black hair and sunken cheeks. There was something insect-like about the mouth. His lips were parted and thin teeth showed. His ears stuck out like dish antennae, and his dark black eyes held no expression I could make out. He was wearing a ragged black suit that looked fifty years old, a white shirt with no necktie.

"I'm afraid I don't recognize you," I said. A blistering staircase of guitar notes poured out of the radio.

"He looks like Franx Kafka," Kathy observed, turning down the volume.

The man got in the back seat and smiled past me at Kathy. His smile was horrible. He was talking rapidly in a high voice. "Gregor Samsa, really . . . though in a reversed sense. I was a giant beetle *before* my unfortunate metamorphosis." He brushed at his suit with rapid Oliver Hardy twitches, his fingers flying in every direction. Suddenly I got the picture.

"You're Franx!" I exclaimed. "You got recorporated at the Truckee dump!"

He gave a bug-like twitch of his lips and flared his nostrils. "I don't know how you humans stand it Felix. All this soft flesh." He plucked at his emaciated cheeks. "Marshmallow bodies with toothpick bones. I really must get back to the Praha section of the Dump and undo this grotesque transformation."

He spotted the beer, opened one and drained it with wet, sucking gurgles. Before I could say anything he was talking again. "I was right, Felix, wasn't I, when I said I'd get my head bashed in. I read the page. I knew the future. This must be your friend Kathy?"

She nodded. "Felix told me a little about you . . ."

"And a great deal more about himself, I'm sure," Franx added. "But he didn't tell you about Ellie, did he?" A moist, clicking snicker.

"Franx, will you cut it out? If it upsets you to be around me, I'd be more than happy to let you out. As a matter of fact I've hardly had time to tell Kathy anything."

"I see you've still got your book," he said, leaning into the front seat. "Tried to read it lately?"

I hadn't actually. Not since I'd passed out on that hot sidewalk. I hadn't even showed it to Kathy yet. She picked it up, let it fall open and squinted at a page. "It's all smeared," she said. "Is it . . ."

I pulled it from her hands and looked for myself. The page ended in a blur, just like before.

Suddenly I realized that I hadn't done any speed-ups since . . . since leaving Ellie's house on the edge of Truckee. I tried to rattle off alef-null La's then, but my touch was gone.

The car made a sharp turn onto a dirt road leading between two of the Dump's mountains of garbage. "That's a no-no," Franx said to me sharply. "Turn around."

"He's not driving," Kathy explained. "It's a talking car."

Franx grunted in fear and yanked at the door handle. It came off in his hand. The road was rutty and twisted, but the car was going faster than ever. It pitched like a boat at sea; the headlights played crazily over the mounds of junk. An icebox. A matress with the springs sticking out. Rotten zucchinis.

I pushed down on the brake pedal. It sank to the floor as if there were nothing behind it. The steering wheel spun as emptily as a wheel of fortune. The radio clicked off then, and in the sudden silence the car said, "GOD KNOWS." Franx began screaming.

I turned in my seat and grabbed him by the shoulders. "Tell me what you know," I said, shaking him.

"I forgot," he babbled. "I didn't want to remember. So you caught me, you and your tumbril, just like the book said. I couldn't face it, and now it's really happening. Oh no! I don't want to leave Cimön! I don't want to go!"

His eyes were glazing over, and white balls of spit had gathered at the corners of his mouth. I shook him again, gently. "Go where, Franx?"

He spoke slowly, painfully. "Into the light,

Over the edge and into the light. I didn't tell you the truth . . . about why I was sad.''

I thought back to his behaviour on the glacier, the things he'd said in the tunnel to alef-one. ''You said you were upset because you couldn't stay in the White Light. But now?''

It took him a minute to answer. The headlights picked out the red eyes of rats by the score. And yellow cat-eyes, and eyes like I'd never seen. Evil-looking fires flickered here and there. Dark forms passed back and forth in front of the flames. The fires seemed to come out of holes in the ground. I thought back to the crack the Devil had opened up in the graveyard.

Franx was talking again. ''I'm scared of the White Light. I love myself too much to dissolve like that. None of the people on Mount On wants to get to the top. That's why they go there. For the people who really want God, there's an easy way. Beyond the Dump. Off the edge.'' His lips were twitching and his hands ran up and down his body like live insects. ''I don't want that, I don't want that . . .'' He began sobbing. I looked away.

The windows had rolled themselves up, and none of the car doors would open. ''What's going on?'' Kathy cried. ''What's supposed to be beyond the Dump?''

''The Desert,'' Franx groaned. ''The edge.'' He fell catatonically silent then. Kathy stared at me with her deep eyes, eyes so like my own. ''What does he mean, Felix?''

''The Dump is a strip seperating the cities of Mainside from some kind of desert. You saw it from the air. Everyone seems to be scared of the desert. Except this car.''

"Who sent you?" Kathy asked the dashboard. But there was no answer. Was the car a devil or an angel? Or just another pawn like us?

The road was worse than ever, but the ride had gotten smoother. We stopped near a huge fire then. The flames were leaping up from a sort of stone well set into the ground. I wondered if we were going to drive in.

There were a number of cars near the fire. They shifted about with fluid grace. Two rushed up to us and began a conversation with our car. They jiggled their hoods up and down and roared their engines. Occasionally a tire would bulge out to gesture plastically.

More cars crowded around. Some stretched up on tip-tire to peer in at us. They took something out of our trunk. After a final roar of conversation they all drifted off . . . all except for a sexy red Jaguard, voluptuously curved and with lidded headlamps.

She seemed to be very familiar with our car. They talked for a long time, occasionally stroking each other with their tires. I let the steady purr of their conversation lull me to sleep.

I didn't have any dreams that I could remember. I was awakened by our car's violent shaking. We were tilted up at an angle and bouncing up and down. The sky was pink.

For a horrible instant I thought that our car was about to jump into the fire. But then I glimpsed a lusciously curving red fender beneath us.

Kathy had woken up too. "Are we stuck on something?"

Just then our car gave a rapid shiver and slid down off the Jag. They nestled side to side with their tires pressed together. "They're married," Kathy exclaimed. "And there's a baby!"

A soft little Fiat 500 came bounding up. It was only four feet long and its features were not fully developed. Its stubby little trunk and hood barely projected past its bulging windows. It called to us with a short toot.

As the parents caressed it, several other cars came up. There was another session of hood flapping and engine roaring. Finally we backed away from the fire. Most of the windshields were wet, and the wipers were running. A battered old Diesel cab sounded an elegiac note on its airhorn, and then everyone was honking goodbye. With a resigned lurch, our car headed deeper into the Dump.

"The car doesn't want to go either," Franx said in a choking voice. The horns had woken him up. "It's your fault, Felix. You're dragging us all over the edge with you. I don't know how I could have been so stupid. I was thinking only of . . ." He moaned and began wringing his hands.

The sky was quite light now, and we could see the Dump all around us. Here and there the Hell-fires flickered, still bright in the daylight. Ahead of us the mounds of garbage were smaller, and now I could actually see through to the flat red Desert beyond.

"We're almost there," Franx wailed. Suddenly his voice took on a terrible intentness. "I don't have to go. There's still a way out for me, there's still a way . . ." He smashed one of the beer bottles against the edge of the case and brandished the broken neck.

I assumed he was going to attack us, and moved

to put myself between him and Kathy. I held my book up as a sort of shield and braced myself.

But he surprised me. With a quick gesture he pressed the jagged glass against his throat and ripped it open. A sheet of blood flopped out, and he was gone.

I stared out the back window as the green light that had been Franx went twisting away. One of those fires was flaring out of the ground nearby, and a sudden tentacle of flame lashed out, snared him. For a second you could see the feeble green light struggling against the orange flames, and then with a thin tweet of agony it was gone. He'd chanced one too many recorporations. I winced and looked at Kathy.

"Those flames," she said. "They're the same color as the fire I saw in the sky."

I nodded. "I've seen them before, too. In the graveyard."

21
Absolute Zero

The car cut off its engines as soon as we got out of
the Dump. A featureless waste spread out ahead of
us. Looking back I could see the Dump stretched
out in an infinite line from left to right. There were
a few figures dotting the landscape here and
there. Hermits, holy-men. But a few miles beyond
the Dump there was nothing but the blank red
Desert. Nothing—as far as the eye could see.

The ground was smooth clay, baked to the con-
sistency of pavement. The gravity vectors must
have been slanting away from the Dump, for we
kept rolling faster. Our passage kicked up a plume
of dust which quivered behind us like a long
straight tail.

As always, the light came from every part of the
sky, but the horizon ahead was particularly
bright. A white line that glared like a crack in a
firing kiln.

It was getting hot, and I pushed at the window crank. Abruptly it gave, and I was able to roll down the window. Kathy followed suit, and the hot dry air whirled around us. We were doing about sixty miles per hour and still accelerating. I tested the brakes, the steering, the gear shift . . . they wagged back and forth unresistingly.

"We could jump out," I said.

Kathy shook her head. "And end up like Franx?"

"That doesn't always happen." The hot wind tore the words out of my mouth and I had to shout. "The odds are very good that you'd just crawl back out of the Dump in your same body." At the rate the hard ground was flickering past there was no question but that the jump would be fatal.

"Are you going to jump?" she called across the wind.

I shook my head. "No. I haven't ever died yet, you know . . ."

"Oh come on, Felix," she interrupted. "Don't tell me you still think you . . ."

"All I know is that I want to get to that white light up there." I shouted, drowning her out. The horizon was brighter than ever, and you couldn't look at it for long. "I'm taking this trip all the way to the end."

She leaned her head and shoulders out the window, tentatively testing the strength of the wind. We were doing a hundred miles per hour now, and the gravity was so steep that I kept sliding forward in my seat. We were the only thing moving in the flat red desert.

Kathy sat back in her seat, then got a beer out of the back. "There's still time to decide," she said. I took a beer too and we clinked a silent toast.

"What do you think it would be like?" Kathy asked. "To be safe in heaven dead."

"Just merged. Merged into the void."

"Maybe Truckee's better."

"For awhile. But not forever." Even though we were going faster than ever, the wind was slacking off. It was as if there was now less air outside. "But I can't tell you what to do."

"You don't think you'll have to stay there," Kathy said suddenly. "You're counting on the White Light sending you back to your body on Earth."

"Well . . . yes," I admitted.

"I wonder if I could go back," Kathy mused. "Maybe I could follow you."

My bottle was empty. I threw it out the window, and whipped my head around to see it explode into dust some fifty feet behind us.

"LAST ROUND," the car said suddenly.

"Are you still here?" I called.

"COUNT DOWN."

Kathy leaned towards the dashboard and asked, "How much longer till . . . till whatever?"

"TIME FLIES."

She looked at me with a shrug. Suddenly the wind caught the cover of my book and riffled it open. The pages seemed more substantial, less densely packed. I checked and it was true. There was no longer a continuum of pages, no longer even alef-null pages . . . it was just a regular book two or three hundred pages long.

I looked at one of the pages and noticed another change. Back at Ellie's the book still had alef-null lines per page. As soon as I'd gone out into Truckee the bottom half had become blurred and smeared. But now most of the blurred part had disappeared. There were a few hundred finely printed lines on each page.

I noticed a sort of flicker at the bottom of the page I was looking at. I watched intently for half a minute and then it flickered again. The lines were disappearing one by one! I flipped to the back of the book and pinched the last page between my fingers. Twenty or thirty seconds went by, and suddenly there was nothing between my fingers.

"Our hair is gone," Kathy cried suddenly.

I ran my hand across my pate and felt mostly skin. I dropped the book and stared at Kathy. She was almost bald. A few hundred long hairs fluttered back and forth on her round, white head.

The pattern came to me in a right-brain flash. "We're going towards zero, Kathy. Nothing. On the other side of Cimön this direction leads towards the Absolute Infinite. Zero and Infinity. They're the same at the Absolute . . ."

The car hit a little bump then and didn't fall back to the ground. Some force pushed me out of my seat and pressed me against the dash. The perspective shifted crazily as I tried to orient myself. The flat red desert stretched back to the endless line of the Dump as before, but instead of coasting across it we were somehow falling down it.

Kathy pushed herself violently back from the windshield. The car tilted forwards and *whumped*. The tires burst and the wheels screamed against the blurred red surface. The rear end raised up then, and the car began slowly to tumble end over end, throwing off showers of sparks every time it scraped the ground which had somehow become a cliff.

The beers fell out of their case and banged around the compartment with us. Kathy was screaming and I managed to wrap my arms around her. The gravity had shifted. We were falling up, or across, or down, the red desert towards that glowing white horizon.

"GOD SPEED," the car said, and abruptly dissolved from around us. It drew itself together into a ball of white light, circled us once, and then in a motion too fast to follow, it flashed all the way out to the glowing crack ahead.

In a way it was a relief to be in free-fall. The air resistance was negligible and Kathy and I, the book, and twelve beers fell across the landscape together. We were spinning slowly and moving parallel to the ground. Suddenly I felt one of my teeth disappear. We must be under a hundred now.

Kathy and I were still clutching each other. "There's hardly any time left," I said to her quietly. Her eyes were wild with terror, and it took her a second to understand me.

Finally it sank in. All except her front teeth were gone and she spoke quickly. "Send me back, Felix. I'm not ready for this." The horizon was brighter and closer now.

"Are you sure? You've got to come here sooner or later . . . or the Devil will catch you." All of our teeth were gone now, and the beer bottles around us were winking out one by one.

"Send me back, Felix," she cried. "Do it fast."

It was easy. I just waited till we had spun to a position where she was between me and the ground . . . and pushed. We drifted slowly apart. The ground got farther from me and closer to her. Our eyes were locked together, four deep pools. And then the impact ripped her to shreds.

I didn't look away. I stared back until I saw the green light flutter up from the ground and circle uncertainly. It was her choice, but I felt guilty for letting her do it. What was it I had promised Jesus? I prayed that she'd recorporate safely.

The beers were all gone, and my book was a thin fluttering pamphlet flying along next to me. The glaring white light shone through the pages. I reached for it with my left hand, but stopped when I saw there was only a stump. All my toes and left-hand fingers were gone. My right hand was still intact, and I used it.

I held my booklet tight. I had five pages left. If there were one more page it would have been . . . been . . . I couldn't think of any numbers higher than five.

Higher than what? My left leg and most of my stomach disappeared. Head, two arms and a leg. That made four. Once I had had something else . . . but what?

My right leg and the rest of my lower body winked out. I squeezed my three pages tight between thumb and two fingers. I wondered what the pages said.

Slowly I brought them up to my face. My left arm was gone. Two. Two things. Me and the book. Head and arm. Thumb and finger. What else had

PART IV

"I think most persons who shall have tested it will accept this as the central point of the illumination:
That sanity is not the basic quality of intelligence, but is a mere condition which is variable, and like the humming of a wheel, goes up or down the musical gamut according to a physical activity; and that only in sanity is formal or contrasting thought, while the naked life is realized only outside of sanity altogether; and it is the instant contrast of this 'tasteless water of souls' with formal thought as we 'come to,' that leaves in the patient an astonishment that the awful mystery of Life is at last but a homely and a common thing, and that aside from mere formality the majestic and the absurd are of equal dignity."

—Benjamin Paul Blood

22
Halloween

The air was filled with a hideous screeching. The bright little figures were moving past me, crowding up to the fountain and circling around it. A man with greasy hair leaned over them, making notes on a clipboard and pressing something into each tiny hand. Why couldn't I remember his name?

I was upright in a crowd of dark forms topped by nodding white spots. Empty white faces anxiously watching the judge. Sammy.

Blue-white lights hissed overhead. They flickered, and the maskers' motions were chopped into scores of stills. A wagon with a dog-house. A silver cube with legs sticking out. Colored cloth, rubber, feathers, paint.

A little red devil bumped my leg as he wriggled past. His face was shining with excitment. He carried a hollowed-out head in his right hand. Orange.

The noise wouldn't stop. It was coming from an electrified horn. Gray metal music of guts and bladders, a voice shouting names. Clicks of static—each just so.

There was muttering around me, words striking each other, sticking together. I needed something to put between. A lump on my chest slid out, opened and my fingers took out a white cylinder. Fire, warm smoke. Between.

They were whispering my name, edging me forward. But I was too fast for them, too rude. I burst out, fought past their angry cries to the ragged fringe of the crowd. I could go where I wanted. I started walking away from the terrible noise.

Footsteps behind me and a hand on my shoulder. "Felix! What happened to you?"

I turned around, breathing smoke between. I studied the face for a minute. Yellowish skin, full lips, intent eyes. It was April.

She took my arm and pulled me back towards the noise. Iris was sitting in her stroller, dressed in a bunny-rabbit suit. Her excited eyes paused on me. "Da-da!" I leaned over to pat her cheek, her stomach. She smiled, then went back to watching the other kids.

April's expression was a mixture of relief and anger. I gestured weakly. "Let's move down the street a little, baby. I can't think with that noise."

Her face tightened. "Of course, Felix. We mustn't let anything upset you."

I tried to put my arm around her, but she drew away. "Are you drunk?"

"I . . . I don't know."

We walked half a block away from the bullhorn

mounted over Sammy's luncheonette, and it was easier to talk. "I was at the Drop Inn . . ."

April's eyes flashed. "And last night?"

I ran my trembling hands over my face. My skin was very greasy, and my fingers were shiny with dirt. "They said I slept there. They said I came in with forty dollars at six o'clock yesterday, drank all evening, passed out, woke up at ten this morning, and spent the day watching television. But . . ."

"I thought so," April spat out. "I saw you sneak in and steal the food-money out of my purse. I saw you and your friend running down the street. And you know what?" Numbly I shook my head. This was going to be bad. "All day I've been hoping you wouldn't come back."

The costume judging was over, and the kids were streaming past us. "I guess it's Halloween," I said.

April stopped walking and I stopped too. She was about to say that she was leaving me. I could feel it coming. Quickly I spoke between. "April, that wasn't me in the Drop Inn. I've been out of my body all this time. I was . . . I was in this sort of after-world. It's called Cimön and I had to get to the White Light before I could come back . . ."

"You're parents called last night," she said, cutting me off. "I had to talk to them and act like everything was fine. Yes, Mom, Felix is at the library. He's really working hard these days." She started walking again and I tagged along, pushing the stroller. "But she knew I was lying. Did anyone see you at the Drop Inn?"

"April, listen to what I'm saying. I've just done something that no one's ever done before. I'll be

famous." It occured to me to look through my
pockets for that little pamplet on Cimön I'd gotten
from Sunfish. But it was gone . . . elsewhere . . .

"Famous for what, Felix?"

"I'll, I'll . . ." My voice trailed off. There had to
be some way to use the experiences I'd just been
through. "I'll think of something."

We were walking up Tuna Street now. April
stopped, picked Iris out of the stroller, and led
her up to someone's lit-up porch. Bunches of
trick-or-treaters were flitting about all up and
down the street. The wet leaves formed a pasty
carpet underfoot. The sky was low and starless.

Up on the wooden porch Iris stared expectantly at the door, her stuffed rabbit-ears leaning
back. A friendly jack-o-lantern glowed on either
side of the white door. It opened, a slender woman
exclaimed over Iris and handed her a candy. Iris
dropped it and April bent over to retrieve it,
graceful and sexy in her tight jeans. They walked
back down the path looking satisfied.

I didn't try to talk anymore, just followed along,
smiling and marvelling at the simple reality of it.
When we got to our house, April went in to hand
out candy and I took Iris to a few more houses.

The Kazars lived two doors up from us, and we
were pretty good friends, although they were a
little older. Marguerite Kazar opened the door as
we walked up. Iris squealed, "Tweet!" and
dumped her candy out on the porch to look over
what she had so far.

Marguerite gave a big laugh, stagy but sincere,
"Isn't she cunning! And I bet her Mommy sewed
that suit herself." I nodded, attempted a smile. It

felt like my face still worked.

Marguerite gave Iris a candy bar and looked up at me.

She was short with a pretty face. "You poor man! You look like death warmed over!" She threw up her hands in mock dismay.

"I've . . . I've been on a trip."

Her eyes widened. "Aren't you worried about your chromosomes?"

"It wasn't really that kind of trip." I bent to reassemble Iris's scattered booty. There was a long, questioning silence, but I left it at that.

"Say hello to your lovely wife," Marguerite said as we left. She was quite a gossip, and I winced inwardly as I thought of stories about my "trip." Eventually—this was the bad part—the stories would get back to April. Oh well. At least it was beginning to look like I might not lose my mind.

The DeLongs rented a small house across the street from ours, and I went there last. Nick De-Long was the only real friend I had in Bernco. He taught Physics and was also new this year. He had thinning blonde hair and the mandatory beard. He worried a lot.

Nick came to the door and waved us in. Iris dumped her goodies out on their tattered living-room rug. Nick's dachshund sped over and snatched a cookie. Iris's face was red in an instant, and tears popped out of her slitted eyes. "Doggy NO!" she hollered with all her strength.

Nick's wife Jessie gave her amazed-at-it-all laugh and locked the dog up in the kitchen.

"Beer?" Nick said, and I nodded. Jessie was handling a fresh group of trick-or-treaters, and he

went to the kitchen himself. The dachshund
wormed out the door, Iris roared, I put the dog
back.

Finally I was sitting in their wooden rocker
sipping a beer. Iris sat on the couch next to Nick,
feeding. Jessie stood behind the couch, observing
Iris with interest. They were expecting their first
child that spring.

"April's really pissed at you," Jessie said without looking at me.

"She came over last night," Nick added with a
worried expression. He took people's relation-
ships very seriously.

I took a hungry pull at the beer. When I'd come
to at the Drop Inn that afternoon I'd had to sober
my body up with Cokes and hamburgers. But I felt
that by now I could handle a few beers.

"It's a long story," I said, "and I've got to get
back to April."

"Why doesn't she come over too?" Nick
suggested. "Call her up, Jessie!"

"That would be good," I agreed. "It might be
easier that way."

Jessie went into the kitchen to call. The dog got
out again, but Iris had all her candy back in her
bag. The dog put his feet up on the couch and
sniffed hungrily. Iris fixed him with a stony stare.
"Gweedy," she observed finally. The dog returned to its bed by the radiator.

I opened the door for April, and she favored me
with the ghost of a smile. There was still hope.
Jessie got her a beer, and she sat down next to me
on a folding canvas chair.

"I hope the kids don't attack our house," she
remarked.

"Did you put the pumpkin inside?" I asked, in an effort to sound like a responsible member of the family.

She blocked the attempt with a cold stare. "*You* wouldn't know if we even *have* a pumpkin."

"I'm really depressed today," Nick put in.

"Why?" April asked responsively.

"Well, first I got an article rejected, and then the Chairman told me that he thinks I'll be terminated next year." He stared glumly at the floor. "I've been working so hard on my lectures, and it's as if no one even cares."

"What was the paper on?" I asked in an effort to forestall a long discussion of Nick's career. If no one stopped him, he would discuss his prospects deep into the night. And April would sit there looking interested. That was what I couldn't stand. If I ever tried to complain, she would just get angry that I could be unhappy when she was making such sacrifices. April had the monopoly on suffering in our family, just as Nick held the franchise in his.

I realized that Nick was talking to me, and tried to assimilate what he was saying. ". . . aether theory. Hell, I made a point of saying that it's compatible with special relativity, but I don't think they even read past the abstract, let alone look at my data. The idea's quite plausible really. There should be two types of basic substance . . ."

Bells were ringing in my head. I'd heard about basic substances in Cimön. Cantor had mentioned a paper of his from 1885, and had suggested trying a physical test of the Continuum Hypothesis. Nick had discussed his work with me before, but of course the significance had never hit me.

I leaned forward in excitement. "You've worked with matter and aether, Nick, but could there be a third basic substance?" I rattled on before he could answer. "Because if there were, then we would know that the Continuum Hypothesis is false. Cantor said so when I was talking to him in Cimön . . . before he went into Dreamland. I just have to read his 1885 paper, and I bet we can work out an experiment. We'll be famous!" They were all looking at me, and I kept talking. "I know where people go when they die, too. You wouldn't believe all the things I've seen . . ."

"Felix just spent the last twenty-four hours at the Drop Inn." April interjected acidly. "And I think he's been tripping on top of it all."

Suddenly I remembered the dream I'd shown April. "I'm high all right," I said, staring at her intently, "But not on false drugs. All I need is a clean windshield, powerful gasoline and a shoeshine." April hesitated. "Do you remember, April? The man in the airplane? You dreamed it right after you dreamed about seeing me passed out on a sidewalk. I'm high all right, but not on false drugs."

"Isn't that from the Firesign Theatre?" Nick put in. "Jessie and I saw them at . . ."

"Please," I cried, waving him silent. "This is so important. I saw April dreaming. I know what she dreamed. It's the only way to prove that . . ." I fell silent, waiting for April to say something.

Finally she spoke. "That's so weird, Felix. As soon as you said that, a dream came back to me. I

took a nap before supper today and it was just like
. . ." She looked at me with wondering eyes.

I filled in more and more details of the two
dreams, and April recognized all of them. By the
time we were through she was really talking to me
again. She believed me.

"Where did you say you were?" Nick said. He
was smiling, happy to see us make up. Baby Iris
had fallen asleep on the couch, and Jessie brought
out some cake.

I talked for the next hour, sketching out the
whole wild ride. They listened spell-bound, and I
realized that at the least I had the makings for one
killer of a surrealistic novel. Nick got up several
times to bring more beer. I waited till I'd finished
talking before I drank my second.

"What was the one word you read at the end?"
Jessie asked.

"I've got to know that word."

"Greetings," Nick suggested with a laugh.
"Like in the Vonnegut book where the robot
brings a one-word message all the way across the
galaxy. Greetings."

"Or Hi," April said with a giggle. They'd heard
me out, but I was still just their crazy Felix. It was
a relief.

"It should only have one letter . . ." Jessie
mused.

"I don't remember what the word was," I said.
"When I got to it, there was only one of anything.
Which meant that the word and I and the Absolute
were all identical. Like there were no more dis-
tinctions, no thoughts."

"But then you still had to reach Nothing," Nick

23
Research

I couldn't sleep for a long time. I was leery of leaving my waking consciousness again. April dropped off to sleep right after we made love. It was a good, thorough sex act . . . even better than with Ellie. There had been some element of physicality missing from all my experiences in Cimön. April was nothing if not physical. I loved her in the same unquestioning way I loved the Earth.

We were lying together spoon-style, and I pressed myself against her long warm body. She made a humming noise and shifted against me. A car drove past and a fan of light swept across the ceiling. My eyes twitched a little as I followed the movement. I kept thinking I saw bloogs.

Walking across the street from the DeLongs' I'd been sure I'd seen one hovering over our chimney. But when I stared it wasn't there. And now I saw something flicker in our closet. I tried to convince myself that it was just phosphenes.

April and the DeLongs hadn't tried to argue with me, but it was obvious that they didn't take my story at face value. Their tacit assumption seemed to be that I had dosed up with some heavy acid and ridden it out at the Drop Inn. It was much easier to account for my knowledge of April's dreams as straight telepathy. Unusual, but nothing to make you question your sense of reality.

My astral body and physical body had run on the same time-line as long as I stayed on Earth. But the two days I'd spent in Cimön had only counted for an hour here. From Wednesday afternoon to Thursday afternoon I'd been ghosting around Bernco and Boston. I'd hit Cimön at about five in the afternoon Earth time, and at six I'd snapped back. The fat bartender . . . Willie . . . had noticed the change at once.

"The dead man walks," he'd bellowed when I stumbled to my feet. I'd been sitting at an empty table staring at the TV. A few people at the bar turned their heads to look at me. "We've been trying to decide whether it was catatonia, autism, aphasia or sheer insaneness," Willie added cheerfully. He'd been a Psych major at Bernco several years ago.

I'd had a couple of Cokes and hamburgers then. I was too wiped out to talk. At seven I'd drifted out into the crowd around the Halloween parade. Tomorrow I was going to have to go back and talk to that barmaid . . . Mary.

Another car drove past. Again I saw a light flicker out of the corner of my eye. A face. I sat bolt

upright on the edge of the bed. It had looked like
Kathy.

I had a bad feeling about her. I should have
taken her all the way to the Absolute. I knew she'd
never go there on her own, and sooner or later
Satan would catch her. That was the one thing
Jesus had asked me to do, to get Kathy to God, and
at the last minute I'd blown it. And he had warned
me to be sure not to bring her back. But how could
she come back? On Earth she was dead.

April and Jessie had both known about the business with her father getting the most expensive
coffin. The fact that I had found this out didn't
impress them. "I *told* you that, Felix," April had
insisted. "You just weren't listening." I wondered
again if Kathy could have followed me back to
Earth. I hadn't really noticed which way her light
had gone after I killed her.

But now everything looked normal. I went into
the kitchen for a sandwich and a glass of milk. I
heard the college bell-tower strike midnight as I
ate. I felt a tremendous sense of relief. Halloween
was over. Maybe everything would go back to the
way it was before.

I looked in on Iris, sleeping on her back with
both arms stretched up by her head. She looked
like she was doing exercise, or like a capital Y. My
eyes watered at her perfection, her solidity. I
thanked God I was back.

I woke up in Dreamland sometime during the
night. I was a red ball of light, moving through the
familiar continuum of possible visions. Urged by
some inner bidding, I picked one, and found myself back in the Temple Hill graveyard with Jesus

and Satan. A bad dream.

Satan is holding a shrink-wrapped package with a styrofoam tray. A supermarket meat package. There is something green in the package. A featherless seagull. Kathy.

He shows his teeth when he sees me. "It's you or her, Rayman. What do you say?" His voice is like rusty iron dragged across concrete.

I look at Jesus for help. There's a crack in the ground like before. He and I are on one side, Kathy and Satan on the other.

Jesus gives off an even, golden light. His eyes are deep . . . black holes. He smiles a little and holds out one of his hands. There's a ragged hole at the wrist, with blood scabbed on it.

I step back, shaking my head. "I can't do that. I'm not you."

Satan laughs, and the laughter echoes.

I woke up covered with sweat. It was dawn. Iris was babbling happily in the next room.

I got up and fed her, and when April got up I made scrambled eggs for the two of us. "And do you know what I dreamed last night?" April asked over coffee.

I shook my head. "I didn't look." April waited expectantly, so I told her my dream. "I dreamed that the Devil had that girl. Kathy . . . what's her name?"

"Kathy Scott. I don't know why you keep talking about her. You never even met her, did you?"

"Just in Cimön."

April lit a cigarette and gave me a worried look. "Maybe we should move, Felix. I don't think it's good for you here. These wild ideas you have all of a sudden . . ." Her face quivered, close to tears.

"You didn't used to be like this."

I went over and put my arm around her. "I wish it was over too, April."

She stabbed her cigarette out. "Last night with the DeLongs it just seemed like a funny adventure. But if you really didn't take anything . . ." She hesitated, then went on haltingly. "I mean, to just forget who you are for a whole day like that. It's not normal." She looked pleadingly into my eyes, "Please, Felix. Go see a doctor. I think you need it this time. You're too far."

From her standpoint it made sense, of course. But the request annoyed me. It annoyed me very much. Fighting for control I said evenly, "The only way I'm ever going to the nuthouse is in a strait-jacket. I got myself into this, and I can still get myself out."

"*Muy macho*," April said bitterly. "Meanwhile you're ruining my life."

There was a hot balloon of anger growing in my lungs, and my solar plexus felt like the tight spring of a wind-up duck. I had to get out before I said something awful. "Please, April," I said as I backed away from the table. "Just give me a little slack. I need to think things through. I don't care what you call my trip to Cimön. But I have an idea, or an idea for an idea, that could really . . ."

Suddenly she softened. "Oh, Felix, don't worry so much." She stood and walked over to me, gave me a hug. We held each other tight for a minute. Iris crawled over to worm between our legs. April scooped the baby up and held the little blond head next to ours. We all stood there kissing for a minute. There was sun on the kitchen floor.

My schedule was such that I had no classes on

Thursday, so my absence had gone unnoticed at school. Friday mornings I had Calculus and Math for Elementary Education. They went pretty smoothly. In the El. Ed. course we reviewed some more for the test I'd scheduled for Monday, and in Calc we covered the formula for the arc-length of a curve.

After my classes I hurried over to the library to look up that paper Cantor had told me about. His collected works are available only in German, and it took me awhile to find and translate the passage I was looking for.*) It went something like this:

The three-dimensional space of our universe consists of a continuum of c idealized mathematical points. There are two types of substance moving about in this space: mass and aether.

We all have a pretty good idea of what mass is, but aether? Aether is a very tenuous sort of substance associated with the transfer of energy. We do not necessarily assume that aether fills up all of the space between the bits of mass. All we know is that some regions of space contain mass, some contain aether, and some are empty.

Now any massive object . . . such as a rock . . . can be endlessly cut into smaller and smaller pieces. In the limit one ends up with *alef-null* infinitely small bits of mass. These indivisible bits are called *mass-monads*. In general, then, any massive object is an arrangement of alef-null point-sized mass-monads.

Aether is also infinitely divisible . . . but even more so! Any aethereal object is to be thought of as an arrangement of alef-one point-sized *aether-*

*)The passage begins on p. 275 of G. Cantor, *Gesammelte Abhandlungen.* A translation can be found on pp. 419-421 of Volume 1 of the journal Speculations in Science and Technology.

monads. Since we have c points in space, and since c is at least as great as alef-one, there is certainly room for all these monads.

At any instant, then, the state of affairs in our universe can be specified by stating which of the c possible locations in our space is occupied by a mass-monad, and which locations are occupied by aether-monads. To put it another way, space contains a set M of alef-null points occupied by mass, and a set A of alef-one points occupied by aether. The state of the universe at any instant depends only on the properties of the two sets of points M and A.

Cantor spends most of the 1885 paper describing a special way of splitting M and A into five significant subsets. He closes with these words: "The next step will be to see if the relations between these distinct sets can account for the various modes of *existence* and *action* exhibited by matter—such as *physical state, chemical differences, light and heat, electricity* and *magnetism*. I prefer not to explicitly state my further speculations along these lines until I have subjected them to a more careful consideration." Cantor loved italics.

When I finished reading, I sat there looking out the library window for a while. The clouds had blown away during the night, and it looked like we were going to get one last taste of Indian summer. The blue sky was like a taut stretched film of color. Dry leaves scuttered up and down the asphalt campus paths.

My mind was exceptionately clear, and I could remember every word of the remark Cantor had made to me in the tunnel to aelf-one. "If there were a third basic substance in addition to mass and aether, then we would know that c has power at least alef-two."

I thought this over. Say there were a third substance . . . call it essence. Mass, aether, essence. What would essence-objects be like?

If mass is like a pile of sand, then aether is like water. Essence would be even subtler, even more continuous. Perhaps the white lights were made of essence. Higher levels.

One thing was clear. To differ from mass and aether, essence-objects would have to be made of *alef-two* monads each. But if there were essence-objects in our space, then space would have at least alef-two points . . . and the Continuum Hypothesis that space has alef-one points would be disproved.

Well and good. But how . . . Suddenly I heard the clock tower strike two. It was time for my Foundations of Geometry class. Hurriedly I gathered together the sheets of paper I'd been writing on. I left the Cantor book on the table by the window and rushed out of the library.

A fitful little breeze was herding things around. Pale orange leaves nipped my ankles. I tried to imagine that there were subtler forms around me as well. Aethereal forms, astral bodies, spirits, bloogs.

It seemed reasonable to assume that most of the things I'd seen in Cimön were made of aether. Alef-one *aether-monads* each. For now, I didn't want to try to think any more about the possibility of essence-objects. Today it would be enough just to grasp the implications of Cantor's original idea about mass and aether.

It was a long downhill walk from the library to

my Foundations of Geometry class. The class was held, due to some quirk of the scheduling office, in one of the phys-ed classrooms connected to the gym. The gym was all the way down at the bottom of the campus.

Lake Bernco floods often, and is surrounded with rich flat soil. Fields jigsaw around the lake and its tributary rills. The largest of the feeder streams is edged with trees and there is a dirt road running along next to the trees. As I ambled along, I could make out puffs of dust from some farmer's car, hurrying along the stream's great curve. There were flies in the air, and their buzzing seemed the very sound of sunshine. I kept asking myself what it would mean for ghosts to be made of alef-one aether atoms each. Two ideas came.

First point. Given a shoe-box you can either fill it with alef-null mass-monads or alef-one aether-monads. Even though both types of monads are vanishingly small, it would have to be that the mass-monads somehow behave as if they are coarser, rougher, less densely packed. Presumably an aethereal body can trickle through the interstices in a solid mass-object. Therefore ghosts can walk through walls. Good.

Second point. A beast with four feet has no difficulty in counting up to three. A physical body has alef-null mass-monads, and is happy with smaller numbers like ten or ten thousand. If an astral body has alef-one aether-monads, then it stands to reason that it can handle alef-null. Therefore astral bodies should be able to carry out infinite speed-ups, but would have trouble with alef-one. Good again.

My students were waiting for me outside the

gym annex. Some of them started laughing when they saw me coming. I put on a friendly professional face as I walked up to them.

The tall kid with the mustache . . . Percino . . . spoke up, "How are you feeling, Dr. Rayman?"

"Fine." I said it as blandly as possible. I recalled that Percino was the boyfriend of that barmaid at the Drop Inn. Mary. I still hadn't had a chance to ask her what my body had done there Wednesday night.

I unlocked the door, and the class folowed me into the quiet hall. Sunlight was slanting in through a window at the end, lighting up a shifting multitude of dust-specks. Something I had read about the Pythagoreans popped into my mind. They believed that there are as many spirits about us as there are motes in a shaft of sunlight. For an instant I could feel an endless hierarchy of spirits teeming around me.

"Mary says you were pretty twisted the other night," came a confidential mutter. Percino was walking along next to me. He waited avidly for my response.

"I had a couple of beers," I said, stonewalling.

Fortunately we reached the room then, and I was spared his follow-up. I could see some half-formed scheme of blackmailing me for a good grade percolating behind his murky eyes. He was the one doing his term-paper on UFO's. I hoped he would get me off the hook by doing a good paper.

The students filed in and sat down. I began to talk, pacing slowly back and forth in front of the blackboard.

24
Teaching

"Last time, as you may recall, I talked about the writing of C.H. Hinton.*) His great concern in life was to make the fourth dimension into something real. I find myself in a similar position today. I want to convince you that infinity is real."

Some of the students looked uncomfortable at this. There was one girl in particular, a tough cookie with blond hair cut shorter than mine. She regularly asked me what my lectures had to do with the geometry she intended some day to hammer into high-school students.

Glancing at her, I lied, "The concept of infinity is crucial for a proper understanding of the Foundations of Geometry." Some of the students sensed a cover-up and chuckled a little. I had already used the same excuse for lecturing on the

*) See *The Selected Writings of C.H. Hinton*, Dover Publications.

fourth dimension for three weeks. "Just give me today," I said with a pacifying gesture. "I've got to talk about infinity today." There were some smiles and some sighs, but everyone looked ready. I began.

"The idea I want to develop today is that the human mind is infinite. I mean this quite literally. If this class is a success, you will all leave this room with the ability to think of infinite things.

"Now, people often assert that it is impossible for us to fully conceive of infinity because our brains are finite. There are two rebuttals to this. First of all, how do you *know* your brain is finite? It is, after all, quite possible that any bit of matter is made up of smaller bits . . . so that any material object actually has infinitely many bits of matter in it. Just before I came here I was in the library reading an article by Georg Cantor. He claims that each piece of matter contains alef-null indivisible bits . . . which he calls mass-monads."

The students looked blank, and I back-tracked. "The point is that maybe the brain *isn't* finite. Maybe it has infinitely many tiny bits in it, so that you really *can* have infinitely complex patterns in your head. Can you feel them?"

My head was beginning to tingle a little. A fat girl in the back row nodded encouragingly and I continued. "That's the first line of defense. Now for the second."

"Suppose the brain *were* completely finite after all . . . just a sort of finite network with only finitely many possible configurations. I want to claim that *even then* it would be possible to experience infinite thoughts.

"The reason is that we are not just made of

mass, of flesh and blood. We have souls, ghosts, astral bodies . . . there is another order of existence. And on that level we are surely infinite."

Some of the students glanced at each other with smiles. One of them spoke up, a physics major named Hawkins. He talked slowly, with a heavy Long Island accent. "That's just your *opinion*, Doctah Rayman. You think you have a soul. I think you're just a complicated machine. We could argue all night about it . . . but why waste the time? There's no way to win."

I was beginning to see green and pink flashes. I tried to collect my thoughts. There had to be a way to bring infinity to Earth. "That certainly seems like a reasonable point," I said smiling. I liked Hawkins for always disagreeing with me. "I guess it's a matter of put up or shut up. Either I show infinity to you right now, or I admit that it's just a convenient mathematical fiction. Now let's see . . ."

I looked out the window for a second, lost in thought.   The soccer team was practicing. Looking at one of the distant players I had a momentary shift of consciousness. I could see through his eyes, feel the ball against my toe. I shifted back and forth between single and double consciousness, between One and Many. I began to feel something. Suddenly I saw bloogs outside. I turned back to the class.

Kathy was sitting in the first row, smiling at me uncertainly. She was made of greenish aether and there were pink bloogs all over the ceiling. Kathy's lips moved. I could only hear the pounding of my heart. She really had followed me back to Earth. And Satan didn't have her after all. I

walked over and tried to touch her, but my hand
went through her head.

I realized then that the students were watching
me curiously. I began again to lecture, talking
almost at random.

"Take self-consciousness. You know that you
exist. You have a mental image of yourself. In
particular, you have a mental image of your state
of mind." I drew a thought balloon on the board
with a variety of shapes inside it.

"Say that this is your mind. Now suppose that
you decide to think about your mind as well as
about the other things." I squeezed a small
thought balloon into the bigger one, filling it with
the same shapes as before. Then I drew an even
smaller thought balloon inside the small thought
balloon. Some of the students began to laugh.

"You see the problem," I said, turning to face
them. Kathy had a bag of something in her lap. I
couldn't let myself look at her for too long, for fear
of falling into her eyes. I picked up the thread of
my argument.

"The idea is that if you form an image of your
mind, then this image has an image of your mind,
which has an image, which has an image . . . and
so on. We are capable of thinking infinite re-
gresses."

Hawkins spoke up. "You can't draw that picture more than about five levels deep."

"But I can *think* it all the way through. That's
what real higher consciousness is all about. That's
the first step to merging with the Absolute."

The girl with short blond hair lost her patience
at that. "Isn't this supposed to be a Geometry

course?" Everyone roared, and I fumbled for an answer.

"Just give me a little slack," I said for the second time that day. Meanwhile Kathy had stood up and dumped the contents of her bag out on my desk. Fuzzweed. A mound of fuzzweed. I nodded vigorously to her. She'd come to help me.

"I've been thinking about infinity a lot recently," my voice was saying, "And you should remember that space is made of infinitely many points . . . though no one knows what the exact level of that infinity is." Kathy took out a cigarette lighter and lit the mound of fuzzweed. It began to smolder like a pile of autumn leaves. Light blue tendrils stretched towards the students.

"I really think there's a chance that some of you could grasp the notion of infinity right now." I walked over and closed the window. "Just relax and try to form an image of your mind." There were titters, but I raised my voice. "I mean it. Let's just meditate together for a couple of minutes, and then we can all go home. I promise to have a more together lecture on Monday."

I sat down and propped my head in my hands. Some of the students followed suit, some leafed back through their notes, and some stared out the window. It didn't matter, though. A blue haze of fuzzweed smoke had filled the room.

I pushed my face forward into the plume of smoke and inhaled. I felt a loosening sensation all over my body. Kathy breathed in some smoke, whited out, snapped back. We smiled at each other.

The students were beginning to look a little

dazed. Percino yawned, then stretched his arms out. Only they weren't his real arms. He realized this, and jumped to his feet in surprise. His body stayed in his chair. Hurriedly he got back in it.

It started happening to all of them then. We weren't whiting out, just comeing loose from our bodies, getting into aethereal consciousness.

There was no time to waste. It's possible to grasp alef-null-sized collections once you're in your aethereal body . . . but you need some to look at. My job right now was to generate infinities.

"La," I said, "La, La, La, . . ." I tried going into a speed-up, but my physical tongue tangled with my astral tongue and I stuttered to a halt. I would have to try something else.

I slipped out of my physical body and began running around and around the room. I did alef-null laps, took Kathy's hand and did alef-null more. Percino jumped out of his body and joined me for the next set, and then the whole rest of the class joined in . . . even the hard-faced blonde.

As the fuzzweed spread its smoke between the two sheets of reality, we slid faster and faster around the room. We started running on the walls. My body had started out as the usual pale-green nude copy of myself, but as I ran I grew more and more streamlined.

There were people all over the walls . . . no one could have said who was first or who was last. Some of the students streamlined themselves as I had, but others added new complexities to their forms. I saw a lobster whizz by, and then gryphons and dodo birds.

All the while our physical bodies sat slack-jawed in their chairs. We whipped through alef-null more laps and fell into a laughing heap in a corner of the classroom, too excited to talk.

I looked for Kathy, but she had disappeared. The fuzzweed on the desk had burned out, leaving no ashes. My consciousness was jittering back and forth between my astral and physical bodies. The gap was upsetting.

I walked back to my body and slipped in, waiting for the tight feeling that would signal I was bonded again. The students—lobsters, turtles, nudes—crept into their bodies too. I wondered what would happen if two of them switched.

Suddenly things lost their aethereal shimmer, the bloogs disappeared, and I was locked back into my meat. I wished I knew how to enter and leave at will. For a minute I tried to bring back that loosening sensation the fuzzweed had given me, but I couldn't quite get it. There was something so simple, yet so . . . so elusive about the transition.

"What happened?" a kid with glasses and dandruff asked. "Did you hypnotize us?"

"It was drugs," the blonde girl said, looking upset. "He was burning something on the desk." She stood up to go, probably to the dean.

"There's nothing on the desk," Percino pointed out. "It was a close encounter of the third kind. Didn't you see that green, glowing being?"

"The main thing is that you saw infinity," I said, standing. "I hope. I'll see you Monday." I had to go find Nick DeLong.

A few of the students left, a few just sat in their chairs, and one or two came up to talk to me. Each had his own interpretation of what had happened. This was, in a way, disturbing—for it made me wonder if there was any reason to believe that my version was the correct one.

The nicest description of it all came from the fat girl who always sat in back. She understood everything and wrote perfect exams, but rarely spoke up. "It was a caucus race," she said to me in a low voice. "Just like in *Alice in Wonderland*."

I walked up through the campus alone, struggling to capture the exact feeling I'd had just before I'd seen Kathy. Percino was walking up the hill fifty yards ahead of me, and as I gazed absently at his back I again had a feeling of shifting consciousness.

I could feel his tight shoes, see through his inexperienced eyes. I was equally present in both our bodies. There were other figures here and there on the campus, and I reached out to them too. I was a jelly-creature with dozens of eyes . . . all equally important. Suddenly I knew how to leave my body. Many to One.

I pulled myself back from the bodies with a sudden twitch. I congealed into an astral body twenty yards away from my physical body . . . about halfway between it and Percino. Suddenly there were two of me on the hillside . . . one made of aether and one made of mass.

We looked at each other . . . that is, the astral me looked at the physical me; and the physical me stared at the spot where the astral me was. "I've got it!" The astral I said. Bloogs were drifting by.

Merging was no longer a problem either. It was just a matter of concentrating both consciousnesses on the One and coming out in the same place. I split and merged several times to make

sure I had it down pat, then walked on up the hill.
I wanted to find Nick.

I met my office-mate Stuart Levin on the path
near Todd Hall. He mimed a pompous mandarin
bow and flashed an ironic smile through his
beard. I hadn't seen him since Wednesday morning.

"How's it going, Felix? Staying clear of the
Devil?"

I smiled slightly. "I think so. He almost had me
a couple of times. I've been gone."

"I can imagine," Stuart said with a laugh.
"Look, let's get together this weekend. I'm dying
to hear about your latest hallucinations. They're
better than television."

"I'm going to be working with Nick DeLong.
Come by his lab tomorrow afternoon and we
might have something interesting to show you."

"I'll be there." He was off with a jaunty wave of
his gradebook.

25
The Banach-Tarski Decomposition

Nick's office was the size of a broom-closet, but he had access to a well-equipped laboratory. The government had bought them all the best equipment in return for a contract assigning them the rights to any inventions. They thought the Bernco Physics department was developing anti-pollution devices. The Physics department thought Nick was doing publishable research. And Nick had all the toys he'd ever wanted.

I found him at work on one of his experiments. The lights were dimmed, and he was studying the screen of a small oscilloscope, his arms elbow-deep in a tub of viscous liquid. I looked into his vat. There were wires in there, arrangements of glass tubing, and several evilly glowing little pyramids. What seemed to be a miniature steam-engine was pumping away at the bottom.

"Charles calls this my *fondue chinoise*," Nick

said without looking away from the oscilloscope. Suddenly the green squiggle locked into a stable saw-tooth curve. He gave a sigh of satisfaction. "That ought to hold for a half-hour." He drew out his dripping bare forearms and went over to a sink to wash the stuff off.

"Is that cooking oil, Nick?"

"God, no. It's liquid Teflon. Only stuff that has the right density and non-conductivity." He dried off his arms and rolled his sleeves back down. "You said you had an idea?"

Before I could answer, a red light began blinking at the other end of the table. "Hold on," he said. "The laser's warmed up."

He walked over and threw a switch. A pattern of glowing ruby lines sprang into life and hovered over the table. A system of mirrors and beam-splitters was arranged to weave a cat's cradle out of his laser beam. The final knot rested on a thin quartz window in the side of his vat.

Nick stepped with quick, sure steps to the wall, threw another switch, and something under the table began to hum. It sounded like a fan. A strange prickling feeling swept over me, and my hair tried to stand on end.

"An air-ionizer," Nick commented. "Can't hurt to try it." The green saw-tooth pattern held steady on the oscilloscope screen, and the tangle of light-beams glowed evenly on the table top. Nick threw one more switch and sat down heavily.

"This run'll take a half-hour. It's on automatic."

"What exactly are you testing for?"

"As you know from my paper, I'm working on a hyper-matter theory." I hadn't read Nick's paper very closely, but I nodded him on. "My idea is that there's a different type of matter . . . gobs of invisible jelly floating around. That net of laser-beams is supposed to herd the globs into the vat, and the little engine at the bottom is to condense them. The rest of the stuff is just to detect the condensed globs of hyper-matter."

"Bloogs," I said.

"What?"

"*Think of black water, think of white sky. Think of an island with bloogs blowing by,*" I recited. "That's from Dr. Seuss. You're looking for bloogs!"

"I guess you could say that," Nick said. "Though I wouldn't want to advertise the fact." The connection struck him then. "Didn't you claim you'd seen lots of bloogs when you were out of your body?"

I nodded. "And I've learned how to control it." I reached out to feel Nick's consciousness, his learning and loneliness. I held the Manyness and made it One, then snapped back with a twist that left my astral body outside my physical body. I looked around the room. There was a little herd of bloogs clustered around a cabinet across the room.

I flew over to them and tried to sweep them towards Nick's fondue. The first time I tried, my hand went right through them. I made myself denser and smaller, tried again. This time there was a slight resistence as I slid through the bloogs. They had moved imperceptibly. I pushed through them over and over . . . combing them along.

I went into a speed-up then, and after alef-null nudges I had forced six of the little gray bloogs through the window in Nick's vat. It took me a couple of minutes. When I was done I merged bodies and told Nick.

He bent over his equipment, his face lit by the dim dials. He turned a knob quickly, reexamined the meters, then broke into a grin. "You really did it, Felix! These are the best readings I've gotten yet!"

I sat back with a smile. "I can get you all the bloogs you want, Nick."

Suddenly his smile faded. "But what good will it do? If anyone tries to reproduce my data it won't work . . . unless you're there. And if I tell them that, they'll just write me off as a crazy psionics researcher." Gloomily he ran his fingers through his thinning blond hair. "I'm crazy anyway to take your stories seriously. Maybe you can get away with it, Felix, but I can't."

My mind was racing ahead, exploring the possibilities. What Nick needed was some physical proof of his theory. Physical proof which was accessible to everyone. And I, too, needed proof. Physical proof that infinity exists. Maybe . . .

"Nick," I said, leaning forward," How good is that condensor you've got in there? I mean, if I shovelled in enough bloogs would you be able to get a chunk of aether . . . of hyper-matter . . . big enough and solid enough for everyone to see?"

Nick shrugged. "I don't see why not. It would take an awful lot of . . . of bloogs, though. And I'm not sure if the hypermatter would look that different from ordinary matter."

"Sure it would," I said excitedly. "It would be made of alef-one particles so it would be possible to cut it into alef-null chunks which were big enough to see." I jumped to my feet. "That's it, Nick! We get a cube of the stuff and I'll cut it into infinitely many slices. Let them try to write *that* off as experimenter bias!"

We worked all afternoon. After I'd rounded up all the bloogs floating around the laboratory, Nick had the idea of my looking in the furnace downstairs. There were plenty of big ones there, and I brought them up through the floors one by one. When it was suppertime we called up our wives and arranged to meet at the local pizza parlor.

Nick did most of the talking at dinner. He was fantasizing about a Nobel prize for the two of us. "They couldn't fire me *then*," he gloated, ordering another pitcher of beer.

April and Jessie were lively, happy to be out on a Friday night. They discounted Nick's optimistic predictions, but were glad to see us working. Iris pounded happily on her slice of pizza, occasionally nibbling at the crust.

I was kind of tired. Several times I thought I heard Kathy's voice . . . somewhere inside me. It took a little effort to keep my bodies together. I kept forgetting which person at the table was me.

We ate and drank for an hour, then all went over to our house to listen to records. There was more beer and some grass. The evening ended in a confused jumble. I fell asleep as soon as I lay down.

I had the same dream again that night, or rather a new installment. This time the Devil stops laughing and sinks his teeth into the package he's holding. The styrofoam makes a snapping noise, and the meat twitches. He jumps into that crack in the ground. I lean forward to see, and Jesus kicks me in after.

I'm hurtling down past solid screams and hoarse light. Somehow it's the Devil's mouth, his throat. Kathy is there, falling too. Her smile is crazy and she locks her legs around my back, riding me like a nightmare.

Ahead there's something like the negative of a fire. All the heat and light are streaming into it . . . flowing out of everything and into that absolute black plexus in Satan's belly.

For the first time I remember what it was like to fall into the White Light at Nothing. But the memory slides away. Flames shoot out of my fingers, black flames, and we spiral around the heart of darkness.

There are others there. They are turned inside out, with festoons of veins and organs decorating them like grisly christmas trees. Kathy is still clinging to my back, and I can't turn my head enough to see her.

I have the feeling that there is some trick of perspective, some four-dimensional reversal I can pull to put everything right . . . turn the people back, make the light flow out, turn black to white. I struggle, knowing that if I stop trying I'll never start again.

I woke up feeling like I hadn't slept at all. It was Saturday. April and Jessie had decided to spend the day shopping, and I was supposed to take care of Iris.

When the women had gone, Nick came over, and the three of us went back down to the lab. We had the building to ourselves. We laid some desks on their sides and pushed them together to make a

sort of pen for Iris. She didn't like it at first, but we
kept throwing things in there until she quieted
down. It was a box of brass weights that finally did
the trick.

When Nick had returned his equipment, we got
back to work. There were fresh bloogs all over the
laboratory . . . especially near the spot where the
radioactive materials were stored. When these
were gone, we opened all the windows and
turned the thermostat up to eighty to keep the
furnace going.

I spent all morning stuffing bloogs into Nick's
condensor. My physical body climbed into the
pen with Iris and fell asleep . . . much to the
baby's delight. Around noon Nick said he thought
we had enough.

For some reason I had a little trouble getting
back into my body. There were some odd, unfamiliar thoughts in my brain which I had to push
away to make room for me. When I had bonded in,
I picked up Iris and went over to the vat of Teflon
to see what we had. The liquid had been clear
before, but now it was turbid with thousands of
little specks. We hoped they were congealed
aether.

We stirred it up good and siphoned the stuff off
into an empty plastic tub to settle. While we were
waiting, we went up to Sammy's for hamburgers.
The same old fat waitress was there. She pretended to be feeding Iris, but kept eating her
french fries. We all pretended we didn't notice.
Iris wasn't very hungry, and she put her hamburger down for a nap in my lap.

When we got back to the lab there was a nice
film of sediment covering the bottom of the white

plastic tub. We siphoned the liquid Teflon off
from the top and poured the sediment into a little
glass beaker. The stuff had an incredibly slippery
feel to it. Nick got a water-powered porcelain suc-
tion filter from the chemistry lab, and we strained
the rest of the Teflon out of the sediment.

We dumped the sediment out onto a sheet of
paper. It looked something like graphite . . . a
gray slippery powder, fine beyond imagining.

"I wonder what it is," Nick said, rubbing some
between thumb and forefinger.

"Aether," I said. "Hyper-matter. Concentrated
bloog."

He sniffed a pinch of it doubtfully. "I don't
know. I've got a bad feeling this is just carbon or
some crap like that."

"Let's heat it up," I suggested. "Maybe we can
fuse it."

Nick found a little porcelain crucible. We filled
it with the gray powder and let it reach white heat
over the burner. After a few minutes of that I
tonged the cover off the little crucible and carefully tipped it over.

A perfect shiny sphere rolled across the table.
Iris was watching from across the room. She
stretched her hand out and shouted, "Mine!"

It was too hot to touch, and we took turns pok-
ing at it with the tongs. In the process of melting,
the powder had drawn itself into what looked like
a geometrically perfect sphere. A big ball-bearing.

There was an insistent hammering from the
building's front door. I went downstairs to inves-
tigate. It was Stuart. I had forgotten that I'd asked
him to come over today. I let him in and led him
upstairs.

"The mad alchemists," Stuart remarked as he looked around the dim lab.

"Look at this," Nick said, walking over with our shiny new sphere. His voice was loud with excitement. "We think this might be a new substance."

At the same moment Stuart and I reached to take it from Nick. Our three hands fumbled against each other, and the precious little ball escaped. But it didn't fall.

It just hung there in the air. It was immune to gravity. It had inertia . . . a heft to it . . . but the gravitational field didn't affect it at all.

Nick was ecstatic. "My God!" he exclaimed. "Just hanging there, that little ball wipes out Einstein's General Theory of Relativity. And think of the applications!"

Stuart rested his finger on the ball and it sank down. "It still won't hold anyone up," he complained.

"But imagine an airplane with no gravitating mass," Nick babbled. "Think of the fuel savings!"

Iris was pointing at the ball and screaming, so I went and lifted her out of her pen. But before I could give her the little ball of hyper-matter, Nick grabbed it and ran across the laboratory.

"I knew it!" Nick cried a moment later. "It's a superconductor too!"

Stuart raised his eyebrows at me questioningly. He had spent a lifetime avoiding physics. "He means that it doesn't have any electrical resistance," I explained. "So you could start a current in a loop of it, and it would flow forever. Makes a good magnet."

Iris was screaming so loud that it was hard to

talk. "Come on, Nick," I said. "Let Iris have the ball."

Grudgingly Nick unhooked his meter from the shiny little treasure and brought it over. Iris snatched it greedily and squeezed it in her fat little hand.

"Ball!" she cried, waving her arm wildly. Suddenly her hand opened and the ball flew across the room. It smacked into the wall and seemed to shatter.

"Oh no!" Nick screamed, his voice cracking. He was a little over-excited.

"Take it easy, Nick. We can always melt it again."

The ball had broken into two pieces, which had recoiled off the wall and were drifting back across the room.

"Ouch," Stuart said, snagging one. "It's prickly." He set it down on the table and I leaned over to examine it.

The piece was a sphere like before, but with some parts missing. It looked something like a cockle burr or a sycamore ball. A collection of radii emanating from a central point. It was not completely even in texture. Here and there the radii were clustered more densely, and the surface had a shadowy sort of pattern like the globe map of some alien world.

Nick caught the other piece and brought it over. It looked quite similar . . . an airy sphere of the same size with dense spots where the first piece had light spots. It was like a negative of the first piece.

"Maybe we can just slide them together," Stuart suggested.

Something occured to me and I stayed his hand. "How about a little Banach-Tarski action, Stuart? Two for the price of one!"

Stuart knew what I was talking about and grinned appreciatively. "Piece A and piece B," he said, touching the two in turn.

I slipped my shoe off and smashed it down on the two little balls as hard as I could.

Nick screamed a hoarse, "No!" and flung himself onto the table to catch the pieces that skittered out. Four of them.

"Are you guys nuts?" he cried, lining up the four pieces and cupping his hand protectively over them.

"Come on, Nick," Stuart said. "Let's have a look."

Nick moved his hand aside a little, and we leaned over the pieces. There were four little prickly spheres now, all the same size as before. Two looked exactly like piece A, and two looked exactly like piece B.

"Bleaze broceed viz za demonztration, Brrofesszor Rrrayman," Stuart said in his best Polish accent.

Iris was tugging at my pants, so I set her on the table to watch. "Don't worry, Nick," I said, reaching for the four pieces. "I'll put them together now."

"Do you think they'll go back to the one ball?" he asked anxiously.

"Eefen batter," Stuart intoned.

"Ball, ball, ball, ball," Iris chanted.

I picked up one of the A's and one of the B's, turning them so that the denser areas on the one were in the same relative position as the lighter areas on the other. Then I began pressing them against each other.

The spines meshed, and for a minute the pieces would go no closer. I kept pushing and gently jiggling them. Suddenly it worked. The two pieces slid into each other and locked together to make a perfect solid shiny ball like before.

I handed it to Iris, who chirped a bright, "Nanks!" Then I put the other two pieces together to make another perfect sphere. I gave it to Nick. We had broken the original sphere into four pieces and reassembled the four pieces to produce two spheres identical to the original one.

"Why don't you mathematicians let me in on the secret," Nick said, wonderingly hanging his ball in the air.

"It works because the hyper-matter sphere has uncountably many points," I said. "Ordinary mass-objects only have alef-null points, but aether objects have alef-one. In 1924 Banach and Tarski proved that any such sphere can be broken into a finite number of pieces . . . which can then be reassembled to make *two* spheres identical to the original one. By Raphael Robinson's 1947 refinement of their proof, we know that only four pieces are necessary."

"You guys are really serious aren't you?" Stuart said, dropping his accent. "Why don't you fill me in on the details?"

"O.K." I said. "How about adjourning to the Drop Inn?"

"I'm ready," Nick exclaimed. "Jesus! We may never have to work again."

26
Bloody Chiclets

The Drop Inn is a square room . . . say forty feet
on a side . . . with a bar along one side of it. The
floor is dirty gray asphalt tile, except for a big strip
of bare concrete the owner never got around to
covering. There's a plate-glass window next to the
sidewalk. If you like, you can sit there, a spectacle
for the Bernco shoppers.

The bar-stools were mostly full, and the four of
us took the window table. Nick went up to the bar
to get a pitcher of beer and an orange-drink for
Iris. I wasn't sure if she was allowed to be there
. . . in New York State you never know if you're
breaking a law. I felt pretty limp from my hang-
over, my bad sleep, and all the speed-ups I'd run
to get enough bloogs into the condensor. Limp but
happy.

It was about four o'clock. April would be back
soon. I resolved to go home after the first pitcher.

Stuart had pried the aether ball away from Iris, and was cracking it into pieces preperatory to multiplying it. Any given piece A can be split into two more identical piece A's . . . and the same goes for the B's. Stuart kept at it till he'd put together seven balls of the bloog-stuff.

He pocketed one of them, gave Iris two and me four. I amused myself by poising mine in the air in front of me. It was fun, the way they'd stay wherever you put them. They were too massive to be very sensitive to air currents. I arranged them to make the four corners of a tetrahedron . . . a pyramid with a triangular base. It looked beautiful.

The afternoon sun was lying like honey on the street outside. I gazed out at the familiar scene with a happy sigh. Things couldn't be better. Just then Nick brought back the pitcher and Iris' orange-drink. Mary the barmaid followed him with the glasses.

She gave a sort of knowing smile when she saw me. "I'm surprised your wife still lets you out of the house."

"Fat Willie said you were in here when I came back on Wednesday?" I questioned.

"Who could forget it," she said shaking her head. "You had two twenty-dollar bills crumpled up in your hand. It was like the death of Janis Joplin." Stuart hadn't heard any of this yet, and was nodding with interest. She addressed herself to him. "Felix comes in like a zombie," she acted out two or three lurching steps, "puts the money down on the bar and just sits there."

"You gave him to drink?" Stuart inquired.

"Sure. And he never said a word. He was loaded

by the time I went off duty, and Willie said they had to lay him out in the garbage shed at closing time." This seemed to strike her as particularly funny.

"I've been wanting to ask you something, Mary," I cut in. "I won't get mad if you tell me, so please just tell the truth. Did you put anything in my beer when I came in after lunch on Wednesday?"

"April thinks you dosed him," Nick explained.

"As if he needed it," Stuart put in.

"Why would I?" Mary asked, in what seemed like genuine surprise. "If I had any acid I'd take it myself."

So there was still no explanation for what had started all this off. The shining tetrahedron hovered over our table. This was real, there was no longer any doubt about it. But why me? Perhaps it never would have happened if I hadn't found that pamphlet, "CIMÖN AND HOW TO GET THERE, F.R." But where was it now? Where had it come from?

A customer was calling for service and Mary turned to go. "Wait," I called to her. She turned back. "One other question . . ." I began. The guy at the bar kept hollering, "Beer, Mary!" so I stood up and walked across the room with her. "Was anyone with me when I came in?"

She thought briefly, distracted by the drunk bellowing her name. "Yeah. There was a guy who might have brought you in. An old hippie in a robe. But he left right away." I could hardly hear her over the noise.

I turned to the source of the yelling, a stocky blond guy in jeans, khaki shirt and a hunting vest.

"Could you just be quiet for about ten seconds?" I snapped.

His fat cheeks reddened with anger. "You own this place, buddy?"

I wanted to argue with him, but suddenly something in me crumbled. I patted his shoulder almost tenderly. "All right, all right. Have your beer."

I went back to our table and sat down. I was a little ashamed of myself for backing down from that fat short-hair so quickly. Something about his face had had a strange effect on me. He was the kind of person I hated on sight. But I'd had an immediate desire to please him, to comfort him. Faugh.

"I was just trying to find out who brought me here," I said to Nick, sitting down. "I figure it was Jesus."

"You certainly get around, Felix," Stuart remarked. "One day it's Satan, the next it's our Lord."

"You haven't heard the half of it," Nick said. He stared at his reflection in one of the spheres hanging over the table. "And I'm beginning to think it's all true."

"Well, let's hear it," Stuart said.

"First a toast." Nick raised his glass. "To the greatest scientific discovery of the century."

He and I drank deeply, Stuart less so. "You guys are due for fame and fortune now, I suppose." He tried unsuccessfully to keep the envy out of his voice.

I could feel Stuart's emotions as clearly as mine. "Why don't we cut him in?" I suggested.

Nick didn't look too thrilled at my suggestion.

He started to say something, but Stuart spoke first.

"Wait," he said. "I just realized. I already *am* in." He pulled his aether sphere out of his pocket. "Anyone who has one of these has access to an unlimited supply of the stuff. I made one into seven while you were getting the pitcher."

Nick winced. I tried to cheer him up. "Look, Nick, we can patent the process. It's going to be a while till anyone else thinks of using the Banach-Tarski decomposition anyway. In the meantime we'll keep it secret and dole out the stuff at top prices. Stuart can be our lawyer."

"Does he have a degree?" Nick asked uncertainly.

"Practically," Stuart said, refilling our glasses with a flourish. "And I'll settle for twenty percent. You guys can take fourty each. Let's drink to it."

"What the hell," Nick said, raising his glass. "Why not."

Iris had put her two bloog balls into her drink. She had a big orange mustache and looked happy to be here with the grownups. I smiled at her and she smiled back.

I drained my second beer and opened my mouth to talk. All of a sudden I felt funny, as if I had no control over what I would say. *"The way the sparkle glow spreads in the belly giving strength and turning the world from a place of gnash-serious absorption into a gigantic gut joy,"* I recited lightly. "That's Jack K."

"I didn't know you read Kerouac," Stuart said. "As a matter of fact, Felix, I'd always had the impression that your idea of stimulating fiction was Walt Disney's Comics and Stories."

"I . . . I did too," I said haltingly. Where had

that remark about Kerouac come from? I only knew one person who . . .

"Oh my god!" Nick exclaimed, suddenly jumping to his feet. "I think I left my machine on. It'll burn out." He looked panicked at the thought. "They'll have my ass for this."

"Relax, Nick, you're going to be so famous you're ass will be all but unhaveable." An unexpected idea popped into my head. "Look, you're just going to run down there and find you turned it off anyway. Let me save you the trouble. I'll split and zap down in my astral body."

"O.K." Nick said, sitting down. "I'll take care of Iris." Stuart watched with interest. I let my awareness flow out to touch everyone in the room. Tiny Iris, Nick, Stuart, Mary, the blond guy at the bar. That guy was so full of sadness . . . he had lost someone, someone close to him.

One part of me wondered fleetingly if it was really safe to go so far from my body again, but then I'd already finished the split. My body lolled stupidly in its chair, and I zipped invisibly out the window.

It took only seconds to get to the physics building. Quickly I found the lab and checked Nick's machine. It was turned off as I had expected. He worried too much. I drifted back up towards the Drop Inn. The sun was low and bloogs streamed out of it. Two blocks away I thought I saw our car turning off Main Street. It was time for me and Iris to go home to April. I went in through the ceiling of the Drop Inn.

Something was wrong. I could see it in Nick's face. My body wasn't in the chair where I'd left it. Frantically I looked around the room. To my relief my body was at the bar. But why?

I spread my consciousness out to the Absolute and flipped back to my body, expecting to bond right in. But something jabbed me and I bounced out. My body, I now noticed, was talking to that stocky blond guy again. How could it talk without me in it?

Without bothering to listen to the nonsense it must be spouting, I tried again to get back in. The same jab and bounce. Again. It seemed like something else had taken over my body . . . some other spirit.

Finally I stopped long enough to register what my mouth was saying.

"Frank. You've got to believe me. I'm your same Kathy, only come back in another body. I can prove it to you."

Frank's fat face was a mixture of sorrow and anger. "You've got a pretty peculiar sense of humour, fellow. Now beat it before somebody gets hurt."

Nick was walking towards the two, a look of concern on his face.

Suddenly my body threw its arms around Frank. "Oh, darling, I've missed you so much. I . . . I could be like a woman for you."

Frank let out a roar like a wounded elephant. "You FAG," he trumpeted, shoving my body away. "You sick, twisted pervert!" He sent a fist to my body's belly, then one to the temple. My possessed form sank to the Drop Inn floor.

Frank was ready to stomp my erstwhile head in, but Nick quickly separated him from the body. Iris was screaming. My body got up and tried to twist out of Nick's grip, but he held it tight.

"Come on, Stuart," he called. "We've got to get him home."

They marched my body up the street, one holding each arm. Nick carried the sobbing Iris in his other arm. Stuart had scooped up our aether spheres, and was carrying them inside his shirt. I floated along after, watching and listening.

"What did you say to that guy?" Stuart asked my body. It didn't answer, and Nick gave it a little shake.

"Come on, Felix, what happened?"

The lips pursed a few times, then spoke. "I'm not Felix. My name is Kathy. Kathy Scott."

April came running out of the house when she saw Nick and Stuart leading her husband's body home. It had taken on an unfamiliar nancing gait, and its features were screwed into an expression I'd never seen before.

"Hello, April," it said. "I don't know if you remember me. I'm Kathy Scott, the woman who was buried last month."

April nodded numbly, believing it. "Felix kept talking about you. He said he . . ."

"He wouldn't leave me alone," Kathy said, raising her voice. "First he dragged me away from Earth, and then he tried to throw me into a horrible white nothing. When he came back to Earth I followed him." Her hands fluttered as she talked.

Somehow none of them doubted her word. "How—how did you get Felix's body?" April asked.

Kathy smiled without showing her teeth. "He kept leaving it alone. Finally I decided to take over. He can go back to his white light now. It's all he really wants anyway."

"No," I cried, "that's *not* all I want. I want my family, my life on Earth!" But none of them could hear.

"Where do you think he is now?" Nick said, looking around. They were standing in our tiny front yard. Iris was dragging her wagon out of the garage. The adults looked at Kathy for an answer.

"*I* don't know," she said. "I'd have to leave this body to find out. But I'm *not* leaving it. Ever."

They had released her arms and she turned as if to go. "Wait," Stuart said, grabbing her again. "This is crazy. It's just Felix having a psychotic episode. We can't let him wander off like this. Nick! Call an ambulance!"

Stuart's sudden conviction broke the spell. Nick sprinted into our house. April took a step towards my body. "Felix?" she said hesitantly.

Kathy whacked Stuart in the crotch then, and broke loose from his weakened grip. She took off down the street, running with her hands switching back and forth at shoulder level.

Stuart straightened up and took off after her. Nick came out of the house then, breathless with excitement. "They're coming," he shouted to April. "Stuart's right. We've got to . . ." He saw the expression on April's face then, spotted the two figures running down Tuna Street, and joined the chase.

It was clear to me they'd catch my runaway body. It was running like a girl. It was depressing to see Kathy jerking me around, and I decided not to follow the chase. I hardly even felt like staying on Earth. They'd haul my body off in a straitjacket, lock it up someplace, give it shock-treatments, tranquilizers . . . and then?

I had a feeling Kathy wouldn't let go of my flesh till it died. I remembered the way she'd acted when I first met her in the graveyard, the way she'd been just before we hit the White Light at Nothing. As far as Kathy was concerned *anything* was better than oblivion . . . even forty years in a nuthouse.

Not that she'd have to stay that long. Sooner or later she would realize that all she had to do was start saying she was Felix Rayman. She wouldn't have any of my memories, but they'd call it amnesia and put her out on the street.

I could hear a siren drawing closer. There were faint shouts from a block or two away. April heard it too, standing tautly at the edge of our little lawn, her face a mask of strain. Iris was loading dead leaves into her wagon, one by one. I never wanted to stop watching over these two, so dear, so real. I made as if to move closer.

A squealing cut the air. The leaves, April's face, wavered and dissolved. Two faces, frightened ovals, upside down. Burnt rubber, gasoline, my throat filling. A horn blasting, stuck. Broken teeth, sliding pieces, no air. The numbness closing in. The noise rushing away. Legs gone, arms, eyes lost in mist, red to black. Just the heartbeat, twitching, once more, still. Rest.

27

(It's Never Really) The End

"I'm sorry," Nick was saying, "I just never bothered to read the fine print."

"Ten thousand *dollars*?" Stuart said again, "Just ten grand and nothing else?"

"That's not really all," Nick said with a nervous tug at his beard. "If we publish anything about hyper-matter we'll be charged with high treason."

"That's a death rap," I put in. It was hard for me to talk louder than a whisper.

"You can still write your novel," April said, squeezing my hand. "Just say you made it all up."

"Or work for the government," Nick said. "They've already offered me a position at Los Alamos. They're hot for Felix to come too, and if you could get a clearance, Stuart . . ."

"Not me," Stuart said with a laugh. "Give me my two thousand bucks and I'm out of the picture." His sly smile gave the lie to this.

"Just don't try selling those bloog-balls to the first Russian spy you meet," Nick cautioned. "Because he's probably going to be from the CIA."

"Oh, hell, Nick, I wouldn't do that. I just want to drop out of sight and build my own UFO's. Felix might want to help me."

I tried to shake my head, but the body-cast made it hard. 'I'll go with Nick,' I whispered. The caps on my front teeth felt funny—numb, and smoother than real teeth. "I'd like to do some more lab-work. There should be a third level of substance, too. Endlessly many. The number of points in space is Absolutely Infinite. It's just a matter of . . ."

"Felix," April cautioned. "You promised me you wouldn't leave your body again."

"Till death do us part," I murmured, meaning it.

"Do you still see things?" Stuart was asking me.

"Not now. But after the accident. I thought I was dead."

"Everyone did," Nick said. "That car was doing 45 and you . . . I mean Kathy . . . ran right in front of it. It was just lucky I'd already called an ambulance."

"Who was driving the car?" I asked.

"It was hit-and-run," Nick said. "They found the car abandoned down on the campus. The horn was still stuck, still blasting. When they traced the plates it turned out the car had been stolen from in front of the McDonald's a half hour earlier."

"I want to hear what Felix saw while he was in the coma," Stuart interrupted.

Nick and April frowned at him, but I began talking. "I was in this big factory, with all kinds of weird machines humming along. They weren't really machines. I mean some were just electronic patterns. But they were all lined up along the walls of this enormous room. There was a real big white-haired guy . . .''

"God?" Stuart said, smiling.

"Of course. Not the Godhead, just the Father. He was showing me the machines. Some were ideas . . . like one was Zeno's Paradox and one was the Continuum Problem. Others were places . . . there was our Universe and there was Cimön. And there were little machines, too, that were just a person or an atom. There was one of everything." This was the first time I'd told anyone about what I'd seen during the coma, and they were keeping still to hear my whisper.

"I noticed that each machine had a wire coming out of it. Like an electric cord. So I asked God what they ran on. He says, 'Do you want to see?'

"All the wires seemed to lead into a manhole in the middle of the floor, and we walked over there together. While we were walking, I noticed that God and I each had wires running out of us and down into the manhole too." I paused for a drink of water. My ribs were cracked and it hurt to talk.

A nurse stuck her head in the door. "The two gentlemen will have to leave now. You can stay another half hour, Mrs. Rayman." I was glad for the interruption. I was too tired to finish.

Stuart and Nick got up to go. "You really mean that about coming to Los Alamos?" Nick said, pausing at the door.

"Didn't you hear?" Stuart asked him.

Nick looked blank, and April filled in. "We have to leave. At Christmas vacation. They're firing Felix for not following the official syllabus for the Foundations of Geometry course."

"He never even covered protractors," Stuart said accusingly.

Nick gave a whoop of delight. "Jessie and I are leaving in December too. The weather's beautiful there. No more Upstate sog! We'll drive out together!"

The nurse reappeared and they left, Nick calling, "I'll tell them you're coming."

April and I were silent for a few minutes. This was only the second day I'd been conscious, and it was the first time I'd seen Nick and Stuart. It would be good to leave Bernco, to make a fresh start.

April sat by me for the rest of her half-hour, patting my hand, talking about Iris, spinning plans for our life in New Mexico. She never bothered to ask me what had been in the manhole.

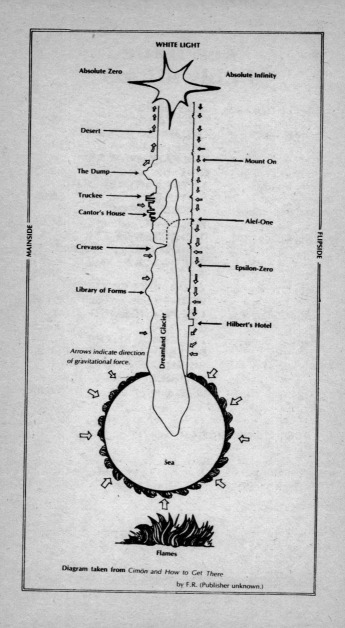

Diagram taken from *Cimön and How to Get There*
by F.R. (Publisher unknown.)

126b

Can't Find An
Ace Science Fiction Title
At Your Local Bookstore?

BOOK MAILING SERVICE can supply you with any Ace Book currently in stock. Just fill out the coupon on the facing page (or supply the information on a separate piece of paper if you don't want to rip out the page) and send it together with a check or money order made out to Book Mailing Service for the cover price of the books you order plus 75¢ each for the first three titles to cover postage and handling. After the first three, we absorb additional postage and handling charges: for three, six or one hundred books, postage and handling totals only $2.25 per order. (No postage and handling required if order is accompanied by <u>Destinies</u> subscription.) This offer is subject to withdrawal or change without notice.

And remember—the Editor of <u>Destinies</u> is also the Executive Editor of Ace Science Fiction. On the following page you will find a list of current and recent ('78/'79) Ace sf titles that he feels will be of special interest to the readers of <u>Destinies</u>. (To order a catalog of all Ace Science Fiction titles currently in stock send 50¢ to Book Mailing Service, refundable on your first order.)

**BOOK MAILING SERVICE
ACE SCIENCE FICTION DIVISION
BOX 690
ROCKVILLE CENTRE, N.Y. 11571**

Ace Science Fiction
Purchase Order

NAME _____

STREET _____

CITY OR TOWN _____

STATE & ZIP _____

Please send me the following:

COVER PRICE

TITLE _____

AUTHOR _____   _____

TITLE _____

AUTHOR _____   _____

TITLE _____

AUTHOR _____   _____

TITLE _____

AUTHOR _____   _____

TITLE _____

AUTHOR _____   _____

POSTAGE & HANDLING   _____

TOTAL   _____

Please enclose a check or money order made out to
BOOK MAILING SERVICE for the total of the cover prices
of the books ordered plus 75¢ per book for postage and
handling. (Maximum $2.25) No postage and handling
required if order is accompanied by <u>DESTINIES</u> sub-
scription.

The Book Mailing Service policy is to fill an order for any
title currently in stock upon receipt. However, delivery is
usually from one to four weeks since postal transit time
must be taken into account. Payments for titles not in stock
will be promptly refunded.